Jogger Girl is closer now, a soft keen coming from her jagged mouth. God, she looks worse than some of the masks we'd wear to scare the audience in the Great Movie Monster Makeover Show.

"Can you hear?" I ask, gripping the Eliminator, trying to keep her occupied, focused on me, on my mouth, my head, not the hand at my side. "Can you talk?"

"Yeah," she grunts, soft air moving through the hole in her cheek where I see her pinkish-white jaw muscles flex. It's a reedy sound but weird because her voice is so Zerker deep. "I just don't like to."

That airiness combined with that hoarseness—I figure probably the gash in her throat nicked some vocal cords when the Zerkers were chewing on her face.

I shiver. "Stop. You don't have to do this. I, I know there are a lot of them, but I have friends too."

She shakes her head, as if even she knows how stupid I sound. "Just don't," she says, limping faster now. "It won't work."

I raise the Eliminator, hoping she'll see it and stop, giving her one last chance. "Don't," I blurt, my voice raw with guilt. "Don't make me do this."

"Do what?" she says, three feet away now. She pauses, giving me that creepy half smile that is her full smile because half her freakin' face is missing. Her good eye narrows. "All you're doing is finishing what they started. What you let them start."

"I couldn't," I sputter, "take them all by myself."

She cocks her head, drool  onto her shoeless foot. "That's not what she says."

"She? Who she?" I growl. "

But she's walking again. " whistly voice croaks from her m time—"when you never helped me?"

ZOMBIES
Don't Surrender

BOOK 3 IN THE
LIVING DEAD LOVE STORY SERIES

Rusty Fischer

MEDALLION
P R E S S

Medallion Press, Inc.
Printed in USA

Reviews from *Zombies Don't Cry*:

"I love zombies books and *Zombies Don't Cry* by Rusty Fischer was an **extremely cool** one. There aren't many zombie books featuring zombies fighting zombies. Fans of zombie teen fiction (one of the coolest genres of all times) will want to pick this up and read it immediately."

~ Night Owl Teen

"**Truly terrifying**, this is filled with action and a sizzle of romance, along with dances, death, and back-stabbing BFFs."

~ Romantic Times

"Rusty Fischer does an amazing job of writing a first-person narrative of Maddy Swift's descent into zombie-hood. Not only does he authentically capture the essence of a teenage girl, but he provides a fun, fresh take on the usual leg-dragging, groaning, brain-craving zombie and pens **a fun and entertaining story** that is often laugh-out-loud and always grin-inducing— although, brains are still required."

~ Renee C. Fountain, Bookfetish.org and NY Journal of Books

Reviews from *Zombies Don't Forgive*:

"Popcorn fun for the brain-munching set."

~Kirkus Reviews

ZOMBIES
Don't Surrender

Rusty Fischer

Published 2014 by Medallion Press, Inc.

The MEDALLION PRESS LOGO
is a registered trademark of Medallion Press, Inc.

Copyright © 2014 by Rusty Fischer
Cover design by James Tampa
Edited by Emily Steele

Typeset in Adobe Garamond Pro
Printed in the United States of America
ISBN 9781605427096

10 9 8 7 6 5 4 3 2 1
First Edition

Dedication

To Martha, as always . . . for always.

Contents

Prologue
The Violent Kind

EVEN FROM DOWN the hall, through the supposedly soundproof walls, I can hear her, shaking the bars of her cage, gnashing her jagged yellow teeth, wailing as if she's in pain.

I wince, subconsciously slowing down as I approach Dad's lab. Well, it's not really Dad's lab, as the Sentinels are always so quick to remind us, but that's how I look at it anyway. I mean, he's the only one qualified to study Val in the first place, so Dad's lab it is and Dad's lab it shall be and the Sentinels can lump it for all I care.

It's nearly midnight, and if we were back in Barracuda Bay, he'd be sacked out by now. But Sentinel City—at least, that's what he calls it, and now it's stuck with the rest of us—has a kind of Vegas feel. Since we zombies don't sleep, there's always as many folks roaming the halls at 2:00 a.m. as there are at 2:00 p.m. And since the place is short on windows, you pretty much never know what time it is anyway.

Sure enough, as I rap on the frosted glass in the middle of the lab door, I hear a quick, "It's open," in between Val's shrieking.

I step in to find the lab brightly lit, as always, the smell of fresh coffee filling the air. Dad, lab coat unbuttoned over his crisp blue shirt and gold tie, leans against the counter across from Val's cage.

He is studying her carefully, the way he did dead bodies back in Barracuda Bay, where he was the coroner for Cobia County. I wonder what he thinks now that he's studying live ones. At least, re-alive ones. From the inquisitive look on his face, I think maybe he likes them a little better. Or maybe, like me, he's just trying to make the best of a crap situation.

I stand there, half in, half out of the door, just watching her scream at him. Dad's face is placid, as if he can't even see her, let alone hear her. Then I let the door shut behind me, and Val starts, as if she thought this was just a private performance.

I smirk. It's kind of nice to see the ice queen

flinch. Moment of shock over, she returns to form, coiled evil at five feet nothing. Val's eyes are Zerker yellow and piercing and, even though I know the bars are three inches thick and solid steel, I shiver and wince and can't even front that I'm not freaked to the bone just being in the same room with her.

She stops screaming, pacing, fanning her fingers out from her cold, dead hand and rubbing them along the bars casually, as if it's the coolest place to be. I avoid her glare, hating myself for looking away but unable to stare back at so much hate.

In the next cage, Stamp leans against the bars as far away from Val as possible. His eyes, yellow too with a tinge of black, are half closed in boredom, as if he's heard it all before, ad nauseum, and doesn't really care if it ever stops. He offers me a weak smile and waves one finger, as if he doesn't want to draw any more attention to himself than that.

I smile, wriggle a finger back, and turn away. "Dad?"

He looks at me, eyes pleading. "Maddy, what are you doing here?"

He asks me the same thing every night. I cluck my tongue and say each time: "Just checking up on you. Aren't you about ready to clock out for the night?"

He shrugs. "Just making a few more observations."

Right, with no clipboard, no pen, no sleek digital voice recorder, or so much as an Etch A Sketch to record his thoughts. I shuffle toward him. "What exactly are you observing?"

"This one here." He juts his chin in Val's direction.

I shake my head wearily. As always, I'm eager to leave five seconds after I walk in. The tension in the air is palpable. I've been in the room less than two minutes, and already my neck is sore from watching my back.

I hate being in the presence of Val, hate talking in front of her, hate that Dad has to spend so much time with her and, what's worse, doesn't seem to mind it all that much.

Doesn't he remember what happened back in Barracuda Bay? The harm she caused? What she wanted to do to him? What she wanted to do to *me*? What she did to Stamp? Then again, maybe that's why he's so obsessed with her. As he always used to say, those who forget the past are doomed to repeat it.

I wave a hand in front of his face. "She'll still be there in the morning."

He looks at me then, gaze far away, face paler than usual, chin covered with two days of salt-and-pepper stubble. "Let's hope so."

Finally, I smile. He has to be kidding. I rap a gray knuckle against the solid bars of her cage, yanking back quickly as she saunters forward to investigate. "She may be immortal, but she's no superhero."

Dad nods, unconvinced. "Did you hear that rage just now?"

"Everyone in Sentinel City heard it."

He's nodding fast. "That's what I mean. You can't contain fury like that. It *will* get out."

"Yeah, with a blowtorch, a forklift, and the cast of *The Expendables*, maybe."

He looks at me, like maybe he's disappointed I'm not taking him more seriously. "Why do you think they keep her here? With me, I mean? Why not just incinerate her in her own device?"

He cocks his head toward the tanning booth from Cabana Charly's in the corner, a dangerous relic where the tubes full of undiluted avotoxia are still hooked up and juiced, just in case the Sentinels decide to do just that.

I shrug. "Sentimental, I guess?"

Dad snorts, a sound from our old life. I think of how many times we stood in our kitchen back home, talking just like this, minus the cages and

Zerkers and rage in the air here. "They want to know how these Zerkers tick. And so do I."

I should care more, I guess, but I know how they tick. The same way cockroaches and spiders and sharks and other killers tick: on cold instinct.

See happy? Squash it.

See good? Kill it.

See Maddy and anyone she loves? End them.

I sigh. "So you're not going to bed, then?"

He smiles, wrinkles creasing around his tired eyes. "Not just yet, dear."

"Come on. You've been at it ever since we got back from Barracuda Bay. It's the same thing every night. She screams, you stare at her, the rest of us get freaked out. How about you skip the 'you stare at her' part and fast-forward to tomorrow?"

Dad nods, clearly with no intention of budging. "I'm interested in what she'll have to say when she stops screaming."

I look back at Val, into these deep dark eyes, so yellow and angry and, after all we've been through, far too familiar. I resist the urge to shiver and instead lean to kiss Dad on the cheek. His skin is so warm I just want to stay there by his side all night, as if I were rubbing my hands over a campfire. But

I can feel the stiffness in his posture, the impatience in his breath. He just wants to watch and watch and watch.

Not for the first time, I regret letting Val live.

I shuffle toward Stamp, steering clear of Val's cage. "Stamp?"

He looks toward me as if he figured I'd just walk on by without even saying good night. "Hi," he says, and I wonder if he's forgotten my name again. His face is blank, with hints of something at the corners of his lips. Happiness? Confusion? Sadness? Gladness? "Maddy," he adds, but I catch him looking at Dad, who's leaning against the counter, pretending I haven't caught him in the act of prompting Stamp.

I turn back, smiling. "You okay in there?"

Stamp shrugs. "I'd be better if this girl would stop screaming all the time."

"She will."

Val chuckles, then clears her throat.

I know what's coming.

Stamp knows what's coming. He inches closer, curling a finger for me to draw near.

I do, even though I know I can't give him the answer he so desperately wants.

"Can you . . . can you get me out of here?"

7

"Soon, Stamp," I say, fake smile fixed on. "Soon . . ."

He smiles, as if he really believes me. As he believed me last night and the night before that.

I smile too because the only good thing about the new Stamp—besides the fact that, you know, he's still here—is that he's too slow to realize when I'm lying.

Chapter 1
Zerker Killing for Dummies

"WHEN DO I get the pen?" I grunt, shoving an-other ice pick into another waxy rubber ear. I follow it up with a lightning-quick slash across the CPR dummy's throat with a six-inch blade.

After a pause and the snap of the last centimeter of grody yellow artificial neck skin, the dummy's head slips onto the floor, joining at least half a dozen more.

Vera shakes her head humorlessly. "I've told you a thousand times: you have to earn the pen!"

I pause, looking at the smattering of heads along the smooth gym floor, some of them literally still rolling. "You're telling me *that*'s not worth a lousy electric pen?"

Vera shakes her head, stiff and serene in her

crisp, blue Keeper fatigues and clearly unimpressed with my mad Zerker-killing skills. Her arm, the arm I broke not long after we met, is better now. Not perfect—you can still see it resting at an odd angle if she's standing just the right way—but better.

"Pens are for Keepers," she tells me for about the two thousand eight hundred seventy-fourth time. "Trainees get the Eliminator. Isn't that enough?"

Eliminator! I love that. She's speaking, of course, about the weapon in my hand. The rubber grip fits perfectly in my palm and, with a quick press of the black button on each end, the scalpel blade and ice pick retract.

It is a nifty weapon, no doubt, and appropriately named. If you're trying to eliminate human-munching Zerkers with their thick hides and general fondness for their heads, yeah, there's no better tool. A quick ice pick to the ear and, snap—out go the lights as the point jams through the brain, shutting one down forever. A razor-sharp blade to dislodge the head, just to be sure, and boom: no more Zerker.

But there's one weapon to rule them all: the supersonic, bad-to-the-bone, James Bondesque electrified ballpoint pen Vera keeps on her at all times.

I put the Eliminator in a pocket of my gray

fatigues. (You don't get to wear blue until you're an actual Keeper, and gray is about the only color left around this dump.) I slump onto the bench along the wall. "Well, not to sound like an ungrateful brat, but how long does this training last?"

I'm not physically tired. That rarely happens unless I go without brains for too long, which is practically an impossibility here in Sentinel City. I'm just tired of waiting.

Always, always waiting. Back in Barracuda Bay, I waited for the Zerkers to strike. Back in Orlando, I waited for the Sentinels to find us. And now, since they brought us here, to this training center for Keepers and Sentinels, I've been waiting to become one or the other, to get out of here and put my Zerker-killing skills to the test. And since the Sentinels are pretty much a sausagefest, as in no girls allowed, it's either become a Keeper or Sentinel Support or bust.

Vera leans against the gym wall, fingering an unnecessary cotton towel absently. "How long do you think your training should take?"

I groan some more, tapping the back of my head several times against the blue cinder block wall behind me. "Not again with the Jedi mind tricks."

She makes that Vera face: head cocked, forehead unlined, eyes nearly closed, lips slightly parted, meaning, *Explain yourself, girl.*

So I do. "I mean, don't tease me with your half answers. Isn't there some chart somewhere that says if so-and-so trains for such and such a time, they become a Keeper?"

She offers a low, quiet chuckle. "If there were, don't you think I'd have told you about it by now?"

I snort.

She's answered another question with a question. I don't know if she's doing it unconsciously or if she's just some mad genius, majoring in reverse psychology.

"Okay, maybe there is no chart but, man, haven't I been doing this long enough?"

"How long do you think you've been doing it?"

"Months now. Years, even."

At last, a smile. Few things are as bright in Sentinel City as Vera's smile. "Six months, to be exact."

God, has it been that long since we captured Val and brought her back here?

She wags a lecturing finger. "But you've been a Trainee for only three, don't forget."

"How could I?" I look at my gray fatigues, where

a big black *T* is stitched on every possible pocket flap, collar, and sleeve.

Vera points to a supply closet full of dummies. "One more round?"

I shake my head and raise my palms in surrender.

"You know, the more you train, the closer you get to your goal."

"I don't know if it is my goal anymore," I say, holding a hand out for her help.

She frowns but takes it anyway. She is small but powerful with all her hidden reserves of fiery anger. Her once-black skin is now ashy like mine.

"What else would you do?" she asks on our way across the gym floor, picking up heads and dumping them in a mesh bag like Coach Potter used to do with the dodge balls after PE back at Barracuda Bay High.

"I don't know," I say, holding up a rubber face for emphasis. "Melt the heads back onto the dummies?"

"Be serious," she scolds, like a French tutor who's not paid enough per hour. "That's not a goal. That's a chore."

"Somebody has to do it." I put the mesh bag into the supply closet, where by magic someone from Sentinel Support will pick them up, melt them back onto the dummies, and line them all up for tomorrow's practice. "Why is that less useful than anything a Sentinel does? Or a Keeper, for that matter?"

She looks vaguely offended. "It's a great honor to be a Keeper. Do you think what I do is unimportant?"

We pause by the locker room door, where we'll part for the day.

"I have no idea what you do, other than ride me all day."

She tut-tuts. "Just as someone rode me all day once upon a time many years ago."

I pounce at the chance to find out how old she is. Keepers, I've found, even regular zombies, are protective of their ages. "Yes, but how many years ago?"

"Finish your training," she says, rolling her black eyes, "and you might find out."

I groan. "Okay, well, can you tell me if I'm at least close to being done?"

She winks, a rarity. "Look at it this way: you're one day closer than you were yesterday."

She turns, her generic black sneakers squeaking.

"Thanks for nothing," I call.

She takes a few stiff steps across the giant gymnasium, dotted now with a dozen headless torsos.

She takes a gray hand out of a pocket and waves backward. "You'll thank me one day," she says without turning around, her voice echoing.

I frown and shoulder the locker room door open. I don't need a shower, exactly. I don't sweat and, by now, lopping the rubber heads off stationary dummies isn't exactly taxing. Still, some things you do just to feel human again, if only for a little while and even if they don't make sense.

I open my locker and slip out of my gray fatigues, carefully folding them on the bench behind me. Inside the locker is a pink towel, some cherry bodywash, and a washcloth with strawberries all over it. I don't know who shops for this stuff, but the girls' supply shed looks like it was stocked by a gaggle of ten-year-old Girl Scouts whose troop leader was either Strawberry Shortcake or a My Little Pony. Not that I'm complaining, mind you. Even zombies need girly stuff every now and then. But they could stand to take the edible-red-fruit theme down a notch or two.

There are eight metal towers in the shower pit, with rounded tops and four spigots surrounding each. I press the cold water button because there is no hot water in Sentinel City.

Even the cold water feels warm on my skin. The cherry bodywash smells supersweet and comes out red, the foam it creates turning pink as I lather it all over my gray skin. I spritz some on my hand and rub it against my close-cropped scalp.

They had my longish black hair cut when I first entered Keeper training three months back. No explanation, no questions, just sit in this chair and watch your hair get snipped off, like something out of a boot camp training film.

They tell me as long as I eat fresh brains on the regular, it will grow back eventually, but it still looks just about the same. It feels good, though, stiff and scratchy under my hand as I wash my skin and rinse it all off. The pink foam swirls around the drain, and I linger under the spray.

This is pretty much it for the day, as far as excitement goes. Stamp is still a little delayed, as Dad so delicately puts it. Dane is distracted, as I like to put it. So that leaves me, myself, and I for the duration.

I close my eyes and shake my head, marveling at how I got to this point, here under this showerhead in a zombie locker room full of gray fatigues, looking at a drain full of pink foam and an afterlifetime of hours stretching before me.

Chapter 2
2 Lunch

DANE'S LAUGHTER BARKS through the canteen door, and I flinch. Not because it sounds harsh, which it does, but because I know who's making him laugh in the first place. And here's a hint: it isn't me.

They're sitting together at a table reserved for Sentinels, and six or seven of them are there as well, black berets on the table, shoulders stiff, but the happy couple huddle away from the others, at the end of the table, hanging on each other's every word. They don't even notice me.

I try not to look too obvious as I quick get in line, which is pretty easy to do because there isn't any line to speak of. Not at this time of day. Well, not at any time of day, come to think of it.

It's like a regular cafeteria line, like you'd have in school, although there are no big-armed lunch ladies in hairnets behind the glass, dishing out carrots and peas and mashed potatoes with yellow gravy.

There's nobody back there, period, not that I've ever seen. You'd think the brain mousse, brain bars (think protein bar but with no chocolate chips), brain smoothies, potted brain, and brain nuggets just appeared out of nowhere, lined up in their little Styrofoam containers all by themselves. But it's like the CPR dummy heads and the cherry soap in my locker and the strawberry-covered hand towels: somebody from Sentinel Support must put them out when we're busy not looking.

I stare at the choices, trying hard to concentrate.

Maybe a dozen people are in here, but the only voice I notice is Dane's. "No way," he's saying, voice supposedly hushed but loud enough for me to hear all the way across the room. "You don't say?"

I cluck my tongue. *You don't say?* That's something a forty-year-old biologist says to his blind date, the thirty-eight-year-old librarian, before he pushes up his foggy bifocals and rubs his sweaty palms against his seersucker pants for the fifth time. *You don't say?*

I shake my head, as if the movement will drown out his husky voice and stupid, stupid, *stupid* come-on lines and throaty laughter.

The kind I hear only when she's around anymore.

I choose a brain bar, a bowl of nuggets, and a smoothie, stuff that'll be easy to down alone at my Trainee table before I bolt away, with Dane not seeing me at all. Hopefully.

Probably.

It doesn't cost anything—yay, free brains!—but I swipe my ID badge at the register at the end of the line. The Keepers like to keep tabs on what I eat—what and when and how much and how often. I put my card in my gray shirt pocket and look for the nearest empty table, sliding onto a plastic molded bench with my back to the Sentinels and my spork at the ready.

I eat quickly and not just to be gone before Dane looks away from his admirer. I'm flat-out hungry. I don't know if it's the constant Keeper training, having nothing much else to do all day, getting older, or what, but the brain hunger is as strong as ever.

The brain bars, nuggets, and smoothie are as much air as they are animal, but I still feel my eyelids flutter and taste buds sizzle with every mouthful. The energy travels throughout my body, filling every cell, as if I've just run a marathon and somebody handed me an ice-cold Gatorade in a Dumpster-sized cup.

I got over eating brains long ago. The disgusting factor, I mean. It's what zombies do, period. There's no way around it. No brains, no energy, no cell revitalization, no nothing. That, and Vera told me months back that we're mostly eating animal brains anyway.

I guess I've gotten too involved in loving the brain juices draining into all my body parts. As I'm nibbling the last corner of the brain bar, the chairs on either side of me squeak out and slide back in, filled.

With Dane.

And Courtney.

He has the barest trace of a limp, his therapy with Dad letting him lose his cane two months ago. I kind of miss his hobble. He's so confident and strong now. Somehow the cane made him vulnerable, I guess. Humble.

Now? Not so much.

"H-h-hey, guys," I say, eyelids fluttery. I cover my mouth as I chew the last grainy morsel and swallow it too fast. "What's up?"

Dane avoids my eyes and looks at my empty tray. "Let me guess: Keeper training making you extra hungry?"

I grit my teeth. Even though I'll never gain another ounce in my afterlife, or so I've been told by everyone I've asked (and I've asked everyone), I don't want to hear about how much I've eaten, especially in front of Courtney.

"Oh, well, you know . . ." My voice is a little high and light. If he were here, Dad would call it my stranger voice, meaning I was putting on airs. I suppose he'd be right.

Courtney is in Sentinel Support, which is kind of like the time Hazel talked me into being a manager for the volleyball team and I spent two weeks folding towels and lining up water bottles on the sidelines before I made up some excuse about my grades dropping in Honors English and Coach let me off the hook.

So basically Courtney provides support for the Sentinels, ordering new black boots when theirs get old, making sure their Tasers are charged before a mission, hemming their stiff black cargo pants if they're too long—that kind of thing.

There are a lot of Sentinel Support members

around Sentinel City. Dane was one, for a time, in the beginning of his training. But now that he's earned his stripes, so to speak, he doesn't have to shine his own shoes or patch up his beret.

Now Courtney is there to do that for him.

"Don't tease her, Dane," she says now, nudging his shoulder. "I hear Keeper training is really hard."

She looks at me for a you-go-girl nod, but I resist the urge to give her one. Maybe if she weren't sitting so close to Dane. But probably not. Instead I rub the dark stubble on my cold head.

She's wearing the Sentinel Support uniform of black pants and a gray top (because everyone must wear a uniform at all times, apparently, even when they're not officially anything), and even though her blonde hair is limp, she's still a new zombie and it's hard not to envy her full face and even fuller figure.

Not that she looks like a Normal. She doesn't. Not really. Her skin is as grayish-white as mine, her eyes as dark, her movements as slow, but her cheeks aren't quite as hollow, her features not as severe. She hasn't lost all her human fat, as Dad might put it, and around here that makes her a cheerleader in a cafeteria full of mathletes.

She arrived at Sentinel City only a few weeks

ago and started sniffing around Dane shortly thereafter. I'd spot her pacing in front of his dorm room, holding a pair of his shiny boots or tossing his fresh-pressed beret like a Frisbee or teasing a lock of hair or licking her thin lips.

I was good with that for a while. (Okay, not really ever.) Every Sentinel needs support, and who would turn down an eager beaver boot licker if she started stalking you all of a sudden with her thrusting bazooms and locks of hair and fresh-pressed socks? But then it turned into something else.

For example, Dane and I used to sneak brain bars out of the cafeteria and to the roof, watch the stars, and talk and . . . junk.

After Courtney showed up, every few nights he'd be a no-show. No biggie. It's not like we're married or anything. But I'd ding him the next day about it, and he'd look way too guilty.

Then one day Courtney let it slip that they'd been hanging around in the media room, and something kind of clicked inside me. What was cold grew colder, and what was warm fizzled out. Ever since then, Dane and I have been drifting steadily apart.

And now he brings *her* to *my* table? And they sit on the same *side* together? Like two lovesick rednecks in their jacked-up pickup truck, blissfully canoodling under the gun rack?

Don't be that dude, Dane. Please. Don't bring your new gal to sit across from your old gal. Be better than that. I know you can.

He reaches over and feels the burr that was once my hair. "I still can't get used to your new do." His voice is so light and infectious—so Dane—that I almost forget the vaguely voluptuous new chick sitting next to him.

"What did it look like before?" Courtney asks, as if she cares. And she asks *him*, not me, which is like three thousand shades of wrong and completely stabworthy.

And then this thing happens: he cocks his head and snorts and says, "Come to think of it, I can hardly remember."

And that clicking thing, that ticking timer dial that's been leaning toward Done for the last few weeks, finally switches all the way over. Ding. It's so loud I'm surprised nobody else hears it.

I stand abruptly and reach for my tray.

"Hey," Dane says, "where are you going?"

I don't answer. I don't even look at him. Much. I just swivel on my sneakers, the ones I have to clean myself, thank you very much, and head toward the tray return area.

I half expect him to follow me, to run me down, chew me out—anything—which would be better than what he does, which is nothing. I hear them murmuring behind me, soft hisses and whispers and not a single boot squeaking on the floor to catch up with me. Not even hers, which might have been a classy touch.

I swing through the red double doors, nearly taking out a squad of Sentinels on their way out. They grumble but note my spiffy Trainee fatigues and let me by without tearing my head off my neck.

I stumble around for a while, muttering to myself, fists clenched at my sides, until I realize I have no idea where I'm going and no real desire to get there.

Chapter 3
"And Many Morgue . . ."

DAD'S DORM IS twice the size of mine and thirty times more civilized. I guess I feel like everywhere I stop is a temporary roof until I figure out what to do with my afterlife, so why bother decorating it? So I don't. But Dad is Dad. He keeps asking the Sentinels for more accessories. You know, like dishes and cups and knives and forks and throw rugs and lamps and clown pictures for the wall (don't ask). Partly it's to make it feel like home, I guess, but mainly he doesn't like the Sentinels much and likes to bug them with as many requests per week as he can.

Unfortunately, the Sentinels don't like Dad much either. Either that or they simply won't—or can't—travel farther than the nearest souvenir stand to grab the items on his list, so his place looks like a cheesy roadside hotel room circa 1974.

I stand in the doorway, a little calmer now after six circuits of the track behind the gym.

Usually Dad keeps office hours, in the sense that he's in his lab from 8:00 a.m. till 6:00 p.m. and then comes back to his dorm suite, where we share a meal (he eats, I watch); then he slips back into his lab coat and drifts away for more late-night studies on Val, the Zerker everyone loves to hate.

I can't blame him, really. What's he gonna do? Watch six hours of *The Lawrence Welk Show* and stumble into the halls looking for a Sentinel to do the polka with?

The lights are off, and I wonder if maybe he's taking a catnap. But, no, I see candles flickering in his kitchenette. Has the power gone out? Has he blown a fuse? I smirk. Maybe the Sentinels finally had enough of his penny-ante requests and pulled the plug, just to show him who's *really* boss.

I don't see him, so I creep in, using my yellow zombie vision. "Dad?"

I hear him chuckle and clear his throat. Then his thin voice sings out, "Happy rebirthday to you.

Happy rebirthday to you. Happy rebirthday, dear Maddy. Happy rebirthday to you."

I shake my head, wondering what's gotten into him.

He comes around the corner, carrying a Styrofoam plate bearing a Twinkie with a candle sticking up from the middle. He's got on a pink-and-green birthday hat, another dollar store wonder that probably took three weeks of constant requests of the Sentinels to secure.

"And many *morgue* . . ." There's a twinkle and something wet in his eye.

There's a small lump in my throat too.

He used to sing that back home, where he was chief coroner for the Cobia County morgue. Every birthday for as long as I can remember, whether the two of us were celebrating alone in the breakfast nook or with a couple of friends and a cake I'd made from scratch, he'd add his little joke: "And many *morgue* . . ."

Sometimes if he wasn't actually carrying the cake, he'd do jazz hands like some bad dinner theater actor and double the embarrassment factor, just for grins and giggles.

But tonight I'm not embarrassed. I'm just plain sad. Or happy. Or sad. Or . . . I dunno. Happysad.

Hasappy? Sadappy? Sappy? Is that what that word really means—a cross between sad and happy?

I figure *bittersweet* is close but not quite right either. It doesn't sound happy *or* sad enough. Whatever. Dad seems happy, and that's all that really matters anymore. He holds the bowl out for me. I blow on the candle, or try anyway, but either he's being nice or we've just plain forgotten that I'm fresh out of breath. He blushes a little, brings it back in front of his face and blows it out quickly. A stream of smoke floats to the ceiling.

He puts the bowl on the kitchen counter, and something comes over me. I give him a giant bear hug and, glad zombies don't cry, whisper in his ear, "But it's not my birthday. Don't tell me you're going senile on me." I let him go.

When he catches his breath, he smiles and straightens his party hat. "It's not your birthday. It's your *re*birthday. I took out the calendar the other day, backtracked, and, with a little help from your friends, pinpointed the day you became a . . . well, a . . . you know—and it's today! So happy rebirthday!"

There's a little table off the kitchen, the fold-up kind you bring out when a couple of extra people are coming over for Thanksgiving or maybe to play cards on a Saturday night. It's covered in a green polyester tablecloth. The folding chairs are not very comfortable, but Dad seems happy as he sits across from me, dragging the Twinkie in a bowl with him like a security blanket.

"I can't believe you did that," I tell him, fiddling with the orange salt and pepper shakers. (No, seriously, they're shaped like real oranges and say *Florida* on the bottom.)

He shrugs. "It's not like I have anything better to do, dear. Besides, I figured you could use a little cheering up."

I give a faraway chuckle.

"Okay, I mean a *lot* of cheering up?"

I look around the empty apartment. "Well, I know it's my first, but I have to say, this is the saddest rebirthday party I've ever been to."

He nods and sits back a little. "It's my first too, you know. But maybe they're supposed to be sad. Like New Year's Eve."

"What? You *love* New Year's Eve." I picture him back home. He'd get us plastic hats and streamers and noisemakers with the date on them, and we'd eat fancy appetizers like brie, *pâté*, papery crackers he said were imported but just tasted stale, and an assortment of butter cookies dipped halfway in chocolate.

We'd sit around and listen to big band Christmas music because Dad said that was the same as New Year's music. Just before midnight, he'd turn on the TV and we'd watch the Times Square Ball Drop. At midnight, we'd whoop and holler, hug, twirl our noisemakers with their funny clatter-clatter-clicks, and then stand there awkwardly for a few more minutes before going to bed.

Lame, yes, but aren't some of the best traditions?

He shrugs. "I always loved the *idea* of New Year's, but the reality is, especially when you get old like me, it's a reminder you've got one less year on the planet."

I rest my chin on my knuckles. "So you'd consider New Year's a sadappy holiday?"

"A what?"

"Go with me here. I'm trying a new word: sad plus happy equals sadappy."

He frowns. "I think *sappy* is the word you're looking for. But, yes, I always got a little sadappy around New Year's."

I nod and open my mouth really wide, making big monster hands. "You know, I can make it so you live forever. That way New Year's will never be sadappy again."

He waves, almost but not quite giggling. "No, thanks!"

He hoists a plastic fork—the Sentinels still haven't gotten him any real silverware—and asks, "So you can't actually eat this, can you?"

I chuckle and slide the bowl closer to him. "It's all yours."

He smiles, digging in with gusto. "Well, it was more ceremonial than anything else."

I nod and watch him go to town. He eats the snack cake in four bites and then sits back, patting his tight little belly. He has on brown dress slacks and a blue work shirt, which is all he has in his closet: five pairs of brown slacks, five blue shirts, and two ties, both the most god-awful yellow gold you've seen this side of 1978. As I said, the Sentinels like him about as much as he likes them. And yet he wears the clothes proudly because every care package or hideous tie they bring him is one small victory, I guess.

He pushes the empty bowl back to me. There's some creamy filling left on the bottom. He nods toward it, sounding vaguely fatherly. "You need to have a little of that for good luck."

He was always big on that luck stuff. Even on New Year's Eve, we'd toast with real champagne, which he'd kill me for any other time of the year. It was just a thimbleful for me and the rest of the bottle for him for good luck. And birthday cake: I always had to have a huge slice, even if I was on a diet, for good luck. And fireworks and lucky pennies (but only if they were heads-up). Suddenly it dawns on me: the dude is completely superstitious.

I nod and dutifully dip my fingertip into the fluffy white cream, then stick it in my mouth for instant sweetness.

Brains aren't sweet. Nothing the Sentinels do to prepare brains is ever sweet, and aside from the occasional soda or sports drink, I haven't tasted anything sweet since I've been here.

It hits my system like a bite of brains—my eyelids fluttering, my tongue sizzling, my synapses firing—and then it's gone. I'd love more, but Vera has warned me, ad nauseum, about eating too much Normal food, as in *any*. I sit back and sigh, almost as contented as Dad after he ate the whole thing.

He has a cup of coffee going, brown smudges around the lip of his mug. It has a picture of a sunrise on it and, underneath, the words *Wish you were here.* It's another Sentinel find from the souvenir shop, but I think he's grown quite fond of it.

"So," he says, putting it down and smacking his lips. "What's got you downer than usual, my dear?"

I shrug, not even denying I've been a full-fledged brat for the last seven days straight.

When I don't answer right away, he smirks. "Well, it can't be Stamp, for obvious reasons, and Vera says you've been getting on brilliantly with your Keeper training, so . . . must be Dane."

I look up too quickly.

He smiles, knowing he's hit the bull's-eye. "What is it this time?" he manages to ask without rolling his eyes, his feelings on the matter of Dane quite on the record by now.

"*This* time?"

He wags a finger. "Don't look at me like that. Last time he was hanging around with that new blonde zombie; the time before that he was still hanging around with . . . That's it, isn't it? They're still hanging around together?"

I nod, then shake my head, then nod some more. Ugh, this is too much to talk about with Dad, particularly *my* dad. I don't miss my ex-BFF Hazel often, but at times like this I do. Heck, right about now I'd settle for Chloe and one of her get-off-your-butt-and-do-something-about-it pep talks.

"I just . . ." I begin, avoiding his eyes. "We used to talk all the time. He's all I have here, besides you and Stamp. And you're always busy with Stamp, and Stamp's not exactly the best conversationalist anymore . . ."

He arches an eyebrow. "He still loves you, Maddy."

"Has he said that?"

"He doesn't have to. I see that look in his eyes whenever you walk into the lab at night."

I frown. "The janitor gets the same look when he walks into the lab."

"But he keeps it longer when you're around. That's an important distinction to make."

"Exactly. My point is . . ." I don't really have one. I'm just mad. And sad. And mad. And whenever I'm around Dad, he makes me think of home, and that makes me think of being Normal, and that makes me remember I'm not anymore. "My point is, I guess I thought we'd be together forever."

Dad shifts in his seat before clearing his throat. "You know, Dane has been a zombie a lot longer than you have. I think . . . Well, maybe he knows a little more about the word *forever* than you do at this point."

I look past him to the poster of a surfer on the wall just over his head. It's so ridiculous, yet he put it there the minute the Sentinels gave it to him. I guess he figured something is better than nothing or maybe he just wanted to spite the Sentinels or maybe he's a closet surf dawg. Who knows?

I refocus on him. "Forever or not forever, I thought we had something special."

He nods. "I could see that. Of course you did. You don't go through something like what you kids went through and not have something special. Have you talked to him about your feelings?"

"I haven't had a chance. Courtney's never away from his side."

Dad narrows his eyes. "He's a Sentinel now. He can certainly choose where and when he roams about."

"That's my point. I'd like to say it was all Courtney's fault, but it's Dane I blame the most."

He furrows his brows, making the birthday hat on his head shift a little starboard. "Who's Courtney?"

"The blonde zombie."

He nods, and it lists. "Oh."

I look in the kitchen and see some extra plates and napkins he never brought out.

His lips purse.

"Did you tell Dane about my rebirthday party?"

"Maddy, listen—"

"Did you?"

"He's very busy. He's not in training anymore, you know."

I grit my teeth and shove the words out. "Did you *invite* him?"

"Yes, I did. He said they'd be by if they could make it."

My dead stomach tightens like a corkscrew. "They?"

Dad looks down into his coffee cup, which I notice is empty. "He and his Sentinel Supporter."

I groan. Out loud. Then I do it again, even louder.

He smiles, reaching for my hand. "I just wanted you to have a nice rebirthday party."

I soften a little; it's not Dad's fault Dane's being a total tool to the nth degree. "I am."

He snorts, standing to pour more coffee. He looks at his watch and reaches for the cream on the counter.

I'm suddenly standing.

"Leaving so soon?" he asks, already grabbing his

lab coat.

I smile. "I thought we could go see Stamp. Didn't you say Zerkers have an easier time eating Normal food? Something about their metabolism?"

He grabs another Twinkie and a spare birthday hat from the kitchen counter. "They pretty much burn through everything we give them," Dad says excitedly, leading me into the hall.

The bright fluorescent lights reflect off the foil in his own birthday hat, which I conveniently forget to tell him he's still wearing.

"So, yes, a Twinkie is certainly not going to clog his pipes, if you know what I mean."

Chapter 4
Stamp Tramp

I KEEP THE Twinkie behind my back the whole time they're moving Val to the observation bay in the back wing of Dad's lab. It takes Dad two random Sentinels plus his lab partner, Hector—a giant Sentinel he recruited his first week in Sentinel City—to wrangle Val from her cage.

There are chains and handcuffs and a big leather muzzle involved. Val watches me the entire time, not blinking, not smiling, not screaming like she was. Even with all the precautions, Dad steers clear.

Suddenly her back is to me and she's doing that awkward ankle-chain shuffle you see prisoners do when they're walking out of the courthouse on *Gavel TV.* She's in hospital scrubs, green and ill fitting, and her white-blonde hair is limp and soft and fine against her scalp. She looks small between the two towering Sentinels, particularly Hector, who is like Lurch on steroids. But I know firsthand that looks can be deceiving and behind those yellow Zerker eyes is a mind burning with ways to tear me—and everyone else in the room—limb from limb.

But not tonight, biotch. Not on my rebirthday!

When Val is in the other room, Dad turns around and nods at me, then shuts the door behind him and locks it tight.

Suddenly it's just me and Stamp in the outer lab. I tap in the six-digit code on his keypad, and the cage door hisses open.

He looks at it doubtfully, as if he doesn't believe I'm here or he thinks it's all a trick.

I sit back on a stool next to the table across from his cage, finally sliding the snack cake out from behind my back. I look at it, frowning. It's all mashed up. I must have gotten a little tense there, watching Val led away, her eyes on me the entire time. I thought I was immune to it, or at least used to it, by now. All these months after she tried to kill Stamp and me, I guess I'm still a little stressed out over the whole thing.

But Stamp doesn't know any better. And, really, can you actually *damage* a Twinkie? I tear open the plastic wrap.

At the first smell of sugar and pastry and God knows how many preservatives, Stamp inches from the cage, no longer suspicious, and reaches for it greedily. His hand stops just above the cake, and he looks to me for approval.

I know Dad and Hector have been working on his manners, so I nod and say gently, "It's okay, Stamp. It's yours. It's for you."

Say no more. He snatches it up, neon-yellow crumbs flying everywhere as he jams it into his maw, smacking and slurping like it's his first taste of brains after I yanked him out of his grave and fed them to him from a picnic basket.

The Twinkie's gone in a heartbeat. Finding nothing left, he licks his fingers, then the plastic wrap. He picks a few crumbs off his scrubs, which are white now to signify he's in recovery.

I don't know exactly how one recovers from being bitten by a Zerker, but if anyone can, it's Stamp. I used to think he was just another jock chump, a pretty boy with good manners and a roving eye, but now I know that beneath his broad shoulders and hairless chest lies a heart that would stop at nothing to keep beating.

Or *not* beating, as the case may be.

I've been through some pretty harsh stuff in the last year but nothing compared to poor Stamp. He stands here, nothing left to lick, looking me up and down as if I'm his next Twinkie. I spot the spare birthday hat Dad left on the slate counter and hand it to him.

He holds it gently, rolling it over in his hand. It's pink and green, all shiny foil with glitter sprayed everywhere. Dad must have asked for birthday hats and the Sentinels came back with the most ghastly, girly, neon, 1970s things ever. That anyone could still be making these horrid hats kind of boggles my mind. I wouldn't put it past the Sentinels to literally build a machine and go back in time just to spite Dad.

But Stamp appears to like it, probably because it's big and shiny and pretty and shiny. "What . . . What do I do with it?"

Lately with him, everything is a question. Don't get me wrong; it's a lot better than when we first got here six months ago, when it was all grunts and groans and later half words and almost words and just plain wrong words. But after months of working with Dad one-on-one—speech and cognition therapy and relearning—he's got to be about as good as he'll ever be.

"Put it on your head. Like this." I demonstrate with an invisible hat. He watches carefully, as if it's the most important thing in the world. It kind of breaks my heart how important things are for him now, daily little chores and habits I take for granted.

"Okay." He puts it over his bristly black hair. It complements his pale face, gaunt cheeks, and half-yellow, half-black eyes.

He's still good-looking. I mean, would he scare a room full of Normals if he walked in right now? Sure, no doubt. But if you sit with it awhile, if you let his features marinate, he's still handsome in a kind of gothic way. What's more, he's here, still kicking, after getting the worst of it from day one.

Why is he still here? The Sentinels don't trust Stamp—that's for sure—but they need him. He's one of the few zombies ever to survive a Zerker bite. Part of the reason they keep Dad around, I suspect, is the work he's done getting Stamp back on his feet, figuratively and literally.

Still, I knew the boy Stamp, and he was funny and bright, his alabaster skin flawless, his lips

45

plump, his hair thick and shiny with a Superman curl dangling in front of his unlined forehead. Now he looks rough and weathered, as if he's aged a decade in the last year.

He will never be a pretty boy again, but there is something ghastly cool about him, particularly in his innocent eyes and gentle gestures. I know the Zerker blood lurks inside him, dormant and unkind. Dad's warned me a hundred times about how strong Stamp is now, how quick he is to anger, how violent he is when upset, but I haven't seen it. Not yet. And though Dad is the only Normal I still trust, part of me just doesn't believe it.

Not Stamp. Not *my* Stamp.

"How's it feel?" I ask, chuckling.

He keeps moving the birthday hat around to center it, even though there's a little elastic string he could fix under his chin to keep it in place. But I know it would take an atlas, three laptops, a topographical map, and a compass to explain it to him, and I don't have that kind of patience tonight.

"It feels shiny," he says without a trace of a smile.

I want to laugh, but I don't because his feelings get hurt easily now that he's more aware he's not like all the other zombies in Sentinel City.

"It *is* shiny."

Well, it *is*.

He smiles. He sits on a bench between his cage and Val's, his long legs splayed out in front of him like a kid's.

"How do you feel tonight?"

"Better." He looks toward the back of the lab at the closed door: beyond the big glass window, Dad's shining a light in Val's eyes; the muzzle's still wrapped around her jaw. "Better now," he says.

I nod, knowing what's next.

"When are you taking me out of here?" He sounds almost but not quite whiny, like a kid the first time he asks if he can open his new toy on the way home from the store, knowing his parents will say no a dozen more times before they finally pull up in the driveway and give in.

"Soon, Stamp. Soon." My face is stony, as always. I avoid his yellowish eyes, as always. I kind of regret coming here. Then I look at the hat drooping off his head and smile.

"You said that yesterday."

I shake my head. "I didn't see you yesterday."

"You said that two yesterdays ago."

Another head shake. Here we go. "Okay, but I'm

not in charge. Remember? Maddy doesn't run Sentinel City. Other people do, and I guess they kind of like it with you in here for now."

Is that insulting?

It's kind of insulting, I know, but Stamp is weird. Things that would insult pretty much anyone else on the planet—you know, like "They want to keep you locked up because you're crazy strong and can't really control yourself anymore"—don't even faze him. But then things you don't think will insult him do. Like when I said, "You look better," and he growled, "Better than *what*?"

This time Stamp just grins. "But you're nice. You could help me if you wanted to." He waits a beat before twisting the knife of guilt just a little more. "If you *really* wanted to."

"I do want to, Stamp. But it's not up to me."

He sighs, looking around the room. I know he'd cry right now if he could. His chin even starts to quiver a little and suddenly I feel like a mom dropping her kid off on the first day of kindergarten. "When will you come again?"

I smile. That's so like him, to ruin a good moment by asking when there will be another good moment. "But . . . I'm still here, right?"

His chuckle is like a dry cough. "I know, but it makes me happy to think of when you'll be here again."

Actually, that's kind of logical. Maybe Stamp's not slow—just very, very philosophical.

"I'll be back soon, Stamp." Before he can ask again, I quickly add, "Tomorrow. Or the next day. But let's enjoy now."

He nods. "Good idea. Let's enjoy now." He looks around again, as if I'm hiding a pony or maybe a Christmas tree. "How do you want to enjoy it?"

I snort. "Just sit here. Talk to me. We have a lot to catch up on."

"Here we go." He sighs.

"How much do you remember?"

"Not much."

"*How* much?"

"I remember you and me. That's how much."

"Where?"

He scratches his head, feeling the hat. He takes it off, smiling at it in his lap. He doesn't try to put it back on, and I wonder if it's because he's forgotten how or because he's punishing me for spoiling his fun. "Away from here."

I nod eagerly. "That's right. Before we came here."

He smirks. "You were fun then. Not like now."

I can't argue with him there. "*Why* was I fun then?"

Stamp looks down, rolling the hat over and over in his bony fingers. "Because I wasn't like this then."

Ouch. "Were *you* fun then?"

"Funner than I am now."

I notice that my voice has become low, probably because it's at its most nonthreatening then. "How come?"

He looks toward the back of the long, sterile room, and I turn, following his gaze.

Val is looking at us through the lab door window, eyes big and yellow over her leather muzzle. One sleeve is rolled up, and Dad's taking a sample of her Zerker blood.

I look away and find Stamp staring back at me.

"Her," he says softly, as if she might hear. "*She* took my fun away."

I grit my teeth, knowing I shouldn't but saying it anyway: "Yes, Stamp. Yes, she did." I meet her stare. "She took *all* our fun away."

The birthday hat is crushed between Stamp's hands. I know from the look in his eyes, he doesn't remember doing it. I stand.

He shakes his head. "A little longer, please?"

I sit back down and open my mouth to say *all right*.

He shakes a finger at me. "No more questions, 'kay?"

I nod. "No more questions. Not tonight."

"'Kay," he says, smiling. "Let's just enjoy No More Questions Night."

I smirk.

We look at each other, knees almost touching, his expression soft and scared. I lean forward and touch his hand. He lets me; he doesn't always.

Maybe he knows tonight is special, after all.

Chapter 5
That's What Friends Aren't For

SUNLIGHT SPILLS THROUGH the high windows and across the gym floor. Vera says Sentinel City (not that *she* calls it that) used to be a community college. Though the walls are painted a generic light blue now, I can look at the sun dappling the crevices and easily picture taped-up signs saying things like Go, Team, Go! and a big American flag hanging from under the clock.

Basketball hoops are at either end, but they're in the raised position now. I've never seen them down, which is kind of weird. You'd think the Sentinels would have a team, maybe even a league. The Sentinels versus the Keepers, and the winners could get a bronze skull trophy. I'd pay to see that happen.

I turn the Eliminator over in my hand, making myself smile at fake team names, like the Sentinel Sizzlers, the Gore Globetrotters, the Crypt Keepers, the Undead . . . Undead . . . shoot. I got nothing basketball related that starts with *U*. Wait: Undead Underhanded? No, they'd never go for that. I don't even know if *underhanded* is a basketball term. Isn't that softball?

See, this is what happens when Vera's not around to stand there in her powder-blue beret, leaning against the gym wall, glaring me into decapitating a bunch of dummies against my will: I spend five minutes naming living dead basketball teams that don't even exist with words that may not even be basketball related.

I stretch in my gray sweatpants and matching top. Even when not wearing the actual Trainee uniform, I still have to wear Trainee colors. The Sentinels are big on uniforms. It's like a prep school where every class wears a different pattern of plaid skirt and matching tie clip or something. It doesn't get confusing so much as just so routine and blah.

I mean, just once I'd like to roam the halls and see some zombie shuffling around in skinny jeans and a faded Iron Maiden concert T-shirt under a flannel shirt, you know? Isn't that what zombies are *supposed* to wear? Sometimes I think Sentinels take being civilized a tad too far.

It was better when we first got here and I could roam in civilian clothes, but then Vera talked me into training to be a Keeper, and Dane went all Sentinel brainwash, and now . . .

It's just hard to believe how much has happened in one short year; that's all.

At first I thought Dad's rebirthday party was pretty lame, but now, a few days later, it's sinking in that I've been undead 365-plus days. Which, if you think about it, since we zombies never sleep, is more like 730 days. My days are twice as long as they ever were when I was Normal and I can do twice as much, although there's not a crap ton to do around Sentinel City besides try to avoid Dane and his Support Sleaze.

In other ways, though, it feels like a *lot* less time than that. I remember every moment of my last few days alive in vivid detail. What the cafeteria served for lunch the day I got struck by lightning (vegetarian chili and Mexican cornbread), where I bought the bra I wore to Stamp's party (at that little Flirt store in the mall, but only because Hazel gave me a gift certificate for my birthday), what the first drops of rain smelled like as they started falling on my way out that last night of my life (rain).

I've replayed that moment so many times in my head. It's like a movie that gets worn down from constant rewinding, but it all feels so real. I can practically reach out and touch it. It's like if I could just go back to Barracuda Bay and buy another bra from Flirt, I could get some great, cosmic do over and try again.

Weirdly, I remember those last few moments of being alive much more than the actual exciting stuff I've done since being undead. Like, you know, saving Barracuda Bay from a Zerker Armageddon. And rescuing Stamp from Val, the witch. And generally trying to keep Normals safe from the brain eaters and cerebellum slurpers, who are *way* more common than I ever thought possible.

And I remember the food! How much I loved food. Real food, junk food, fast food, hot food, Normal food. Dad being the typical workaholic single parent that he was, I did a lot of the cooking, which meant a lot of ordering in or picking up or driving through, and I got to know the value menus of most places in town on a first-name basis.

Sure, okay, I *tried* to eat as healthy as possible, but being lazy and rushed for time and always, always hungry, I pretty much ate whatever was fast and hot or greasy or iced or just plain *sounded* good. Still, there were some major standouts over the years.

What I wouldn't give to have a ginger and pine nut smoothie at the Shake Shack or a batch of sweet potato curly fries at the Burger Barn or even a basket of fried mushrooms at Dad's favorite rib shack, Sloppy Sam's. Now all I get is preshaped brain bars and chunky brain smoothies and seared brain nuggets.

I sigh and tighten my grip on the Eliminator. It looks so dull in my hand, just a black tube about the size of a kid's bike handle and, like a bike handle, with grips for my fingers on one side.

I look at the dummies scattershot throughout the gym. They're affixed to metal stands, their heads about the same height as my own. But they seem funny, these mostly realistic fleshy, rubber dummies on top of these stands that look like bar stools or something.

They're tougher than they look. You hear *rubber* and you think rubber ball or rubber raft, but these are more like rubber cement. I asked Vera once why we trained on such tough mannequins when

Zerkers are, after all, human flesh.

"You've battled them before," Vera said, conde-scendingly. "You know better. The older the Zerker, the tougher the hide."

"But why?" I pressed, just looking for a little rest and knowing the only way to get it was to lure her into a diatribe. For once, it worked.

"They're scavengers," she spat. "Murderers and grave robbers. Their diet is inconsistent and com-prised mostly of animal flesh, not brains. While we strive to eat brain regularly, their hides are more like sedimentary layers of their diets. The less brains they eat, the less alive their cells are and the more they petrify. The more they petrify, the tougher their skins. Which is why we train on these CPR dummies, who are as close an approximation to Zerker skin as I've ever seen."

I stretch my neck, at least as much as I can, then bend at the waist to touch my toes. Fat chance. I haven't touched my toes in at least nine months; I've gotten that stiff since my heart went offline. Still, Vera keeps me as limber as possible with these daily workouts.

Today she's meeting with the other Keepers at Sentinel City, so I'm alone in the giant gym. It's quiet. No one around but me and the dummies, literally. I focus, taking my place under the basket-ball net at the far end of the gym and crouching.

I'm in running shoes, which took the Sentinels three months to order for me. They're a little big, so I've tied them real tight and am wearing two pairs of socks. Pink socks because the Sentinels think all girls should wear pink socks all the time. Either that or they must be inexpensive, because the Sentinels are way cheap.

The sneakers squeak on the shiny gym floor as I move forward, pressing the button at the top of the Eliminator so that the ice pick slides out. With a thick, gassy pop, it plunges into the first dummy's ear. I pull it out, pressing the other button so the switchblade thwacks out.

Still moving, eyes open and wary, I slice the blade through the neck, straight through the PVC pipe up the middle, which Vera says replicates a spine, until the blade comes out the other end and—slurp—the head slides off the rubber chest, plopping onto the floor and rolling at my feet.

I'm about to move on to Dummy #2 when I hear stale clapping behind me. I turn, Eliminator held high, to find Dane standing just inside the double doors. He sees me wielding the lethal weapon and puts his hands up in a mock don't-hurt-me pose.

I smirk and press both buttons at the same time, sliding the sharp ends in so I'm not tempted to do just that. I lean against the dummy I've decapitated and watch Dane walk toward me.

His black beret is on tight, sticking like glue to his close-cropped hair. His cheeks are hollow, his eyes brooding, his shoulders looking broader than usual in his black fatigue shirt. The rubber boots give him a few inches of height and make him that much more impressive as he stalks in my general direction. As usual lately, he's not smiling at me.

Not even a little.

"Nice moves." He nods toward the fallen dummy head, lidless rubber eyes staring back at me mournfully.

"Thanks." My voice is as dead as if the dummy's head just said it.

He's close enough to extend a hand now, and I almost reach for it just as he says, "May I?"

And I know he's not asking for a dance. I hand him the Eliminator.

He turns it over affectionately in his hand. "They gave us these the first week of Sentinel training," he brags, fingertips caressing the buttons on either end. He pushes them both—snap! snap!—and the blades come out, one after the other, catching the waning sunlight in the gym. "Before we got the Tasers."

I roll my eyes. Stupid Sentinels and their Tasers, like it takes a ton of skill to stick an electric socket into a person's neck and squeeze a trigger until their eyes bug out and they slump, slack jawed, to the floor. I'm pretty sure even Stamp could do that. I'd say something clever, like *Whatever*, but I'm not really speaking to him at the moment.

He holds up the blade, looks at the row of dummies, and heads for the nearest one, sticking the switchblade into the ear and trying to slice through the neck with the ice pick. I snort and cover my mouth, but luckily the sound of him butchering the poor dummy's face covers up the sound.

Two minutes later, he's still chopping away at the PVC spine like it's a giant block of ice and he's an 1890s housewife trying to keep the milk and eggs cool.

I walk up behind him, careful to avoid the rain of rubber dummy chunks and say, "It's okay. You're just out of practice."

He smirks and gives up.

If only to put the poor dummy out of its misery, I grab the Eliminator and use the scalpel end to slice the rest of the head clean off, just like that.

"Guess so," he mumbles, shuffling over to the bleachers and taking a seat on the bottom row. He pats the seat next to him.

I roll my eyes and remain standing, thanks very much.

He leans back, resting against the bench behind him. "What's going on with you?"

"Me?"

"Yeah, that deal at Z-lunch yesterday, huffing off like that? Rude."

"What's rude, Dane, is that happened *three* whole days ago. You've waited this long to chew me out about it. Used to be a time you couldn't wait three *hours* to chew me out. Wait. That didn't come out right . . ."

His face is frumpled, almost like Stamp's for a minute there. "Three days?"

"Yeah."

"Wow. Well, still, friends don't treat friends like that."

"I agree."

Surprise slowly forms across his face. "Really?"

"Absolutely. Friends don't bring their new friends to sit with their old friends and practically lick tonsils at the lunch table. No, they don't."

Suddenly, it dawns on him. (And I thought Stamp was the slow one.) "That's what this is all about, then, is it? Courtney?"

"You tell me!"

His eyes get big.

I look down to see the Eliminator, locked and loaded, in my hand. When did *that* happen?

"Take it easy," he says, waving his hands.

I shake my head and click the blades back in, sliding the weapon into my pocket to avoid the temptation to stick an ice pick in his ear.

"I'm just saying, I can't believe you'd think there's anything between me and Courtney."

"I don't," I snap. "There isn't anything between you and Courtney, because she's always stalking you so hard there's not even room for air between you."

"Very funny."

I shake my head, emotion choking me. "That's just it. It's not funny. Whatever you're doing or not doing, it's not even anywhere near funny. You don't just drop people like that. Like . . . like . . ." I sweep my hands toward the corners of the gym, then back at myself. "Like *this*!"

He looks up at me, sad. "I'm not dropping you, Maddy. How juvenile. Things are different now.

I'm a Sentinel. You're a Trainee. Stamp's . . . Stamp. Everything's changed. Forever. You can't expect it to be like it was back then."

His words hit me so hard I take a step back. Literally, I stagger as if one of these dummies has come to life and nudged me. "What the hell does that even *mean*?"

He avoids my gaze again, making things even worse. "I just mean things change. People change. We're changing. Right now."

I can't believe this. Is he dumping me? Out loud? Without actually saying he's dumping me? Can he be that ludicrously chicken? "Have *you* changed? 'Cause I certainly haven't. Have you changed so much that you can't even come right out and tell me what you're talking about right now?"

Holy crap, this just keeps getting worse. How is this happening? Is this some joke? Is he sorry he didn't come to my rebirthday party the other night so he's punking me and any minute he'll smile and pull a Twinkie with a flickering candle out of one of his cargo pants pockets?

And he's so cool about it all, just sitting there, back against the bleacher, like we're talking about who gave the best pom-pom at the pep rally. "What do you want me to say?"

"Say the truth!" I hate the high, panic-stricken sound of my voice as it echoes off the gym walls. "Who *are* you all of a sudden? You're acting like we're strangers or something!"

Just then the gym doors open and Vera walks in, blue beret in hand. Dane is kind of obscured from her view by a dummy, and she's looking at just the one head on the floor.

I know she can't see him when she says, "Maddy, everything all right?"

"No," I blurt, voice cracking, something it hasn't done in months. "No, it's not."

Vera flashes me a quizzical look.

Dane stands then.

She looks at each of us. Slowly, as she does everything. Then it seems to click, and the fire comes into her severe eyes. "May I help you, young man?"

Dane takes off his beret quickly, and suddenly I remember. As a Keeper, Vera totally outranks his ass!

"No, no, I was just leaving."

"I'd say so," she huffs, watching him go. She turns back to me as the double doors crash in his wake. "Don't you have some heads to lop off?"

At first I'm kind of disappointed that she's not

all girl talk and women's lib and *We are family* and asking me about my man, but I nod and release the blades from the Eliminator.

Slicing through flesh-colored rubber up and down the gym floor, I realize a little decapitation is just what the doctor ordered.

Chapter 6
Scapegoat

I'M IN THE library, guiltily reading one of those *Why Women Like Men Who Don't Like Them Back and Never Will* books behind a women's magazine when a Sentinel team shows up. In the library. The quiet library. Loud and clacking and clomping.

Like . . . one of these things is not like the other.

At first I think they're friends of Dane's coming to break up with me on his behalf, since he never actually said the words the other day, or maybe even to sing me one of those he's-so-sorry-he's-a-dead-guy sing-a-gram viral video things, but they're in full battle gear with Tasers pulled and gleaming black shoulder pads (Dane once bragged they were his idea, and back then I believed him) clattering in the silent library.

The shortest one steps forward. His eyes are so glossy I can see myself in them, his cheeks so hollow I could cut the pages of my magazine with them. "Come with us."

I take an involuntary step back, shielding myself with the self-help book I've been hiding. "What? Whoa. What for?"

They're not playing. They lurch forward, and I freeze like some clueless chick in a B movie. Just like that. All my Keeper training bolts the minute I'm faced with three Sentinels and their snapping Tasers and cold eyes.

In seconds they've got my hands behind my back, one of those plastic zip ties slapped on so I can't move except to shuffle as they lead me out of the library and down the hall. The short one's out front; the taller ones are on either side of me. It's an easy formation, and I can tell they've practiced it a million times.

Dane too, probably, and I wonder why they didn't send him to get me. Or did he send them to get me? Does he have that power yet? To order Sentinels out to pick up his ex-girlfriend and scare her into forgiving him? And why does part of me—the dumb part, obviously—think that would be kind of a romantic gesture?

Out in the clamorous halls Sentinels are everywhere, all with their stun guns at the ready, all glowering at me like I've stolen the brain smoothie machine from the mess hall or something.

But this is no joke. Even the air feels serious, like the atoms themselves know not to play games. No one speaks, not so much as a word. Or grunts, which is the preferred means of Sentinel communication. Even their rubber boots barely squeak on the linoleum floor.

I've never seen it like this before. There must be some kind of drill all through Sentinel City, but did they have to actually cuff my wrists? They could have just said, "Here—wink-wink, nudge-nudge—walk with us and put your hands behind your back and pretend to be cuffed. It'll all be over in a minute." I would have been all over that. But no. Stupid Sentinels have to do everything by the book.

I see a blue blur of Keeper uniforms ahead of me in the midst of all the black Sentinel suits, but there's no Vera. I don't know any of the rest of them, and nobody's looking at me anyway, and it wouldn't matter if they did spot me, because my escort is just speeding along, stopping for nobody and nothing at all.

We pass the empty cafeteria, media room, gym, and locker rooms. Just as we're heading toward my dorm wing, we turn toward a hall I've never been down before.

It's quieter here, with fewer Sentinels and no Keepers in sight, but I soon see why. Half a dozen tall cages are at the end, gleaming metal like the ones inside Dad's lab that they keep Val or Stamp in.

But these seem creepier. Spending so much time around Val has made me feel like the only good cage is a full cage, and seeing an empty one—let alone a row of them—makes me feel very creeped out indeed.

My sneakers screech as I stop—or try to. It's like one of those cheesy tween TV shows with their canned laugh tracks and bright colors, where two friends are dragging the cool kid on a blind date where he just knows the girl is going to have braces and pigtails and freckles and glasses and he does everything in his power to stop from being delivered to his doom, like he's some kind of catch and that would be just so horrible or something, hanging on to open locker doors and clinging to the water fountain and . . . hilarity ensues.

You know the type.

But there are no locker doors or even water fountains to cling to, and we just keep streaming ahead, the Sentinels yanking my arms as I struggle to lean back, knowing there can be only one reason for the cages.

"What . . . Where are you taking me?"

In reply, the Sentinel to my left pulls me faster down the hall. The one on the right goes even quicker, more gung ho than the first, so I get a little turned around like when you're rowing a boat and your right hand rows faster than your left and you keep going in circles just a little bit until you get the hang of it.

The short one pulls out a jingling keychain and opens one of the cages. They toss me in face-first, slamming the door before I can turn around and press them for answers.

"Wait! Please. Just . . . just tell me what's going on."

They don't even look at me, clomping down the hallway and leaving me in the cage, fuming, worried now because what the hell kind of drill *is* this where they not only strap your hands behind your back but throw your butt in a cage?

I pace, looking to my left, farther down the long, dark hall. Nothing but cages as far as I can see, and I look pretty far. To my right, a few more cages, all of them empty.

My Eliminator is in one of my front pockets, heavy on my calf. There's no way I can reach it with my hands behind my back or I'd use it to cut myself loose right now. The cages are built of heavy wire mesh, stiff and sharp. It might work if I backed against one side and ran the plastic tie up and down, but I could take off half my wrist in the process and, really, what's the use? There's no way I'm getting out even with my hands free. If Val hasn't been able to do it in all these months, as ticked off and full of Zerker rage as she is, how am I supposed to do it on my first try?

Why couldn't they have sent Dane to get me? He's an actual Sentinel now. At least he would have told me something. Possibly. Or not. I don't know anymore. Maybe being a Sentinel is more important than being a boyfriend. Hell, more important than being a friend. I hear more footsteps at the other end of the hall, crane my neck, and see a field of blue: Vera!

She's followed by two more Sentinels. No, one Sentinel Support in her black-and-gray uniform and one Sentinel in black, clattering battle gear.

Dane! At last! And Courtney, of course. What is this? Some elaborate prank? *Hey, yeah. Sorry. Dane didn't break up with you badly enough the first time, so now we're going to include all of Sentinel City in it, 'kay, thanks, bye!*

"Vera! What's going on?" My voice is high and harsh in the long, echoey hall.

Vera looks paler than usual, which is saying something. Her expression is tighter than usual, which, again, is saying something. "Maddy, listen to me. Before you say anything, listen to what I'm saying first. Can you do that?"

"Not if you keep talking in riddles," I half joke, but the awkward pause that follows and her no-nonsense zombie librarian face make me swallow. Hard. "Okay, yes, of course. Just . . . tell me something!"

I flash a helpless look to Dane, but he's gazing at the ground or his shoes or something cute Courtney wrote on them (like maybe *Snuggles to my Sugar Bear*) while she was shining them this morning.

I glance at Vera, who inches forward as if she knows Dane is distracting me, forcing me to look into her deep eyes. Finally, she speaks, and what she says makes me wish she'd kept her mouth shut: "Val is missing. And your father."

I crouch at the very back of my cage, rocking to and fro as shaky images flicker before my eyes. "Not again," I hear my squeaky voice say. "Not . . ." I focus on Vera's face, which looks slightly angry, slightly sad.

I rush toward the front of the cage. "How could this happen? She's locked up 24/7/365."

But she's not. Even as I say the words, I know they're a lie. Just the other night, during my rebirth-day party, Dad had her out, muzzled and chained and shackled and all. Sure, there were three Sentinels guarding her, but she was still out of her cage. How many times did he do that a day, a week, a month?

I think back to my rebirthday and how she acted while I was there. So quiet, so docile, her yellow Zerker eyes on me the whole time, even as they led her away into the back room. Had she been plotting something all along? Watching me?

Warning me?

I'm staring past Vera, at the off-white wall over her head, when she rattles some keys and opens the cage. I start forward and she puts a firm hand on my chest.

"I need you to behave, Maddy. The Sentinels are

on high alert, and they're blaming your father for what happened. I'd tread carefully if I were you."

So that's why every Sentinel has been giving me major stink eye.

"Dad? Why?"

I guess I push forward a little, jutting my chest out, not even realizing it until she slips the electric pen from her top pocket.

"I said behave. We can do this the hard way, you know." She waves the pen, and I freeze. "But I'd rather you be conscious for this."

"Okay, okay." I back away instinctively, having been on the pen's receiving end one too many times. "I'm sorry. I just . . . Why Dad?"

We start walking, right past Dane and his concubine.

"He's been in charge of Val since the day we brought her back here," Vera explains, leading me through a sea of Sentinels, all going in the opposite direction. "Who else would they blame?"

She has a point. Why the Sentinels—or the Keepers, for that matter—trusted a mortal, the only Normal in all of Sentinel City, with the proper care, feeding, and study of a Zerker-killing machine with spiky hair and the worst attitude on the planet is beyond me. I guess it wasn't such a great idea. And of course no one's going to blame the folks at the top, just the guy with the heartbeat.

We head toward Dad's lab. My hands are still tied tight behind my back, making it awkward to walk, especially with Sentinels flying by at the speed of sound and joyously bumping into me every few feet.

A group of Keepers approaches, waving Vera down. She pauses, partly ignoring me for 6.2 milliseconds, and I bolt toward Dad's lab.

Dane catches up, putting a hand on my shoulder. Strange that after all we've been through together in the last year, it already feels so unfamiliar. "Careful," he says, looking back at Vera, making a phony smiley face in her general direction, waving a fraudulent it's-okay-all's-well hand. "You don't want to give her a reason to use that pen."

"What do you care?"

He ignores me. "Listen, before she gets back, there's something you should know . . ." He inches close.

Courtney's off to one side, looking nervous or jealous or both or neither—but who cares?

"What? Hurry, Dane. What?"

"Your dad's not exactly missing. Not. Exactly."

"Where is he?"

"They don't know for sure." His eyes are wide but sympathetic, which scares me because he kind of only looks that way when something has gone horribly wrong and he's powerless to stop or fix it. "They're taking you . . . to identify his body—"

"Or what's left of it," Courtney interrupts.

He shoots her a look, but it's not half as hard as the laser beams I'm shooting her from my searing eye holes. "Shut up," we both shout.

It takes all of Dane to stop me from head butting her into the next afterlife or the nearest wall, whichever comes first.

Vera comes up then, yanking me away by one arm. "Here now, what's all this?"

"Why didn't you tell me about my dad?" I huff, following her toward the lab.

She glares at Dane.

He glares at me.

But what's the difference? Normal dads who might be corpses trump all the living dead, period, ad infinitum.

"You didn't give me time," she sputters.

We're almost at the lab now, Sentinels filtering in and out like they know what the hell they're doing.

The lab door is off the hinges, hanging half in,

half out of the hallway.

Vera wades in, says a few words from her tight lips, and the Sentinels scram, just like that.

Dane and I look at each other, impressed, until I notice half of his face is covered by Courtney's wilted blonde hair since they're standing so flippin' close together.

I step into the lab, not wanting to.

The first thing I notice is the smell: part chemical, part fleshy rot. The second is the big puddle on the floor. "What is that?" I ask, stepping over it to follow Vera into the lab.

She points to the open door of the tanning booth from Cabana Charly's. "It used to cover this. Remember?"

The glass door is open, the bottom of it leaking something slimy onto the ground. That's the smell. Avotoxia. Val used it to turn some poor Zerker into bones and goo back home.

"Why is this open? Who would use it?"

"That's why you're here. We think . . ." Vera turns to me, actually putting her hands on my shoulders—and not to zap me with her pen. "We think your father's in there. We need you to identify the body."

"What body?" The floor of the tanning booth is covered in white slime, greasy foam dripping down the walls, bone fragments in a heap rising out of the sludge in the bottom.

She has an Eliminator on her and presses one of its buttons, using the switchblade side to snap my bonds. I rub my wrists, even though they don't hurt. Having watched every single season of *Law & Disorder: CVU*, I just feel it's the thing to do. Besides, I'm none too eager to find out what's in that decomposing guck at the bottom of the tanning booth.

I look around for something long and metal to use and find an old pointer Dad uses to teach his assistant, Hector, about chemicals and cells on the big whiteboard in the corner. (It never really works, but I think it makes Dad feel better to be sharing science with someone again and probably makes Hector feel pretty good to not have Dad yelling at him for a few minutes every day.)

I kneel, and Vera follows, snatching my hand back. "Careful, Maddy. The avotoxia is still strong enough to turn your hand into . . . that." She nods toward the steaming soup.

I flip the metal pointer up at her. "That's what this is for."

She nods but passes me some industrial-strength black rubber gloves just the same. Looking around the room, I see a few Sentinels wearing them as well. I slip them on, then take the pointer and dig around the mush.

It makes smacking noises as I shift the pile, and the smell is overpowering. It's like the bones have been marinated in hell for six months and then spray painted with skunk funk, a million rotting banana skins, and Dumpster juice. I gag repeatedly on the avotoxia fumes, flashing back to when I was in a booth like this one not so long ago but very far away.

I smear the bones around, looking closely, then stand, sighing.

Vera's lips are so thin by this point they're almost nonexistent. It makes me kind of happy to think she's sad about losing Dad.

"So?" she asks.

"That's not my dad in there. He had a hip replacement a few years back, pure titanium, about the size of a tennis ball. It's not in there."

"Thank God!" Dane blurts, and I don't even think he realizes he's doing it, which makes my dead heart do whatever a dead heart can do when it feels like beating out of its chest but can't.

80

Vera just puts a hand on my arm, squeezes, and then lets go, her own personal version of *Thank God!*

The relief is overwhelming. I lean against the long lab counter and let the pointer clang to the ground, quickly followed by the rubbery flop-flop of my gloves.

And I realize as I stand there, smiling, looking at Val's empty cage, that Stamp is gone. And that I've been so worried about Dad, so focused on finding out what happened to him, that I never even stopped to ask Vera where he might be.

It's not Dane or Vera who ends the celebration.

Courtney clears her throat. "So if that's not her dad in there, then who *is* it?"

Chapter 7
Better off Dead

A SUDDEN COMMOTION stops me from almost wringing her neck for a second time as a team of Sentinels wrestles something out of the back supply closet.

I hear that telltale Fourth of July snap-snap-snap of Tasers going off and the whump of a body falling to the ground. Rushing to join them, Vera at my side, I see Dad curled in a fetal position on the floor, a yellow tie shoved in his mouth, his hands secured in front of him with his own belt.

He's ticked off. I can see it even from halfway across the lab. His forehead is sweaty, and whatever hair he has left is damp and smeared around his high forehead and he's kicking and shouting through his tie.

"Get him out of there," I shriek, snatching Vera's Eliminator and sprinting toward him.

A Sentinel tries to stop me.

Rather than fight him, I literally dive past his outstretched arms like I'm sliding into home plate. I land next to Dad, turning over with practiced precision to slice his leather belt in half.

He takes his hands, both of them, and claws at his mouth, dragging the tie out with a gag and a cough and another gag. He rises to one knee, Tasers sputtering all around him. We look up to find ourselves surrounded by just about every Sentinel in the room and some who came in from the hall just to join the fun.

"Get after her," he shouts, first thing, looking at them. "What are you wasting time on me for? Go. Now! She can't have gone far."

"Dad, what happened?"

He slumps onto his rump, breathing heavily, face red. He looks up.

I hiss at the Sentinels, "Give him some room!"

Amazingly, they shrink back a step or two, letting him rest against a set of cabinets. He looks at me and Vera, who's crouching by my side. "We were taking her out of the cage for some more tests," he wheezes, sliding an arm across his sweaty forehead.

"Who was?" Vera says.

"Hector and I. We . . ."

"*Just* Hector and you?" Vera's eyes narrow.

He flashes her an impatient look. "Yes, we had called for the Sentinels, as always, but when they didn't show after a few minutes, we decided to move her ourselves."

Vera shakes her head. "But that's not protocol."

Dad and I both look at her.

"Are you kidding me?" he blurts. "Is it protocol for the Sentinels to take so long? Is it protocol for me to have to check with them every time I tie my shoe or zip my pants? I'm doing important work here, and they've never respected it. Not once. I can't test Val properly if she's in a cage all the time."

Vera stands, smirking. "Well, she's not in her cage anymore, Dr. Swift."

"I know that." Hand on his scalp, he shakes his head miserably. "Don't you think I know that?"

"Dad," I say, reaching out to touch his knee, "who is that back there in the tanning booth?"

"Hector," he moans, looking at me through swollen eyelids. "He tried to put the muzzle on her while I put her handcuffs on, and she bit him, tore his thumb clean off, and swallowed it whole before she had him on the floor, his Taser in hand. She made him take the tarp off the tanning booth and get inside, and the second the door slammed shut, she sprayed him, sizzled him down to the bones. I thought she'd do the same to me, but she tied me up and shoved me where nobody could see me."

I look up at Vera. "See, it *was* an accident."

"Of course it was an accident," he sputters, looking from me to her and back at me again. "Who said it wasn't an accident?"

"Dr. Swift, when exactly did this happen?"

"At 10:17. I noted the time on her chart before we opened her cage."

Vera turns to the Sentinels.

They snap to attention before she even speaks.

"Alert the border patrols that she's been gone for over two hours. Clear the halls. I want every available Sentinel after her immediately, no excuses."

They grumble, and one finds a walkie-talkie and relays the message.

While Vera coordinates, I lean in. "Dad, the other cage. It's empty. Where's Stamp?"

He smiles, then nods toward the second supply

closet.

I feel another wave of relief shudder through my dead cells, a distant Normal emotion trapped in there somewhere like phantom adrenaline haunting my veins.

I stand and make a move to open the closet.

Vera yanks me back. "Let them do it. When will you get it through your head that he's still a Zerker?"

"Not as much as he used to be," Dad croaks. "That's . . . What do you think I've been doing here? Why do you think Val was so important to me, to you, to everyone here? By studying her cellular structure, I've been able to isolate some of what makes zombies and Zerkers so different from each other. I've been working with Stamp, giving him regular injections at his brain stem to phase out the Zerker cells, healing him, in effect. Not curing him, exactly, but as close as he'll ever get, I'm afraid."

He looks at me, almost apologetically, before turning back to Vera. "I think that's why she left him behind this time. She could tell they had nothing in common and he was of no use to her anymore."

The Sentinels have the door open and Stamp is there, not tied up, not gagged, just standing quietly in the corner of the supply closet, waiting next to a yellow mop handle. As if he knew we'd be there all along. He looks so shy and sad.

"Stamp," I cry, lurching for him.

Vera yanks me back again.

"It's okay, Stamp," I say from the sidelines. "You're safe now. It'll all be fine."

He offers me a small smile before the Sentinels gather him up. They are rough, and the anger starts in the back of my throat, a kind of low, dull hum.

Dad notices and reaches for my hand.

"Maddy, I'm sorry."

Vera looks down at us both, a note of sadness in her voice. "Dr. Swift, I assure you, you have no idea what sorry means, but you will."

I stand, turning to her. "What does that mean?"

She swivels, signaling to the Sentinels. In less than ten seconds, I have my hands behind my back again, my wrists tied. We all do: Stamp, Dad, and I. They lead us out of the shattered lab. The Sentinels in the halls pause, letting us pass, watching us with hooded eyes.

They take us back to that long passageway, the dark one with all the cages. They put Dad in the first one, skip one, put Stamp in the third, skip one, and put me in the fifth.

I notice Vera's not with us. She must've stayed behind in the lab.

The Sentinels lock us in and storm off.

All but one. A tall, grim specimen who looks like he's been dead a long, long time. He watches us carefully, looking from one to the next, then back again.

I look down the hall, to the first cage. "Dad?"

He mumbles something that sounds like *sorry* twice, then nothing more.

"Dad!" I need him to talk to me.

After the third or fourth "Dad!" Stamp turns to me, eyes yellowy black. "Leave him alone," he hisses, inching as close to me as his cage will allow. "He'll talk when he's ready. Can't you see he's not ready?"

Chapter 8
"Be Careful What You Wish For . . ."

THEY COME FOR Dad first.

It's night. Or day. I can't really tell anymore. I tried counting for a while but gave up after I got all the way to 4,987 seconds and Stamp said something pointless to wreck my concentration.

We've been showered and fed in preparation of our appointment, as Vera keeps calling it. Now we're in gray hospital scrubs, all of us, even Dad. His are a little snug, and he keeps fussing with his shirt where it rests awkwardly on his little potbelly. Every time he does, my eyes go to the plastic ties around his wrists and I wince, half guilty, half angry.

Guilty for bringing him to Sentinel City in the first place; angry that they think he had something to do with Val escaping. It's been less than a day since the first team of Sentinels yanked me out of the library, which means this must be a pretty big deal. I don't think the Elders usually move this fast.

The Elders don't stay here at Sentinel City all the time. They're too valuable to keep all in one place— in case the Zerkers ever found out. Dane says they're from all over the south—Florida, Georgia, Tennessee, South Carolina—so they must have some pull to get here this fast. Either that or a few private jet pilot zombies on standby at all times.

"Maddy?" Dad says in a trembling voice, the first word he's spoken to me since they caged him.

It's hard to hear over the clanging of the keys and the door and the clattering of the Sentinels' shoulder pads.

"Honey," he shouts, high and strange. I can't tell if he's mad or scared. "I'm fine. Don't worry. I didn't do anything wrong. Nothing's going to happen to me. To Stamp. To you. Nothing at all."

"I know," I shout, wishing Stamp would move out of the way a little so I could get a better view of what's happening. I hear the clomping of the Sentinels' boots, the jingling of keys, Dad grunting as they drag him out roughly, the way they do everything all the time.

I see a shock of gray hospital scrubs amidst all the Sentinel black, the back of Dad's balding head, but that's about it.

"Vera," I shout, seeing a flash of powder-blue beret in the mix. But as I inch closer to my door, I see it's not her at all, just some other Keeper who doesn't even look back as Dad's pulled away.

"Dad! Say something."

But he never does. Or, if he does, they have him muzzled or, worse, a Sentinel is clamping his dead hand over his mouth, which isn't much fun when your lips are the same temperature but has to be absolutely grosstastic when you're 98.6 degrees Fahrenheit.

The Sentinels never frisked me. I don't know if that was Vera's doing or if it was because I'm a girl or if they're just lazy, but either way I still have my Eliminator on me, wedged into the little fold at the top of my hospital scrubs. Although I can't reach it with my hands tied in front of me this time, I can rub my wrist against it every so often. I know it probably wouldn't help against a team of Sentinels, but it makes me feel good just to have it there, slim, sturdy, and violent.

I pace my cage. The hall's empty except for Stamp, who paces with me.

"Quit doing that," I hiss.

He gives me his surprised look, as if he didn't think I'd get ticked off at him matching me step for step. "I will when you will."

So I stop, thinking he'll lose interest, like a kid you've played peekaboo with too long and now they want to play Marco Polo and then hide-and-seek. But I can't stand still and start pacing again. He follows, loping with his long cricket legs.

God, how I wish he were the old Stamp, even the jerk Stamp I lived with in Orlando. At least I could talk to him then, in between the living skanks he rotated through like a rock star. A cup of coffee here, a morning walk there, a break between performances of the *Great Movie Monster Makeover Show*. We could at least converse, share a few civil words, even a smile, though we were exes.

I try, just to see what might happen. I stop pacing and lean toward the bars of my cage that are closest to his. "What do you think they're doing to him, Stamp?"

He stops too, leaning in. "Doing what? To who?"

I stare back at him, unblinking. "To Dad. To

my dad, who's been taking care of you all this time."

He nods, eyes growing small. "I know that." Then, a few seconds later, "I knew that already."

I grunt. So much for that. I turn to pace again.

He mumbles something.

"What'd you say, Stamp?"

He glowers at me. "I said, I wonder how *he* likes it in a cage."

I smack the bars, close to his face.

He doesn't flinch. Not even a little.

"That's not nice, Stamp. Not nice at all."

He doesn't say anything.

I turn, afraid I will. Then I turn back: "He was just trying to protect you. That whole time. Me too."

He glares back, indifferent, unmoving.

I wave him off and walk away.

We pace some more, maybe a few minutes, maybe a few hours. It's hard to tell with no windows or watches or doors. I hear the clomping of Sentinel boots down the hall before he does, so I'm watching his face until—pop—his eyes open wide when at last he hears them too.

"Hey," he says, moving closer. "Hey, Maddy, I'm . . . I'm sorry." His fingers are out as far as they will stretch from his side of the cage.

I push mine out until our fingertips touch the outside of the empty cage between us, barely. It's almost like we're really touching. Better, probably. Less sad this way than feeling his cold skin against my own.

"I know you are."

"Away," a Sentinel says, rattling his keys to open Stamp's door.

I back up, thinking it might be better for Stamp, but now he clings to the bars of his cage, looking at me, eyes wide as the Sentinels pry him off and drag him out the door.

I expect him to cry out, but once he leaves the cage, a sense of calm seems to wash over him and he never turns back.

The blur of black Sentinel shoulder pads and Stamp's bristly hair masks a quiet blue presence lurking at the end of the hall.

It inches forward after Stamp's removal.

"Vera?" I ask, sagging against the bars as if the afterlife's just gone out of me.

I told myself I'd be strong. That whatever was happening, I'd be tough for Dad and Stamp. I'd act like I knew what was going on, that it was all normal procedure: nothing to see here, move on. But after

Dad left and didn't come back, and now Stamp, I've got nothing left.

I just slouch there and wait for her to say something, anything.

"Yes, Maddy." She appears across from my cage door, leaning against the off-white cinder block wall.

"Where's Dad? Where are they taking Stamp?"

"For sentencing. The Council of Elders is giving sentence. You know that. I told you."

I stand up straight, pacing again. "And what's the sentence?"

She shifts against the wall. "You know I can't tell you that."

"Then why are you here? If you can't tell me anything, I mean."

"I came to check on you. Before . . ."

I stop pacing.

She pushes off the wall, steps closer.

We both hear the Sentinel boots trudging down the hall toward us.

"Before they come for you." She sounds almost glad.

I look to the right of me, to the empty cages where Dad and then Stamp once stood. Before they came for them.

"I'm not coming back here, am I?"

She shakes her head, looking toward the Sentinels' footsteps.

"Good." I'm pressed against the bars now, her face an arm's reach away if only I could fit more than a few fingers between these stupid bars and wire mesh. "Because whatever happens, Vera—outside these bars, down that hall, with the Elders, whatever it is, whatever the sentence—no one's ever going to put me in a cage again."

Vera looks at me as she opens the door, voice as cold as her ashy skin. "Be careful what you wish for."

Chapter 9
Vanished

THERE ARE NO CPR dummies in the gym this time. The air of finality that fills the vast room means there probably aren't going to be a whole lot of CPR dummies in my future.

Midafternoon sunlight filters in from the windows high above the raised basketball hoops. Vera and a team of Sentinels lead me inside so slowly, as if we're at some kind of funeral or something. And maybe we are. Who knows?

As always, I shiver at the sight of the withered Elders seated at the far end of the gym at fold-up picnic tables well below their station in life, or afterlife. Behind them, just as with the first time we were introduced, stands an elite team of what I call Super

Sentinels, kind of like Elder Bodyguards. All they do is follow the Elders around.

The Elders watch me approach, hands tied in front of me. The room is eerily silent except for the squawking of my shoes on the varnished gym floor. There is a single chair set up in front of the Council, and the Sentinels lead me to it.

I picture Dad walking in, sitting in this same chair. Looking at the Elders' skeletal faces and long, veiny necks, their coal-black eyes and popcorn-yellow teeth. What did they say to him? How did he respond?

Knowing Dad, he probably approached the meeting in a clinical manner, studying their skin, their nostrils, their eyelashes, wondering if I might look like that in three or four hundred years. The thought of Dad analyzing the Elders even as they chastised him almost makes me smile.

And then I think of Stamp. Right here in this chair. Did he know what was happening to him? Has he figured it out yet? And the $64,000 question: where did they both go after the Elders gave sentence?

The six Elders stare back at me, glossy eyes bulging out of their shrunken heads, frail but menacing in their identical white pajamas. I know they're probably not really pajamas, but that's what they look like—either that or karate uniforms, and why would they wear those?

Vera stays standing by my side after the Sentinels have shoved me into the chair and stepped away. She looks down at me, but I ignore her, so I don't know if she's scowling or shaking her head or what. Eventually, she approaches the Sentinels.

She turns and points to me (as if she could possibly be talking about anyone else; the bleachers, maybe?). "The third and final prisoner, gentlemen." That sounds so Vera. So precise, so clipped, so accurate.

They nod slowly, some imperceptibly.

One of the Elders in the center grunts. "What is she accused of, Keeper?" His voice is crackly.

I squirm a little and look away, but I can't miss any of this, because who knows when I might see the Elders again? Or anyone else, for that matter?

I sit up a little, hoping to hear Vera better.

"Maddy is the reason Dr. Swift, who allowed the Zerker to escape, is here, Elder."

"How is that possible, Keeper?"

"Elder, he is her father."

The Elder, who is obviously the ringmaster here, is fleshier than the rest, which means that rather than being 500 years old maybe he's only 300. He wears a blond wig. A good one but a blond one. I'll call him Blondie for that.

Blondie says, "How is it that she brought him here?"

"For protection, sir."

"You know all this," I shout, rising.

Sentinels come out of nowhere to shove me into my seat.

"This is *not* news! You *allowed* him to stay here with me. He's a doctor! Even better, he's a coroner. You wanted his help studying the Zerk—"

"Silence," says Blondie, never raising his voice but implying all kinds of violence with those buggy eyes and bulging veins. "Prisoners are not to speak unless spoken to. Keeper, what of the girl? What did she do to help the Zerker escape?"

Vera turns to me, looking hesitant. Then she turns back to Blondie. "Elder, Maddy knew her father took the Zerker out of her cage at night for additional studies without the consent or consultation of trained Sentinels assigned to guard her. Maddy knew the danger and, despite being in Keeper training, never reported it."

Blondie nods, looking left, then right. One by one, though it takes a while, the other Elders nod.

"Maddy," says Blondie, pointing to me, his

finger skeletal and bone pale just like the Ghost of Christmas Future in that old movie Dad made me watch with him every December. "Rise."

I jump up and stand in place, but something's not right. Everyone is still looking at me funny. Nobody's saying anything, and it feels like I'm forgetting something.

Vera cuts me a look and nods toward the table.

I gulp and nod back and walk to where she's been standing this whole time.

Up close, Blondie looks even worse. The skin of his nose has pulled back so that he has almost no nostrils, and his lips are gone, showing giant yellow teeth even when he isn't speaking.

"Maddy, for the crime of aiding and abetting the Zerker's escape, you are hereby Vanished. I can't say I wish you well out there, but I can say I'm sorry things turned out this way. We had high hopes for you. Good luck on the outside."

With that, the Super Sentinels move in, helping the Elders up and scooting them outside. Before I know what's happened, I'm looking at a row of empty tables.

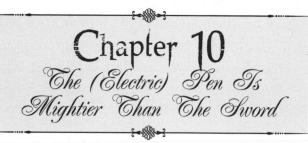

Chapter 10
The (Electric) Pen Is Mightier Than The Sword

"WHAT'S VANISHED, VERA? What does that even mean? Why can't anyone ever just say what they *mean* around this stupid place?"

I'm leaning against the empty picnic table where Blondie and his skeletal friends just sentenced me to . . . something.

Vera has pulled the single chair up next to me and is sitting in it, as if she's the one who just got Vanished or whatever. She seems more relaxed now that the Elders and Super Sentinels are gone.

She looks up at me. "It's kind of the same as being banished."

I knew it. Stupid Elders and their stupid Elder words. "So why don't they just say that? Why are they always talking in code?"

She frowns, looking at the pocket flap on the side of her thigh and trying in vain to get it to lie flat. "It's an Elder thing."

"So what, then? We're banished from Sentinel City?"

She looks up and makes a crumple face. "Where's that?"

I sigh. "Here. It's what Dad always called it. And Dane and I picked up on it. And Stamp and even Courtney. And I dunno. It's kind of a thing."

"Sentinel City. I think I like that. I think the Elders would like that, too."

She smiles but doesn't answer my question. I ask it again: "We're all banished?"

"Just you and Stamp." She shakes her head. "At least you'll be together."

"And Dad? What about him?"

Her eyes grow darker right in front of me. "Maddy, he's a Normal. We can't very well let him wander around grumbling about Zerkers and Sentinels and whatever else he learned while he was here. Besides, he's learned more about Zerker physiology and rehabilitation in months than we have in decades. He's being transferred to ZED, where we can keep a closer eye on him and his studies this time."

"ZED?"

"Zerker Education and Dismemberment."

Gross. "Sounds cheery."

"Believe me, it's better than the alternative. Although he'll basically be a prisoner there, at least he'll still be working in his field. In fact, as a coroner he's one of the most qualified physicians at ZED."

"I'm sure that will make scrubbing up in handcuffs all the more worthwhile."

She opens her mouth to speak but bites her lip.

I wish I had that kind of self-control. If I did, I probably wouldn't be here, on the verge of being Vanished right now. I look at my feet. "And Dane? What about him?"

"Seriously? He's a Sentinel now. He's been out on patrol since after you and Stamp and your father were apprehended."

"Doing what?"

"Doing what Sentinels do. Looking for Val and any other Zerkers she may have befriended or created since your dad let her out."

I glare at her, but it's too late to defend Dad now. Besides, that's only half of the equation. "And Courtney? Who's she going to support now that Dane's out in the field hunting for Val?"

Her eyes get big, and she slaps her palms onto her knees. "I can't believe this. You just got Vanished by the Council of Elders and you're worried about Courtney?"

I shake away the shame and press her. "Courtney. Courtney. I'm not tired. I can do this all night. Courtney. Tell me: what's going to become of poor Courtney?"

"She's Sentinel Support. Where do you think she is?" Before I can answer, she adds, "Out in the field, supporting Dane."

I don't know which fact hurts more: that I won't get to say good-bye to Dane or that he'll be too distracted by Courtney to notice I never did.

I shake it off and glare at Vera. "So explain this banishment business. What is it? Temporary, 200 years, what?"

"Incredible," she says, almost to herself. "It's forever. That means you are banished from Sentinel City, as you call it, but also from anywhere Elders, Keepers, and Sentinels gather. You're banished from our shelter, from fresh brains, from our uniforms and order and, most of all, from our protection. You are no longer one of us."

"But I *am* one of you. Look at me; look at you.

We're the same."

She shakes her head, not smiling, not frowning. "We're not the same. I'm not Vanished."

I stomp one foot. "So, basically, you're saying I'm no better than a Zerker at this point."

She cocks her head and studies me. "That's exactly what I'm saying."

I shake my head. "Good, whatever, fine. If that's all it takes to get kicked out of Sentinel City, then—"

She's on her feet and in my face in seconds. "All it takes?" She paces, boots squealing as she pivots with military precision. "You're lucky you're still re-alive. I know you think we are violent creatures, but look how we live. Look what we've built. You may not think much of Keepers or Sentinels, but believe you me, this planet would be overrun with Zerkers if it weren't for us."

Her tone softens. "You could have been a part of that. You were so close to finishing your training and joining us. To joining *me*. I would have loved to work with you, watching you grow and evolve. You could have helped us keep the world safe from them. Instead, you . . ."

"You can't think of anything, can you? All that crap you sold the Elders, whatever BS you dragged up on me, you can't say it to my face now. You probably can't even remember it, because I didn't *do* anything. I was sitting there in the library, trying to figure out how to get Dane back, when all this happened to me. So if it's that easy to get kicked out of your zombie tribe, well, good luck saving the human race!"

I walk away and she reaches out, yanking me back with both hands on my shoulders. Her grip is both firm and tender, if that makes any sense. Like one hand wants to toss me out on my ear and the other wants to pull me in for one last hug.

She does neither.

"Listen," she hisses, face close to mine. "Once you walk out those doors, the Sentinels take you and you're no longer under my protection. I want to give you this."

She reaches into a pocket and slides out her pen. *The* pen. The electric one. The one I've been begging her for since, oh, I dunno, forever.

"But why?"

She looks away, then back to me. "Every spare Sentinel has been out hunting for Val. Every one. And we still haven't found her. I think she's out there, waiting for you. I think you'll need this more than

I do. Besides, there's more where that came from."

I take it, but my hands are still tied in front of me, so I hold it awkwardly. "Won't they wonder where yours went?"

She avoids my gaze. "By the time they ask, you'll be gone and out of our reach. I'll wait until then to blame it on you."

"Gee, thanks."

She releases me, but I don't walk away just yet. "I would have made a good Keeper. You know that."

She nods, but that's as far as she's going.

"This is all BS. You know that too."

That's too much. "Your father let a violent Zerker escape. He cost the life of a valuable Sentinel. He put this whole facility and every Normal within the next three counties in danger. And you're the one who brought him here. I don't think I overstated my case to the Elders at all when I said you were partly to blame for Val's escape."

I nod. "Then I have nothing more to say to you."

Apparently she has nothing more to say to me either.

I walk toward the double doors, awkwardly sliding the pen down my gray granny panties in case the Sentinels search me on the way out. This way, even if they catch the Eliminator, they might miss Vera's pen. I wait for her to say something, to warn me or apologize or even yell or maybe thank me.

Nothing.

She says not a word, and I'm too proud to look back to see if she's waving or even watching me with a sad look on her face.

Beyond the glass window in each door, I see the Sentinel shapes waiting for me.

I pause just before pushing through, watching them watching me, waiting until they inch forward just enough, and then—slam—I whip open the doors and conk them on the foreheads, just for the hell of it.

Chapter 11
Thing 1 and Thing 2

STAMP IS WAITING in the back of one of those tacky tan vans, hands on his knees but no chains, cuffs, zip ties, or even duct tape binding them.

The van is sitting there, backed into the motor pool at the end of Sentinel City. It's idling, as if it's been waiting for me.

"Hi," Stamp says as the Sentinels dump me in next to him like last week's garbage. "Where you been?" He sounds perturbed but upbeat, almost as if he can't wait to get started on some big adventure and he's kind of glad I'm along for the ride.

"Sorry, Stamp." I move across from him so I can spread out a little. "I was busy getting Vanished, you know?"

One of the Sentinels takes an Eliminator and pops the scalpel side open, slicing through my plastic zip ties before turning around without a word.

"What's that?" Stamp crinkles his nose.

The Sentinels slam the back doors, and a few seconds later, I feel their heft as they climb into the front seats. The van pulls out right away, tires spinning, as if they can't wait to get rid of us.

I study Stamp, spiffy in his hospital scrubs. He's thin and wiry, like Dane was when we first met back in Barracuda Bay. He has the same shrunken cheeks and hooded eyes too, as though he's seen too much for someone so young. "What's Vanished?"

I sigh and consider how to explain it to him. "It's kind of like getting expelled from school."

His eyes get big. Then he gets that crooked smile. "Good. I hate this place."

I look out the tinted back windows. Sentinel City, drab and isolated, slips away with every spin of the van's tires.

"Me too," I realize.

He nods.

We have something in common again.

It's a bumpy, fast ride, and I look around the back of the van, figuring maybe there'd be some backpacks full of brains, clothes other than these medical scrubs, something.

"Did they give you anything?" I ask, nodding toward the front of the van, where a grate separates us from the Sentinels.

He shrugs. "Just a hard time."

I chuckle. I never know if he knows he's making a joke, or if he just says funny stuff sometimes. "Did Dad say anything to you?"

"When?"

I count to ten so I don't lunge at him and shove Vera's pen up one of his nostrils, leaving my finger on the trigger until what's left of his brain is chopped steak, medium well. "Back there." I sigh. "In Sentinel City."

Another shrug. "He said good-bye to us."

"To *us*?"

He looks at me the same way I probably look at him most times. "Yeah, you and me. *Us.*"

I sit up a little. "*What* did he say to you and me?"

An impatient groan, like I'm the dumb-dumb. "I already said. Good. Bye. Is what he said. To us."

I shake my head. "Did he say anything else? Think, Stamp. I may never see him again. This is important."

So he looks at his lap, his thinking pose, I guess.

We're slowing down now, skidding to a stop in what feels like sand. Lots of sand. In the middle of nowhere.

"Please, Stamp."

He looks up from his lap. "He said something, but I can't remember."

The van is stopped now. The front doors slam, and the Sentinels will be opening the back doors any second. "Please," I whimper, begging him with my eyes.

Then the doors open, and we're pulled out, dumped in crusty Florida sand at dawn in the middle of a field dotted by sickly scrub pines.

By the time I scramble up, the Sentinels are retreating to the front seats. I chase them, yanking on the driver's sleeve.

"Hey," I shout as he spins around, giving me his best bored zombie face. "Hey, what are we supposed to do out there?"

His partner, the passenger, chuckles. "Didn't you hear the Elders?" He walks toward the van. "You're supposed to Vanish."

The driver nods and tugs his sleeve away.

I let him go.

He looks over his shoulder and cocks a smile. "Have a nice afterlife."

The front doors clang, the engine kicks into drive, and the tires spin, spraying us with sand.

I watch until the taillights blink at the end of a long dirt road, turn left, and disappear.

Stamp is still sitting in the sand.

"Get up," I huff, holding out a hand.

He raises a hand but is dead weight as I yank him up.

"I remember now." He looks down at me.

"Remember what?"

I walk toward the road, hoping to find out where they've dumped us.

"Your dad," he says, loping beside me, threatening to overtake me with his long legs.

I stop, but he keeps going, and I have to take two quick steps before I can reach his sleeve to twist him around. "*What* did he say?"

He looks at me. "He said I should take care of you until he can find us. And that's what I'm gonna do."

He nods and reaches for my hand. I think it's kind of sweet until I find out it's just to haul me along behind him.

Chapter 12
Are We There Yet?

STAMP SITS ON a tree stump by a pond while I wash the grime off my face. It won't improve my looks, but keeping clean makes me feel better. The pond is clear, and the water is warm on my skin.

It's been a few hours since the Sentinels left us in their rearview mirror, and we're just off the main road, which is hardly a road and far from main. Near as I can tell, they dumped us in the middle of some ranch in the center of the state in a town where nobody has raised cattle for decades.

I haven't heard a car the entire time, and it's nearly noon. I don't have a watch, because I guess that's not part of the Getting Vanished Package, but I can guess the time from the sun beating down on my neck.

"Dane's not coming?" Stamp looks at me as if I promised him a birthday party and took him to the dentist instead.

I try to keep the spite out of my voice. "Not this time, Stamp." It's like Dane and I got divorced and he left me to tell the kid.

He digs the toe of a cheap black sneaker into the sand. "But Dane always comes." His disappointment is actually kind of sweet, and I have to admit he has a point.

Ever since this whole thing started, with me sneaking out to meet Stamp in the dead of night and the rain falling and the lightning flashing, Dane has never been far behind.

For good or bad, even when we didn't want to be around each other anymore, we've always been there, the three of us. Living together in Orlando, scaring the audience in our monster show. And then, suddenly, Stamp was gone, taken by Val in the dead of night. And that was the beginning of the end for the three of us.

After she bit Stamp with her Zerker teeth, and made him what he is now, it was like she infected the rest of us. Dane became obsessed with becoming a Sentinel, and I started training with Vera, and

Stamp was in a cage, and then there was Courtney, and now we're all . . . done.

Vanished, just as the Elders said. And they weren't kidding.

We're miles from anywhere, without a brain in sight, with just the clothes on our backs and no idea where we are, where we're going, or what we'll do when we get there.

"I'm hungry." Stamp kicks a pebble, and we both watch the ripples through the pond water.

"Me too." I can't remember the last time I fed. I suppose it was when Dane and Courtney showed up at my table goofing and smiling like something out of an *Adventures of Ozzie and Harriet* rerun.

"I get mad when I'm hungry," he warns, eyes big, like he's telling me something I don't know.

"Yeah," I grunt, standing up. "I've seen it." I reach for his hand.

But this time he stands on his own. "So we should probably eat."

"Yeah, we're gonna."

"Like, soon."

"Yeah, I gotcha." I wave my arms toward the wide, flat landscape, nothing but lone palm trees and scrub brush and waves of heat as far as the eye can see. Florida, the world's longest putting green. "Do you see any grocery stores around here?"

"No," he grumps.

We start walking. As far as being Vanished goes, Stamp is a good guy to do it with because he's not a big talker. He can walk for an hour at a time without saying anything. Half the time, I think he forgets I'm here. We follow the road, just along the tree line in case some farmer in a pickup drives by to feed his imaginary cows.

I know it's hot, but it doesn't really faze us because being undead is like walking around with your own refrigerator in the center of your chest. We don't sweat, we don't really get tired, and the stiffness I usually feel in my legs wore off about two hours back.

So we just walk, like Energizer Zombies, feet falling and arms swinging and eyes scanning the horizon. Quietly. Me thinking, and him, well, doing whatever he does in that head of his.

And then he stops, turns, and touches my shoulder to get me to halt. "Where are we going anyway?"

I jerk my thumb over my shoulder and look back. "See how the sun is going in that direction?"

He looks. "Yeah."

"Well, a few hours from now, the sun will set. In the west. We're going in the opposite direction. The east."

He nods, impatiently, as if he already knows all this, which I know he probably totally doesn't. "Okay, but why?"

"Because Florida really has only two sides, east and west, and I want to get to the other one."

"But why?"

I cluck, open my mouth to answer, then shut it. I have no idea. Honestly, I have no idea why. "I just . . . I grew up there. That's why."

He looks down at me, shading his eyes. "We can't go back there. Not again." He sounds almost scared.

"We're not. We can't. But I want to go somewhere like there, get my head right, get some clothes and some money together, get to a computer, check out ZED and figure out how to get there."

He turns, like that's enough for him, and we start walking again. Then he stops. "Who's Zed?"

I stop too. "Not who. What. Zerker Education and Dismemberment. Z-E-D. It's where they took Dad before we got Vanished."

He smiles. Or maybe he's just squinting at the

sun. "So then, when you find where it is, we can go rescue him?"

"That's the general idea."

He nods, and now I see the smile for sure. "Good."

We walk till I kind of miss talking to him. "Why good, Stamp?"

He shrugs. "I guess I miss the old man; that's all."

I chuckle. "I thought you hated him for putting you in a cage all that time."

"Not really. If I were him, I'd put me in a cage too."

Chapter 13
My Dogs Are Barking

I SMELL THE first dog at the same time I see the road sign just ahead:

Seagull Shores   10 miles

I whisper to Stamp, "Stop."

He just keeps stomping along, leaving me in the dust.

So I have to say it a little louder: "Stop." And then harsher: "*Stop*."

He turns, irritated, once-boyish face now a mask of gray lines. "Let's just keep going!"

So help me, I take a step back.

We stand here, his neck out, face frozen in rage, me wondering if now would be a good time to retrieve the electric pen, just in case.

His eyes are clear but seem unfocused, as if they're looking just to the left of me.

"Stamp?" I wave both hands at him.

"Yeah, what?" he growls, but he stands up straighter, blinking rapidly. Then, as if to make up for totally reaming me out, he smiles and says it again: "Yeah, what?"

"Whoa," I say, hands still up. "That was . . . unpleasant."

He shakes his head, vaguely unapologetic. "I told you I'm hungry, Maddy. Let's go."

I inch closer, grabbing his arm before he can turn. "Do you think I stopped you for no good reason?"

His lips curl. "Yeah, why else?"

Ugh, this is going to be a freakishly long ten flippin' miles.

I try another approach since, clearly, polite conversation isn't getting the job done. I sniff the air, and now the dog scent is stronger. "Do you smell that?"

He is nearly a head taller, and his neck is long,

so he supersniffs the air in all four directions before looking back at me. "Kinda funky. What is it?"

"You mean, you don't know?"

Eye roll. "Let's go, Maddy. I'm starving and . . . dog!" He suddenly brightens, eyes bugging out of his skull like an Elder's. "I smell dog, right?"

I walk on, dragging him with me. "Yeah, but I was hoping you'd have a stronger sense of smell now or something."

"Me? Why?"

How do I put this delicately?

"Well, you've got a little extra . . . zombie in you now, right?"

We're walking slowly toward the town, this *Seagull Shores* place, and between waves of dog funk, I can smell ocean, salt, seashore, sand, palm trees, and coconut oil. Just like back home, in Barracuda Bay.

He wrinkles his nose and not because he's sniffing the dogs at our backs or tan lines up ahead. "Why? Val bit me, so now I'm more zombie than you are?"

"Well, yeah. A little, sure."

He's not as mad as before but still mad. "Well, I don't. I can't smell better than you, and what's to smell anyway?"

I keep my voice calm, which I figure is what he needs now. "Dogs."

He turns, looking around, like this is the first he's heard of it. "Where?"

Seven. Eight. Nine. Ten. "No, there are dogs to smell; that's what. That's what you asked."

"When?"

"Jesus!" I can't help it.

"All right, then."

We go like that, bickering and trying to communicate as best we can as I sniff and he sniffs and we sniff. There are four or five distinct smells. I can't explain it. I haven't been outside of Sentinel City in months, and everyone there smells the same, if at all, so maybe I'm misreading it now that I'm back in the world, but the smells are differently, and definitely, pungent.

Like one smells sweaty, one angry, one dirty, and one foul. Each uniquely and grossly fragrant. Each with a personality. The closer the smells get, the more distinctive each is.

"Stamp," I hiss as the sign for Seagull Shores shows eight miles. "Stamp."

I stop. He keeps walking. I'll catch up if he

doesn't notice soon enough.

I hear footsteps, different from Stamp's. Smaller, faster, closer.

"Stamp!"

The wind is coming from behind me. Not a breeze, exactly, but moving air just the same. And the smells are changing. The five smells shift to four, then three. Then, suddenly, the smells are replaced by sounds. First comes the dry grass rustling underfoot to my right—no, my left. A twig snapping over there—no, over there.

And then stronger sounds. The first howl is a soft, low keen. I can tell Stamp doesn't hear it because he doesn't flinch the way I do. He's too far away to talk to now, not even looking back at me anymore. Not even worried about me.

I pause and reach into my scrubs, unwinding the drawstring from my waistband around the Eliminator. But I never finished my training and, even then, I fought rubber dummies who didn't move and never fought back and didn't have teeth or smell like boiling, rancid bat pee.

I drop the silent treatment and flat-out scream, "Stamp!"

Finally he turns. He looks down at his side, as if

he knows I'll be there, and then he gets this look on his face when he can't find me. It's not a concerned look, exactly. Just impatient. And when he turns to find out where I really am—twelve paces behind his giant praying mantis legs—he just shakes his head and holds his hands up in a *Really?* gesture.

"Stamp, I—"

The growl is loud and near, but still I see nothing. It's like something you'd hear on a nature channel with the sound turned low in the background.

We're in scrub brush and tall, dry grass. Nothing towering like in *Children of the Corn* or anything but enough to hide a stray dog looking to sneak up and tear your calf muscle out before you can stick a handy ice pick in his ear.

I was hoping to make it to town before they attacked. Hoping that, if there were cars and surfers and some bad cover band singing Jimmy Buffet songs on the back porch of some raw bar, the dogs would give up and we'd be safe. But I guess they're not going to patiently wait for us to walk those last six or seven miles into town after all.

Stamp turns, waving me to him. There's a football-field-sized patch of sand and scrub between us.

I frown. Let him and his cricket legs do it. So I

wave him back.

He waves harder.

I wave faster.

We could do this all day, but finally he takes a step toward me just as a blur flits across the field in front of us. Black fur, with flashes of white mixed in. I see four legs, furry paws, wide eyes, and white teeth.

Stamp freezes.

I press both buttons on the Eliminator, just in case.

The smells are mingling now, hot and wet and rich.

Something steps on a dry twig behind me.

I jerk, Eliminator raised in my right hand, ready to do what it does best. I pivot, just for a moment, to see nothing but waving grass behind me. I watch it, waiting, listening.

I hear a yip to my right. Not a playful yip. Not at all. And not designed for me to hear but for someone to follow: a signal. And just like that, three dogs creep from the tall grass. One stands directly in front of me, one to my left, and one to my right.

With everything at my disposal—zombie vision, double the smell, and nothing but the sound of my own footsteps to distract me—still they crept up on me like a squirrel in a full-on nut-gathering frenzy.

Chapter 14
Crunch Time

THE DOGS ARE snarly and foul. God, they stink. Like it hasn't rained in weeks and they've been writhing in each other's waste the whole time.

They are a motley group of mutts and feral dogs, a scabby and toothy pack on the hunt. That's what this is. There's no mistaking it. A hunt. The one directly in front of me is a German shepherd, big and bad with greasy fur and ribs showing and giant paws and eyes that never look away from my throat. His tongue lolls to one side, and his low growl is the kind you feel more than hear.

To my left: a terrier of some kind, black fur and brown paws and ears. Mouth open, jagged white teeth, sniffing with a moist snout.

To my right: a bony mutt that can't stop panting.

I crouch, as Vera taught me, but I know it's useless if they go all pack mentality and rush me. One at a time is okay. Maybe two if I'm quick enough. But three?

From behind, in the distance, I hear another yelp, followed by a low growl. I want to turn and see what Stamp is doing, but I know the minute I do, I'm toast. As it is, the German shepherd is stealing forward, the slimy snout rippling above his teeth as the growl gets louder. The two stray dogs on either side of him follow suit.

Screw it. I'm not waiting for them. Behind me the yelping gets louder, and I realize it's Stamp growling, not some stray dog. I leap at the German shepherd, startling it momentarily but not for long. I bring the ice pick down hard and fast but miss his ear and jam it in his shoulder instead.

He's no dummy. Literally, this dog is no CPR dummy. He yelps, in real pain, squirming and squealing, and I try to yank the Eliminator out of his tough hide, but the dog blitzes out of range, taking my weapon with him and leaving me standing there, defenseless.

Well, not exactly. I'm reaching for Vera's pen

when the terrier leaps. It's blinding fast, and I'm strong but slow. I manage to pound its flat, bony head with my fist, and he yelps as I kick out, launching him five or six feet away.

The third dog tears into my scrubs, slashing at my thigh with his rabid (probably) teeth as I reach down and break his neck with my icy grip. He yips once, wiry and foul in my hand, then goes limp against my leg, sliding down the rip he made seconds ago.

The terrier comes charging, a blinding black bullet, and I jerk left just in time to see it zip past, landing in the dirt and spinning around to blitz me again.

He never gets the chance. I turn, crouching when he darts at me.

Even faster is Stamp, lunging for him, catching him in both hands and twisting his furry little body like a dish towel you'd ring out over the sink.

No time for a yowl, just a snap and a twist, and Stamp throws him to the ground at his feet, standing tall, teeth bared, dripping fists at his side.

"Jesus," I say again, cringing from the look of pure rage in Stamp's eyes. I'm half expecting him to come and wring me out like a towel as well.

I look beyond him to the carnage: two dogs lying broken and bloody in the vacant field, their heads torn—no, cracked—open. He stands above me, still and silent, eyes filled with rage, chin slick with fresh blood.

I hear growling and turn to find the German shepherd standing his ground, listing a little to the side where the Eliminator sticks out of his shoulder, blood dripping from the wound.

God help me, I have to say it smells *delicious*. I inch forward, and the wounded stray winces, taking a step back, limping.

Behind me Stamp walks forward, and I yank him back. He turns, mouth open, and now, up close, I notice for the first time the gore wedged between his teeth.

"Stop!"

He shakes his head, turns away from me. "You do it then!"

I hear crunching behind me and find Stamp, well, you don't want to know what he's doing to the wrung-out dog. When I turn back to the German shepherd, he is limping away into the brush. I look down to see a big puddle of blood where he stood, too much to recover from.

I follow him at a distance, giving him his space. I ignore the crunching sounds of Stamp feeding behind me. Walking along, quietly, slowly, I think about life and death, the strong and the weak, animals and humans, and what I've become.

I asked Dad once, about what happens to an animal when a zombie bites it. Does it reanimate? He thought about it for a moment, then smiled: "Not if you consume the brain, which is the only reason I can think for a zombie to bite an animal."

From the sound of what's going on behind me, there won't be much dog left to reanimate when Stamp gets done with it. And I wonder if he'd even think to save any for me.

I hear panting and, a few seconds later, the sound of a body slumping to the ground.

It's approaching now, close at hand. I can smell the fear and the weakness and the coming nothingness in the air. It's stronger than the dog's sweat and funk, stronger even than the fresh blood trail I've been following so eagerly.

I sit down a few feet away and watch the dog take its final few breaths. They are ragged and unpleasant and far from peaceful, the way I've been taught that dogs die from after-school specials and morning cartoons. But then, so little of what I've been taught holds true anymore.

I gasp when at last the life goes out, leaving the dog's body long and limp and flat, like a duffel bag after you've taken everything out and shoved it in your hotel room drawers. It's so final and fast, as if a string has been cut, letting out all the slack and, poof, instant dog carcass.

I rise and look behind me, finding Stamp standing still, gore on his chin, looking for me. I sigh and reach over, yanking the Eliminator from the dog's shoulder. Then I turn it, scalpel side down, and do what needs to be done.

Chapter 15
Seagull Shores

I FEEL BETTER having fed. What's more, I feel better having fed myself, if that makes any sense. I've been in Sentinel City too long to remember what it was like to snag brains on the fly, to take care of myself without attracting attention. I've been fed and clothed and sheltered and trained and zombie coddled, and now I'm Vanished.

So I guess I better get used to it.

I tuck my chin as we walk. The sky is dark now, or mostly so. A thin orange line sizzles along the horizon. Fiery red glows like a racing stripe across the distance. I've missed the sky. I've missed the sand and the sea to one side. But now that I'm here, I find I can't enjoy any of it.

"Buck up," I grunt to myself as Stamp scratches his ear. I've done this. We've done this before. In Orlando, we all passed every day. Driving to work, earning money, renting an apartment, living in the open, finding our own brain source, making do when we had to. And we did have to.

But it was easier then. We had clothes and money and a car and licenses and identities. Now I know why the Sentinels call it being Vanished, not banished.

Banished is just a mindset. You don't belong anymore. Big deal.

Being Vanished is the real deal. We are basically naked, like prehistoric savages in a distinctly modern world. We have no identity, no paperwork, no Social Security numbers, no drivers' licenses or voter registration cards, no photo IDs. All of that was taken from us when we entered Sentinel City, and at the time I didn't think twice. I handed it over gladly, in fact, figuring we'd never need it again.

Now I know why Vera didn't explain it better when I asked her point-blank about it. Why she didn't foreshadow what was *really* to come. If she had, I would have fought harder, maybe too hard, and wound up worse than Vanished.

I look at a sign near the road:

Welcome to Seagull Shores, Florida!

You're not going to believe this, but there are seagulls all over it. I know, weird—and original and not expected or predictable at all.

Stamp comes to a stop next to me, like a dog trained to heel. He's happy now, having fed—a lot. I mean, he's fed so much he's almost dopey. Brain drunk, Dane used to call it.

"What?" Stamp says, but he doesn't snap at me like before. He's mellow.

"This town . . ." I point to the sign, wooden and purposefully distressed and brown with white lettering and blue seagulls flying all over the place as if it was placed here in 1972 and, like a zombie, never aged a single day since. "What do you think?"

He makes a frowny face like he's really thinking, but I can tell in his eyes he's just making it look like he is so I'll be impressed. "I think I'm tired of walking."

"So we'll stop here?"

He shrugs.

I nod and walk on.

This time he's the one who grabs my sleeve and yanks me back.

"We should wait." He nods at his own suggestion, as if maybe that will make me nod too. He's still looking at the sign, his feet firmly planted by the side of the road.

"Wait? Why wait?" I look around. The sun is done setting, the street lights are flickering on one by one, and it must be a weeknight because the place is dead.

Barracuda Bay was the same way. Dad used to say they rolled the sidewalks up at 9:00 sharp every night.

Stamp nudges my shoulder not so gently. "I don't want to get caught. We should wait a little while, see what it feels like."

Almost on cue, headlights flash in the distance followed by the sound of an engine.

We dip, low and fast, among the palm trees by the welcome sign and watch as a police cruiser passes slowly. Not slowly enough to make me think he saw us, but the lights on top of the cruiser remind me of where I stand: barely hidden, wearing grungy, bloody hospital scrubs, no ID, no purse, no good reason for being here.

Suddenly I realize why Vera gave me her pen.

We're alone, stranded, abandoned, betrayed, and cursed, and if we don't get off the street, lie low, and figure out a game plan fast, there's no telling what the Normals will do with us.

We would not be the first zombies discovered by Normals. Barracuda Bay was never the first or the last outbreak on the planet. I know that now that I've been in Sentinel City long enough to watch them go out on patrol, sometimes every single week and at least every month. They're not heading out into the world, suited up and clutching Tasers, for their health. They're out there putting down a little infestation here, checking out a zombie sighting there. I know that now. I know how it works.

But without the Sentinels' protection, without the Keepers' cooperation with local authorities, without that little cushion between us and the real world, the Normals will do what they want with us and make no apologies later. Lock us away, tear us apart, ship us off to Washington to be studied or out into the sea to be lost and forgotten.

Vera was right when she said I was no better than a Zerker now. This is how they live, I figure: crouched and gory and avoiding human contact unless they get hungry enough to seek and snuff it out.

Long after the cruiser is gone, I stay crouched behind the skinny trees, shaking my head at the insanity of what we're doing and how and even where we're doing it. The weight of our reality shoves me to the ground, where I sit, no idea what to do or where to find ZED, let alone how to get Dad back.

Stamp slides down next to me, sitting cross-legged like a kindergartener by my side. "What are we thinking?" he asks, leaning in and whispering as loud as he normally talks, but he's so serious about it all I can't even shush him.

I reach for his hand and he lets me hold it. "I'm thinking we're scared."

"Me too." Then a few seconds later: "What are *you* scared about?"

"I'm scared of getting caught. What are *you* scared about?"

He nods. "Me too."

We sit quietly like that, hidden by the welcome sign's shadow. There again is the sound of ocean in the distance and the salt air for the first time in months. Scratch that, nearly a year.

I never thought what life would be like outside of Sentinel City. Between Dane joining the Sentinels and Vera's training, I was content to live out the rest of my days fighting Zerkers, keeping Normals safe, and laughing with Dane over brain bars in the canteen, visiting Stamp in his cage on the down low, and watching the Sentinels fill Dad's dorm room with souvenir crap every time he handed them another shopping list.

And now, here I am in the wild again. What am I going to do? What are *we* going to do?

"We should get walking," Stamp answers, pulling me up as he stands.

"Wait. Was I talking out loud? Just now?"

"Sure. Why?" He drags me into the shrubs, and we find a scruffy path into town, parallel to the road but not on it. Close enough to see the asphalt with our zombie vision but not close enough to be seen by mere mortals.

"I'm losing it, Stamp."

He chuckles softly, and I realize we're still holding hands. "Welcome to the club."

Chapter 16
Zombie Squatters

Now I know what it feels like to be a Zerker. To hide in the shadows, to live in the dark, to not come out in the light. Every snap of every twig, every tree rustle, every moaning branch I stop, crouching and dragging Stamp down with me. We follow the tree line all night long, down one residential street after another, looking closely at the For Sale signs; there are a lot of them.

The streets are all the same: suburban and long and neat and clean. Pumpkins flicker on the front stoops, reminding me that fall is here once again and that means I'm an undead year older.

The houses are mostly new or refurbished or just really, really clean. Most streets have about eight or nine houses on one side, eight or nine on the other, with a cul de sac featuring three or more at the far end. Each driveway has one or two cars, nice ones, a fine layer of dew already misting the windshields, though we're still a few hours from dawn.

Every fifth or sixth house seems to be for sale, but I don't find what I'm looking for until we're half-way down our seventh street of the night: a postcard Florida street called, naturally, Lumpfish Lane.

"Here," I hiss, pulling Stamp behind the plastic trash cans and recycling bins lined up in front of the garage. "This one."

"Why?" he asks, not whispering at all.

I point to the For Sale sign. "That's why."

He looks up and down the street, pointing at three identical signs. "Why not those houses?" His face crumples as he tries to figure it out, but I don't have time.

"Because they don't have that . . ." I point to the magnetic yellow Foreclosure banner slapped kitty-corner across the realtor's sign.

He wrinkles his nose. "What's that mean?"

I forget about his scrambled brain and curse the Zerker that Dad couldn't bleed out of him. "It means no one lives here," I say, dragging him up. We walk along the side of the house toward the backyard. "It means we can stay here and nobody will bother us if we don't do anything stupid."

He stops me halfway down the side of the house to turn back and look at the sign, squinting so he can really check it out. "It says all that? But it's so small."

I chuckle and jerk him forward again. "Kind of," I mutter. "I might be paraphrasing a little."

There is a wooden fence, leaning a bit but in pretty good shape otherwise, with a door where the wood meets the back wall of the house. I unlatch it pretty easily, popping my scalpel out of the Eliminator and sliding it through the crack until the latch pops and the door creaks open.

I lug Stamp inside and shut the door quietly. There is a lap pool featuring some questionable water, leaves floating on the calm, black surface.

The house is on a canal, and there is a dock and, lapping quietly next to it in the water, a small sailboat. Every so often there is the soft clink-clink of metal on metal, rigging against mast. Next to the pool is a screened porch with no furniture and beyond that a sliding glass door to an empty living room.

I stand there, finger on my chin. "Now to get into the—"

Stamp wrenches the screen door open, and I figure it was probably locked and he just broke it, but you know what? I'll replace it once we're able to pass better and I can walk into the nearest hardware store in something other than draggled scrubs.

The big patio is tiled, and I think how nice it would look with wicker furniture and cute red throw pillows. Not too red, maybe even maroon with oversized black buttons down the middle. And a little table for two where you could sit on cool nights and eat chips and salsa and listen to the river lap against the dock pilings or maybe even some steel drum music oozing from your iPod.

Crunch goes the sliding glass door lock as Stamp forces it open as well. I sigh and look at the Eliminator I was going to use, retracting the blades and sliding it back into my waistband.

The house smells musty, as if no one has been here for months.

Just to get rid of him for a few minutes so I can clear my head, I tell Stamp, "Go check upstairs. Make sure no one else is squatting here."

He nods eagerly, as if I've sent him on some spy mission full of danger and intrigue and martinis. I hear him clomping heavily up the stairs, the very opposite of secret. I rush through the rooms downstairs: kitchen, dining room, living room, guest bath, two-car garage, laundry room, and guest room in the back.

Not a stick of furniture was left behind, not a leftover fork or sponge or battery or refrigerator magnet or bottle of bleach. I check the locks on the front door and lower all the blinds.

I clomp up the stairs to find Stamp looking out a guest bedroom window, peering at the street below. He looks so peaceful I hate to bug him.

"What's up?" I ask, touching his shoulder gently.

He doesn't even flinch. "I thought I saw someone under that street light."

I scoot him out of the way and look through the blinds. A street lamp sends down a cone of orange light in the predawn darkness, but I don't see anyone now. Still, we both know that doesn't mean anything.

"Did it look like one of us?"

He studies me and thinks for a second. "No, not really."

We watch for a little while more, but nothing happens. "It could have been someone out walking their dog," I suggest, backing away from the window. The space is small, like a child's room, and I think it's a good fit for Stamp.

He furrows his leathery brow. "Without a dog?"

I shrug and drift away to see the rest of the upstairs: another small bedroom right next to Stamp's, a guest bathroom, a small loft overlooking the downstairs, and then the master suite, twice as big as Stamp's room with its own little balcony and master bath.

It has hardwood floors and lots of room, and the balcony overlooks the pool and river. Again, I find myself decorating in my mind, wondering if I'll ever be able to walk into a Pottery Barn and buy a throw pillow and bring it to a home I live in and put it on a chair I own.

Stamp trudges in and taps my shoulder, a mischievous smile on his face. "How do you like my room?"

I look around at all the space and frown. "*Your* room?"

"Yeah, I called it." He sounds indignant, like how dare I even ask.

"When?"

He avoids my gaze. "When you were downstairs. Didn't you hear me?"

I shake my head and shrug. It's the perfect end to one of the worst days of my afterlife.

Chapter 17
B & E and ME

I KEEP TRACK of everything in a little notebook I found by the cash register. Yes, I feel bad for breaking and entering. Yes, I feel terrible for stealing. But if we don't get regular street clothes, we may never be able to pass among the Normals, and this thrift shop was the only place within walking distance of the house on Lumpfish Lane that looked like it didn't feature sixteen surveillance cameras and a silent alarm and booby traps on the fire escape out back.

Stamp is at home, sitting in his room, waiting for me. At least, I hope he is. God, please let him be. I made him promise not to go anywhere, but he's so unpredictable now.

We've been sitting in that silent house on Lumpfish Lane for almost two full days. I couldn't take it anymore. After talking Stamp out of coming with me, which took half an hour, here I am, a felon, skulking around in the dark.

I hurry through the thrift shop, grabbing a backpack and a duffel bag, stuffing them both to the gills with anything that looks like it might fit, writing it down in the little notebook, tallying the little cardboard price tags dangling off each sleeve or cuff or shoelace or belt loop.

As I work, I picture Stamp getting restless cooped up in the house, ignoring my instructions and walking outside, knocking on the neighbors' front doors, asking everyone on the street where I might be and could he come in and wait a while and, oh, by the way, do they have any brains, and if not, that's okay; the ones in their skull cages will do just fine, thank you very much.

I bring some clothes into a dressing room and slip them on. Yes, I know I could stand naked in the middle of the store and no one would see me at this time of night, but old habits die hard.

It's nothing fancy, just some fresh underwear, an olive tank top, maroon track pants, and a gray-and-black-striped hoodie. I slip on some of those footie socks and a pair of off-brand walking shoes, a little snug but they'll do. I'll wear them in while walking around Seagull Shores in the dark for the next few nights, I'm sure.

Outside of the dressing room, I spot a rack and grab a few hats, remembering my burr head and what it might look like to the Normals. There's a ball cap for some local team, the Seahorses or whatnot, and I slip it on and shove the rest in my pack.

There are sunglasses by the cash register, and I grab some of those as well, just in case. By the time I tally everything up, and I keep rounding up because I'm sure I missed a few things along the way, it all comes to $126. Yikes.

It's gonna take a lot of picking pennies up off the street and checking soda machines for spare change to pay that back. Or who knows? Maybe I can pawn the sailboat behind the house on Lumpfish Lane or something. I'll figure it out one way or another before we leave town.

I slip the backpack and duffel bag over my shoulders, climb on top of a shelf in the middle of the store, and slip through the ceiling tile opening I entered through forty minutes ago.

I replace it, hoping no one will notice the stuff I took. Okay, maybe they'll catch the three twenties I took out of the deposit bag from the manager's office, but maybe the bank will blame the manager and the manager will blame the bank and it will all end in a draw: he said; she said. No harm, no foul.

I just don't want anyone mad at me is all. I may be Vanished, one level of zombie above a Zerker, but that doesn't mean I have to turn into some lawless punk taking good money away from innocent Normals just trying to run a business.

The air-conditioning vent on the roof is a tight squeeze, but I'm smaller than I used to be and not so panicked about the side of the thin metal tube pressing against my chest as I pull, pull, pull myself up and out of it. When I'm standing on the roof again, I slide the round top back on the vent and walk to the edge.

I'm in downtown Seagull Shores now, standing above something like a main street or just off it. There's a post office at one end, a bank at the other, a drug store and a men's store and a women's store and an ice cream parlor—and no one is around. The clock on the bank says in big, red digital numbers that it's 4:43 a.m., and that feels about right.

I smell the salt air and hear the crash of the waves to my right as I step down the fire escape to the street below. I grab my bags' straps atop each shoulder and look both ways before slinking through the same alleys I crept up to get here.

There is a convenience store between the thrift shop and the house on Lumpfish Lane. A bench sits out front between two newspaper machines. I shove my bags under it, pull down my Seahorses ball cap, and walk inside, the three twenties from the deposit bag crisp in my hoodie pocket. The lights are bright, which is good. Not because it makes me look better, but it makes everyone else look bad, so hopefully I won't stand out too much.

The clerk is tall and thin with short, red hair and big, black glasses and a tan-and-red Stop N Go vest. He barely looks up from his girly mag as I walk in and head for the drink aisle. I grab some generic grape soda, something sweet and cold, and make for the pet food aisle, looking past the name-brand stuff to the cut-rate cat food, smiling when I see lamb brains down the long list of ingredients on the back of the can.

It'll do for now.

I walk to the register and slide the items next to

the guy's magazine, which isn't full of naked girls, as I first thought, but muscle cars. I stand there, money out while he reads the last paragraph and looks up.

"Oh, hi," he says, meeting my gaze.

I wait for him to grimace, but he doesn't. I can't imagine he gets many supermodels in the joint in the middle of the night, and even undead I probably look better than half of his regular customers.

He rings the stuff up so slowly I have time to notice the pumpkin-scented candles on display by the cash register. I ask him to add a few of them to my bill and then grab two 99-cent cigarette lighters at the last minute.

It comes to $12.79, and I hand him one of the stolen twenties, taking the change while he double-bags my stuff. "Quite the midnight snack," he says, shoving everything in one bag.

"My cat Trixie got hungry."

He doesn't even flinch, just slides the bag across the counter and goes back to his magazine.

I nod and take the bag, divvying up the items between the backpack and duffel bag so they're easier to carry through town. I save one bottle of cheap grape soda, sipping it slowly on the way back to the house on Lumpfish Lane, my dry, dead cells welcoming the sugar rush that will last a few minutes until, like everything else we eat, it evaporates in the endlessly hungry wastelands that are our innards.

I finish it under the street light beneath our window, looking up. When I shield my eyes against the weak orange light, I see Stamp looking out between the slats.

He seems happy to see me. Or maybe it's just the soda bottle I have in my hand.

Chapter 18
Ground Rules

"Feel better?"

Stamp burps, wipes the cheap grape soda off his lips, and nods.

We're in the kitchen, sitting cross-legged on the tile floor, a pumpkin spice candle flickering between us, and it looks so '80s B movie that I half expect one of us to whip out a Ouija board any minute. The shades are drawn in every room, as tight as they can clench, but still I don't want to risk being seen on our third night in the house on Lumpfish Lane.

A few seconds later, he adds, "Much."

And it's been so long since I asked him, I think, *Much what?* Then I realize he means much better. I shake my head. Talking to Stamp is like being on a seven-minute delay.

I wonder, as I watch him tidy up his cat food tins and empty soda bottles, if he and Dad ever just sat and talked like this back in the lab. I bet they did. Speech therapy, as Dad called it, was a big part of their work together.

He's kind of in a trance, moving slowly but purposefully. When he catches me looking, he smiles shyly, as if we hardly know each other. "Do you think she'll find us?"

My back is to a row of kitchen cabinets, and he's in front of the kitchen sink. "Who, Val?"

He nods.

"I don't know. I imagine she's far away from here by now." Half of me truly believes that, or at least wants to, and the other half just doesn't want to worry him.

Too late. He shakes his head pretty adamantly. "No, she isn't."

"What do you mean, Stamp? She broke out of Sentinel City almost a week ago by now. Why would she stick around that long when she knows every Sentinel in Florida is looking for her?"

"Stop talking so fast." His tone is soft, but his words are hard.

I blink a couple of times. "What?"

"I mean, I can't keep up with you when you talk like that."

I nod. That makes sense. "I'm sorry, Stamp. I'm used to talking to . . ."

He nods. "Dane, I know. And Dane is fast, I know. But I'm not anymore, so slow down please."

"Okay, I will."

The pumpkin smell is strong. I don't know if it's my zombie sense or a really strong candle, but I blow it out. We don't really need it anyway. I just thought it would be nice to live like Normals for a change, lighting a candle in the dark, having a picnic on the kitchen floor.

Guess not.

We sit silently while our eyes adjust. In a few seconds, the room glows a soft, gentle yellow even without the flickering of the candle. Zombie vision, I call it. Dad could never explain it, said there's no good reason why a dead thing's eyes should see better than a living one's, but here it is just the same. It's been this way ever since Barracuda Bay.

Stamp moves his hand in front of his face. "I almost forgot we could do this," he marvels, like a kid on Christmas morning.

"We can do a lot," I remind him. "We're the good guys, remember?"

"Not me." He's pouting. I can see his features, harsh in the hazy yellow glow. "Not anymore."

"That's not true. You're here with me, and nothing's gone wrong, right?"

"Not yet."

I raise my voice. "Stamp, listen to me. Look at me." I wait until he does. "You're a good zombie. You're not like Val. You never could be, even if Dad hadn't sucked half the Zerker out of you."

"You say that now, but just wait. You don't know."

"I don't *want* to know. If a guy like you can go bad, then . . . I don't want to know. Don't you remember, back in Barracuda Bay, how you saved me from Val?"

He leans in, as if getting a better look at me will help him remember. Finally, he rests his back against the cabinet and shakes his head. "I was all bad then. I forget a lot."

"Well, I don't. I remember, and if it weren't for you, I wouldn't be here today."

"Really?"

I reach across and touch his knee. "Really. If you hadn't saved me, Val would have torn me limb from limb."

He nods but scoots back a little, so that my hand falls to the floor. "Maybe, maybe I can save you again when Val comes."

"She's not coming," I hiss.

He nods. "You're right." Then, after another seven-second delay that feels like two minutes, he adds, "She's already here."

"You saw her?" I'm ready to get up, grab my Eliminator, and cut the next tiny blonde witch I see.

"No, but I feel her. She's part of me, remember."

"She bit you. You're not linked or something."

He shrugs. "You don't know that."

"I pretty much do. That's not how it's supposed to work."

He cocks his head. "This isn't how dead is supposed to work either."

I open my mouth to argue, but then I give up. He's right. More often than not. More often than me.

"Okay, so you feel like Val is here?"

He nods.

"So we have to be careful," I add. "Extra careful. Which is pretty much why we haven't left this house in three days."

He gets to his knees and crawls to me. He seems

a little faster now.

"What are you doing, Stamp?"

He sits next to me, facing out of the kitchen toward the living room and the foyer. "Being more careful."

I chuckle. He always was a sly one. "Gotcha. Right."

"Can you hug me?"

I inch away to get a better look at his face. "How is that being more careful?"

He smiles. "It's not. Sometimes you just need a hug at night. Your dad would give them to me sometimes, when Val wasn't around or even if she was and he knew I extra needed one."

"He would?" Sweet as he is, for the life of me I can't picture Dad hugging Stamp.

Stamp shrugs. "Yeah, he was a good hugger."

I snort. "Yes, yes, he was." Then I wonder how long it's been since I've had a hug from Dad. "Okay, come here."

He leans in, head on my shoulder, and I have to put my arms around him while his arms stay at his side. Has he forgotten how to hug? Or is he just afraid of what might happen if he does?

Chapter 19
Stranger Danger

"**W**HATCHA DOING?"

My fingers fly to the Eliminator in my front pocket. I'm creeping out of the back gate, looking left when a voice comes from the right.

I turn and find a short Asian girl standing casually just outside the door. I'd jump back inside if I could move that fast.

I shut the fence door behind me just the same, the plastic Stop N Go bag full of empty grape soda bottles and cat food tins dangling in my free hand. "Nothing. Just taking out the trash." I try to sound defensive.

She puts her hands up and takes a step back. "Okay, yeah, I see that now."

She is pretty, in a tomboyish sort of way. Short and stocky, straight black hair clipped severely across her forehead, very little makeup but a soft, clear complexion. She has on long black jogging shorts with white stripes down the side and a Spider-Man T-shirt. Her black-and-white basketball shoes are untied, and her white socks go up to her knees, which is about where the hems of her shorts end.

"You must have moved in when I wasn't looking," she says cryptically, nodding toward the back gate as if wanting to be let in. "I've been waiting forever for some other kids to move onto this street."

I wasn't expecting to see anyone so soon and don't really have a cover story down yet, but she's kind of just given me one. I add to it quickly: "Uh, yeah, my brother and I didn't get here until just a few days ago. We were supposed to be here last week, but the bus broke down in Tallahassee, so . . . here we are."

"You moved . . . by bus?"

Um, yeah, she's right. That was kind of stupid. Well, hell, they never covered being Vanished in my Keeper training. I keep it going: "Well, not exactly. My parents won't be here until next week, but they wanted my brother and I to get checked into school early, so we came ahead so we wouldn't miss much more of the school year."

That goes down a little better.

She looks at the house, up and down and then up again. I wonder if Stamp is back upstairs, studying her through the blinds. I try to follow her gaze and see nothing but closed shutters and pulled drapes and a normal Florida suburban house.

"So, cool, like, you have the whole house to yourself all week? Party time!" She pumps a fist.

But I don't join her, for obvious reasons. "Yeah, no, it's not really like that."

She takes another step back. "Cool, okay, you're straitlaced; I get it. Me too. I mean, I'm not really the party type, you know. I just thought, if you were, well . . . I didn't want to make a bad first impression."

I lean on the fence, trying to be casual but wanting to run. But I've come this far, and she hasn't bolted away screaming *Zombie* yet, so maybe it'll work.

Maybe.

"So where's your brother?"

Man, this chick. If I can pass with her and her wannabe crime scene investigative skills, we may get out of this re-alive after all.

"Still sleeping. Have you ever tried sleeping on a

bus?" I yawn for effect.

Her curious eyes tell me I'm overdoing it more than just a little. Then she stands at attention and juts out a hand. "Oh my gosh, I can't believe we haven't even introduced ourselves this whole time. I'm Lucy Toh."

I pull my hand from where I've been warming it against the back of my sweatpants and take her hand. I haven't had much time, so I hope the temperature isn't too bad. She doesn't say anything, so maybe I did all right.

But then she pulls her hand back. "You sick or something?" She reaches into one of the pockets of her shorts and pulls out a travel-size bottle of hand sanitizer, something pink and cherry scented, splotzing it all over her hands and sliming them together.

"A little," I say, taking the bait. "Like I said, two days on a bus, you catch a lot of germs."

Her hands now dry and clean, she taps a foot.

"What?" I say.

"I showed you mine; you show me yours."

I blink a couple of times.

"Name. You never told me your name."

"Maddy," I say on instinct, as I did a thousand times in Orlando without thinking twice. "Maddy Swift."

She smiles and looks more girly that way. "I like that. Sounds kind of like a superhero name."

"Really?"

"Yeah, you don't think so?"

I shrug. "I've never really thought about it before."

She looks at me—specifically, at what I'm wearing. Black sweatpants, too-tight sneakers, gray pullover with a zipper collar. "So you're not going to school here yet?"

"Not yet. Like I said . . ."

"Your parents, yeah, got it. So, well, when do you start?"

"I dunno. I guess when my parents get here and bring my paperwork and stuff."

She seems busy all of a sudden. Restless, as if I'm keeping her, when she was the one stalking me. "Okay, well, maybe I'll come over later. After school, I mean."

My eyes get big. "Oh well, really, I mean, the place is a mess and the furniture isn't here or anything, so . . ."

But she's already running on her stumpy legs to the house next door, up the steps and stopping on the front porch, hand on the doorknob. "Cool. It's a date. See you then."

I watch her walk inside, cursing myself while smiling, waving like an idiot. A big, Vanished, zombie idiot. The door shuts behind her, and a light goes on inside.

I'm about to turn around when I notice the divot in her front yard. I inch a little closer, not wanting to be seen but needing a better look.

I fiddle with the trash can, like maybe I'm throwing something away, and steal a glance. Sure enough, I see fresh grass, kind of a different color, on a square divot of lawn. It's a little lower than the rest. Fresher too.

I creep inside the gate, pretty sure there was a For Sale sign in front of that house just the other day.

Chapter 20
Street Cred

THE DOORBELL RINGS later that afternoon, right on time. I curse as Stamp peeks out the dining room blinds while I crouch behind the front door, Eliminator close at hand to decapitate any and all comers: traveling Bible salesmen, Zerkers, SWAT teams, whatever. Bring it.

He makes his crumple face. "Did you order Chinese?"

Jesus. It must be Lucy. "Don't *say* that, Stamp!"

He lets the blind down, face blank and hurt. "Why? What'd I say?"

"Not all Asian people deliver Chinese food . . . I mean *Asian* food, Stamp."

His eyes get wide, like this is big news to him.

"No, I know that, but this Asian person has Chinese Asian food. She's waving at me. I think it's for *us*."

Holy God. Have I screwed up that badly? *Already*? Four days in town, and I've already blown our cover?

I open the door and, indeed, Lucy Toh has come bearing Chinese food. "It's from my parents' place," she says as I slip the door shut right behind her. "They own Lop Sing's in the Breezeway Strip Mall. Right by the Family Value Mart?"

She says it so casually, as if she thinks I should know where it is, and I think I do. Wasn't the thrift shop where I stole the clothes I'm wearing right now in the Breezeway Strip Mall?

Or was it in the Sailfish Shopping Center?

The Grouper Galleria?

"It smells so good," I say, standing in the doorway so she'll see she's not really welcome. "Thank you so much, but our parents don't really want us to have people over while they're not . . ."

Forget it. Too late. She's already breezing in.

She's in a gingham skirt now and high knee socks and shiny black shoes and a maroon blazer with a school crest on the outside of the left lapel. She must go to a private school.

"When did you say your parents were coming, again?" she asks, walking right into the kitchen, where she puts the food on the counter.

Stamp follows her like a puppy.

I think she kind of likes it.

"Next week," I say, trying to remember what I said just this morning. Ack, I'm no good at this being Vanished stuff! I'm going to get us nabbed before I ever have a chance to find out where ZED is and, more importantly, how Dad is.

"So what are you going to do until then?" She's busy taking out the food, lining it up precisely.

Stamp lurks, sniffing over her shoulder, glancing at me with a look on his face that says, *Is it okay?*

I shake my head. Half Zerker or no, he knows we can't eat Normal food. A little meat, maybe, but very little and cooked rarely. Then again, who knows what Zerkers can and can't do? I should have asked Dad more about them while I had the time.

He ate that Twinkie all up on my birthday and didn't keel over, right? Could Chinese food be much different?

"Thanks for all this Asian food, Lucy," I stumble. "But we—"

She smirks, looking at Stamp. "Asian food?" She

looks back at me. "It's Chinese food . . . It's okay. You can say it. Chinese. Food." She chuckles.

Stamp chuckles too, but I know from the glazed look in his eyes he's just being nice to whoever brought him food.

"Oh, okay, well, I never know what I should call it. I mean you . . . I mean . . . Oh, man . . ." I bury my face in my hands, hoping when I look up Lucy and her food will be long gone.

No such luck. She turns to me with a half-skeptical, half-disappointed, half-superior look (yes, I'm aware that's too many halves). "You must not hang around a lot of minorities."

I give her the same look back and cluck. *Honey, if Val gets her way,* I think, *the human race is about to become one giant minority.*

She arches a smooth eyebrow.

Out loud I say, "Sorry. It's just, where I come from, everybody's pretty much the same."

And it's true. White, black, red, or brown, we all turn up the same shade of freshly poured concrete, gray after a week or two of being undead. Shoot, the Council of Elders could be the original Temptations, for all I know.

She leans against the counter, studying me more

carefully. "I guess you were just trying to be polite."

I don't say anything more.

She looks up at Stamp, who stands next to her like a giant lap dog begging for scraps. "What's up with this guy?"

"That's Stamp," I say, because what else can I call him? I'm me and he's him—and if Lucy keeps pushing, I don't know what will happen.

Obviously I'm not going to decapitate her like a CPR dummy.

I'm no Zerker, but it will mean gagging her with her own prep school tie and going out to the back-yard for a bunch of garden hose to tie her hands while Stamp and I make our way out of Seagull Shores for good.

"Hi, Stamp," she says, sticking out a hand.

I gasp.

Even though Dane and I taught Stamp the whole sit-on-your-hands trick back in Orlando, I'm pretty sure he's forgotten it by now.

Sure enough, on reflex, he just holds out his hand.

Lucy takes it almost greedily. Her eyes get big, and she looks at me, not Stamp. "My, how cold your hands are."

"He's been sick," I state flatly, because suddenly

this witch is on my last nerve. "So if he can't eat any of your food, just forgive him."

"Oh, he can at least eat the meat, right, Stamp?"

Stamp looks at me, but I look at her. "He can have a little."

She pulls out white boxes with red dragons on the sides and little aluminum tins with white lids. "This is moo shu pork," she says, opening one and filling the kitchen with wafting steam clouds of hot, Normal goodness. "Lots of meat for you."

"Not lots," I interject, leaning against the counter so I can keep one hand close to the Exterminator. "But maybe just a little."

Stamp nods, and a part of me is happy to see she hasn't completely lured him away with the promise of hot animal flesh. She undoes a Baggie and hands him a plastic fork.

"Okay?" she says to him.

He kind of nods and digs in.

While he's busy, an awkward silence grows between me and Lucy. She breaks it first.

"So, look," she says, gazing past me. "Let me just put this out there: I know who you guys are."

As I blink rapidly, she finally looks at me. "Or, should I say, *what* you are."

Chapter 21
Brain Busted

S HE SLIDES TWO sheets of paper out of a red-and-black plaid messenger bag covered with sew-on pink-and-black skull patches. She sets the pages facedown on the kitchen counter.

It's pretty hard to hyperventilate when you can't breathe.

Hard but apparently not impossible.

"That's not us," I spit, tapping the counter but not touching the papers. "It can't be us."

She cocks her head, straight hair leaning with it. "I never said it *was* you. She turns the sheets over, and I can tell right away from the big, bold letters on the first one: they are Missing posters.

I look at Stamp, but he's still digging for strips of

meat in the moo shu pork.

Idly, not even really conscious while I'm doing it, I warn him, "Not too much."

He nods at me just as robotically, as if to say, "Stuff it, lady. I'll eat as much as I want."

Meanwhile I'm transported back to Barracuda Bay where, in every shop window, taped to the side of every mailbox, stapled to every tree, the same kind of Missing posters littered our beach town during my last few weeks as a living, breathing human.

Three girls had gone missing from my own Home Ec class before I became one of the living dead and learned they weren't missing at all but dead, their brains food for the Zerkers.

I slide these new posters toward me.

Lucy watches me carefully, Stamp munching indiscriminately.

The first poster is for a boy, slim and handsome in his yearbook photo. They always use a yearbook photo for these things. His name is Armand Suit, and he was captain of the swim team up until three days ago when he went for an early morning jog and never came back.

The second poster is for a girl. She's blonde and sun-kissed in her yearbook photo, the kind of girl you see all over Florida beach towns, slim and pretty in a bikini or short shorts, hair pulled back, zinc on her nose, always on the way to or from the beach.

Her name is Cecile Brigham, and she's an honor student, captain of the volleyball team. She, too, went missing the other morning while running with . . . Armand Suit.

I look up at Lucy, narrowing my gaze. It's my new thing. It's kind of like a laser beam squint, but it doesn't seem to faze Lucy much. "I thought you had to wait at least a few days before reporting someone missing," I say. "This could be some senior skip day prank or 'Let's run off to Make-out Point and make out all day.'"

She nods. "You're probably right, except Cecile's dad is the sheriff, and she hasn't missed a school day since second grade. She's been gunning for the perfect attendance award since the first day of freshman year and, as lame as that sounds, if you knew her, you'd realize that if she's not at school twenty minutes early on a weekday, then she's missing."

I slide the posters back. "You said you know what we are. What does this have to do with us?"

She eyes me coolly. "Nothing, or you'd be locked up by now."

I lean a hand on the counter, peaceful, cold, and pale. The other is about two millimeters from my Eliminator. "Quit playing around, Lucy. Spit it out or hit the road and take your food with you. Stop now, Stamp. That's enough!"

They both flinch.

While I've got his attention, I wrench the tin out of his grip. Half of it is gone. "Stamp?"

He shrugs and uses a sleeve to wipe the oily brown moo shu juice off his lips.

When I look back at Lucy, she's pulling something out of her messenger bag. I swear I almost click the button on my Eliminator and shove the ice pick through her wrist just for kicks, but I give her a second.

Out comes a book. Well worn, dog-eared, as if she's been studying it for quite some time. Weeks, at least. The title leaps out at me in those cheesy blood-dripping letters, like the ones in those bad late-night horror movie titles: *The Living Dead for Losers*.

She flashes those superior eyes at me. "I'm not stupid, you know. You show up in the middle of the night, in a foreclosed home, wearing bloody hospital scrubs, and—don't look at me like that, Maddy Swift. I'm a light sleeper, heard the back gate slam the other night and couldn't sleep. You couldn't either, I guess. Walking around in the house all night, eating—what was it—grape juice and cat food by candlelight?"

She thumbs through the book, finding a dog-eared page. She scrolls down it with maroon-painted nails until she finds what she's looking for, reads it out loud as if we're in Reanimation Reform School or something:

"The living dead cannot partake of humans' food, except in the rare cases of sugary sodas, which replenish their decaying cells with much-needed liquid energy and the occasional can of pet food, many varieties of which feature brains as a main ingredient, especially those off-brands found in all-night convenience stores. While such food cannot sustain the living dead indefinitely, in periods where fresh human or even animal brains are scarce, the latent brain tissue found in the processed product can keep their energy levels high enough to keep them alive for up to two weeks . . ."

She actually has a pleasant reading voice. You can tell she's good in school.

Still, I make a sneer face. "So, because we like grape juice and fed a stray cat for a few nights, we're . . .

what does it say?" I make a big show of snatching the book out of her hands, slapping it shut to gaze at the front cover. "The living dead?"

Lucy rolls her eyes and does a soft golf clap.

I'd blush if I could.

"Very nice performance, Maddy. Maddy Swift, did you say?"

I nod, dreading the decision to use my real name as she digs into her messenger bag. That stupid bag! What is it, bottomless or something? Magic? Did Hermione herself give it to her?

She pulls out a few printed pages, and when she holds the first up, the afternoon rays filtering through the blinds spotlight the banner page from the *Barracuda Bay Bugle*.

". . . tragic news from the horrible fire that claimed the lives of dozens of students when the gym ignited due to faulty wiring during this year's Fall Formal," Lucy reads in her pleasant, Honors English voice. "The body of Madison Swift, daughter of Cobia County's chief coroner and junior at Barracuda Bay High, was found amid the rubble, along with her date to the dance, Stamp Crosby. Also a junior, Stamp was the kicker for the football team and new to the varsity squad. Details are still coming in from the—"

"What do you want?" I interrupt. "Why are you here?" My voice is lower now.

Even Stamp's eyes grow wide. He clings to the oven, at a loss for words.

My hand is on the Eliminator as I round the counter.

Lucy still looks confident, but she hasn't seen either the blade or the ice pick yet. How she answers will determine if she ever will.

"Believe it or not," she says, "I want to help you."

"Why?"

"Because you're not the only zombies in Seagull Shores."

Chapter 22
Three's a Crowd

"**V**AL?" STAMP AND I say it at the same time.

Lucy makes her own crumple face and reaches into her messenger bag once more. I swear to God, if she pulls out another library book about zombies, I'm going to use it to knock her block off. Then Stamp and I can fight over her brain, which, judging from her voluminous knowledge of the undead is probably pretty big.

Instead of a book, she slides out a thin tablet like an iPad but not quite. She taps the screen a couple of times until a slideshow starts. I watch a few grainy shots of a street light shining on a sidewalk. "You know how I've been watching you guys creeping around here for the last few nights? Well, that got a little boring, so in between, I started watching the end of our street. And when I saw this, I started snapping pictures."

The screen shifts to a second picture of the sidewalk, and in the right corner of the screen is a faint shadow. No, not a shadow at all. A foot. The picture changes, and now the foot is attached to a leg, bare and hairless but definitely masculine. A guy's leg. From the looks of it, a young guy's leg. Sleek but also firm. The picture changes again, and now there's more leg, plus some running shorts and the fingertips of a hand, just out of frame.

I look closer and see blood on the running shorts, on the pale fingers. Another screen, another picture, more of the bloody jogger. A hoodie appears, unzipped to a narrow waist, navy blue over a plain white T-shirt also dotted with blood. A strong chest, broad shoulders, and a shadowy face.

Lean and haunted, almost feral.

"Can you stop it?" I ask, but I'm not really asking. "Freeze it, I mean?"

I've got my zombie voice on, and as tough as she's acting, as if maybe she's holding all the cards, I get the feeling Lucy knows I'm being polite out of curiosity and, if I really wanted to, she'd be joining the anonymous bloody jogger wandering around town at night looking for fresh brains on the quiet streets of Seagull Shores.

Either way, she gets it and taps the tablet twice.

"Can you zoom in on the face?" I say.

Lucy doesn't say anything, doesn't look up or give me attitude; she just does it. A click here, a scroll there, and the legs, bloody running shorts, and half the background disappear. In their place hovers a grainy young face, distinct but imperfect.

I slide the Missing poster across the kitchen counter and compare it to the grainy picture on the iPad that is not an iPad. The bloody jogger in the picture is definitely the missing boy—what's his name?—Armand Suit.

And he's definitely no longer one of the living.

"When did you take this?"

"Two nights ago. Or, if you're keeping track, a few nights after you two showed up in Seagull Shores."

I'm still staring at the photo. It's a good quality shot, not great, but good enough, and I can see the telltale shadows under his eyes, the yellowy glint in his gaze, the shady teeth, and the thin lips.

"We didn't do this," I add, almost as an afterthought.

"I know that," she says, tapping the screen again.

It returns to normal size and progresses a page, still in slide show mode. This time there is someone else entering the frame, just behind Zerker Armand. I see half a hand, half a pink hoodie, half a thigh, all blood-splattered. A girl. Hairless legs, lean and long, thin and soft.

"I know it because I was watching you, sitting right here in this kitchen, when these two went missing."

Another frame passes, and the girl comes into focus. I don't even need Lucy to blow it up this time to know that it's the girl, Cecile something or other, Armand's girlfriend. I look down at the poster and find her last name: Brigham. Cecile Brigham. Lucy blows the photo up anyway, and it's the same thing all over again: hooded eyes, thin lips, gnarly teeth, blood on her collar, splatters on her chin.

"What are they doing?" I ask out loud. But I'm not really asking Lucy, and I'm certainly not asking Stamp. It's a habit.

She looks at me like I'm crazy. "You're asking me?"

I wave her concern away. "It was rhetorical."

"My guess is they're feeding." Her voice is certain and steady, but her eyes seek mine for approval. I still can't tell if she's being helpful or setting a trap, but either way what she knows or doesn't know, what she is or isn't doing here, doesn't really change the fact that two kids have gone missing in the last 48 hours and, apparently, are now undead.

I harrumph. "But then there would be more people missing. If they're feeding and they're new, they're not going to be subtle about it like whoever turned them apparently was."

Lucy shakes her head. "Not if their victims don't get reported."

I shuffle the Missing posters around the kitchen counter for emphasis. "Who wouldn't report someone missing? I mean, look how quickly these kids got reported."

The slide show over, the tablet slips back in her pack. She shrugs. "Lots of old people in Seagull Shores. It's Florida, you know?"

I nod, biting my lip.

Barracuda Bay was like that too. Lots of quiet houses you thought nobody lived in anymore until one day you caught some blue hair stooping over in the front yard, digging the morning paper out of the bushes, and looking at you like you invented loud music or something.

I slip the Eliminator back in my jeans pocket

without her ever knowing it was cocked and ready to slice open her jugular if she kept up with the attitude. Then I lean back against the counter. "You said you wanted to help us. How can *you* help us?"

Lucy considers the question. "You tell me. Then I'll let you know if it falls within my skill set." She's so funny, this schoolgirl, and she talks so old. If I couldn't see her, right in front of me in her school uniform, I'd swear she was in her midthirties or even older.

I ignore her overconfidence—I'm kind of used to it by now—and answer, flat out, "We need to pass among the Normals."

She stands there, fiddling with the bottom of her thin, black tie.

"What? That's not in your book?"

She shakes her head.

Finally, it's my turn to smirk. "Normals are you. You're a Normal."

"So you mean humans? You need to pass among humans? Like, mingle and stuff?"

"Right. We need better clothes, we need IDs, and if someone's making kids in Seagull Shores go missing"—I look at Stamp, who's busy studying his teeth in the microwave's reflection—"one of us needs to go to school and find out who's doing it."

While he's not looking, I point at myself. "Like, I need to go to school. Not Stamp. Stamp no go to school."

It's kind of a girl moment. She looks at Stamp and back to me, then nods, all conspiratorial, wink-wink, nudge-nudge. Then . . . nothing. She doesn't say anything for a while.

"So can you help?"

"I can do that."

"Which part of it?"

She smiles, shoving everything in her bag and slinging it over her shoulder. "All of it."

Chapter 23
Pass or Fail

L UCY COMES BACK later that night, knocking on the fence door.

Stamp and I are sitting, feet in the pool, enjoying the warm water on our cold skin. Well, *enjoying* is probably a pretty strong word, but when you're undead, you take what you can get. Anything to take my mind off what might or might not be happening in Seagull Shores and who might or might not be causing it.

When I don't get up right away, Stamp sighs. "My turn?"

I shrug. "Not really, but I'd appreciate it."

He frowns, and I think I should have used a simpler word than *appreciate*, but it's too late now.

He's already up, tromping to the gate.

"Who is it?" he asks.

Lucy's voice is playful on the other side. "George Romero."

Stamp looks at me, face crumpling.

I snort. "Let her in. At least she knows the password."

This chick! Since it's nighttime now, she's changed out of her school uniform and is wearing a lavender track suit with a black T-shirt underneath the tiny jacket. Covering her basically flat chest, the Superman symbol is plastered in glittery purple bling.

I shake my head as she sits, cross-legged, next to the pool.

"Do you live around here?" Stamp asks, putting his feet back into the pool. He's in thrift shop boxer shorts, and his legs are unbelievably long.

I expect Lucy to snort. I would snort, and she's twice the witch I am. But she doesn't. She cocks her head and says slowly, but not too slowly, "Sure, Stamp. I live right next door." For emphasis, she points above the gate to the second floor of the neighboring house, the window facing us bright behind closed purple drapes.

He smiles, and I can't tell if it's because he's happy she's our neighbor or because she answered him without yelling. Probably a little of both.

Then he gets very serious. "And your name is?"

She cuts me a look, a half smile on her face. "My name is Lucy Toh." She enunciates her last name very carefully. It sounds like *toe*.

He nods. "I know you! You deliver Chinese food!"

She snorts, and I'm kind of amused. Other than, you know, being mortified.

I open my mouth to correct him.

She waves it off. "Among other things, yes. Today, Stamp, I'm delivering something I think you'll like even more."

With that, she slides a manila envelope out of her messenger bag. Only, it's not a regular manila envelope with a metal clasp that always digs under your fingernail; this one has two red circles, and she unwinds red thread from them. It's all very James Bond, and that's probably a big part of why she chose it.

During the unwinding, Stamp kind of forgets he's supposed to be interested and goes back to watching his pale legs wriggle under the water's brackish surface. I like watching him this way: quiet and soft and innocent. I wish he had more time to stay happy and clueless. I wish that, wherever we went, trouble wasn't always chasing us. Maybe one day he'll never have anything more to do than wriggle his legs in the deep end of his own pool. And I wonder idly why I don't see myself in that picture with him. Why both our feet aren't dangling in the deep end—

Lucy clears her throat. "Ta-da."

In her hands are two Florida driver's licenses and two slips of paper.

I take them from her and look at the license with my photo on it. "But how—?"

"Look closely."

So I do. The picture is from my old license, the one I got back in Barracuda Bay when I could still sweat bullets over parallel parking and four-way intersections. But the name is Madline Swift, not Madeline Swift. And the address is 1465 Lumpfish Lane, Seagull Shores.

"It's amazing what leaving out one letter can do," she says. "Now if anyone looks close enough to search for Madline Swift, they won't find out you're—you know—dead."

I ask again, "But how?"

She shrugs. "Mostly it was my brother, his laptop, and a website it's probably illegal for me to even say the name of, plus a laminating machine he uses all the time making his buddies fake IDs. But whatever. It'll be good enough for you to go to school with, even drive with. If nobody looks too closely."

I look at Stamp's and gasp so loudly even he looks up from the wading pool.

"What is it?" Lucy asks.

"Maddy?" he says, about to get up.

I wave him back down. It's just his picture looks so different from what he's become. It's like another whole person. His original photo shows the old Stamp, the real Stamp, the Stamp I fell in love with and snuck out to meet, and I guess died and came back to life for.

Thick, black hair with that little Superman curl dangling over his forehead. Alabaster skin except for the apples in his hollow athlete's cheeks. He's wearing a sweater, something his mom probably picked out for him, black with a kind of high, stiff collar and a zipper down the front and, underneath, an almost blindingly white T-shirt.

His name has been altered too. Stamp Crosbie, it says on his new Florida ID, rather than Stamp Crosby. And we share this address.

"Are they okay?" Lucy asks, the first sign of

insecurity I've ever seen rippling across her face.

"They're fine. They're beautiful. I just . . ." I cut a look toward Stamp, who's gone back to watching his wet feet. "I haven't seen him like this in, well, over a year."

She nods, looking at him now and then down to his license. "I just kind of whisked them out of the laminating machine," she says slowly to me. "I didn't really take a close look, but hubba-bubba."

"Yeah." I chuckle.

Then I shake the thoughts out of my head and turn my attention toward the slips of paper. They are school schedules, one for each of us.

"Just in case," she says, when she sees me still looking at Stamp's.

I nod and focus on mine. According to this, I'm an eleventh grader at Seagull Shores Prep School, locker number C-1601, combination 35, 5, 22. I've got PE fourth period and Chem Lab sixth and B-lunch.

"Ooohh," I joke. "I've always wanted B-lunch. I always got A back home." I look down at the future in my hands and then back up at Lucy. "Why?" I ask her.

"What, you want A-lunch?"

I shove her playfully but not so playfully. "No, I mean . . . why are you doing this? Why are you our neighbor, and what were you doing looking in our windows, and how did you get this done so fast, and why are you not freaking out over what we are?"

In the second it takes the blush to rise to her cheeks, I realize two things. One, she's *definitely* not a zombie. And, two, she's not being entirely truthful.

"I told you, Maddy. I know who you are and what you're doing. Trust me, if I thought you were here to eat me, I'd be calling the cops right now. But since I saw you sitting here while the Missing posters say Armand and Cecile were going running that morning, all I can figure is maybe you can help find whoever, whatever's doing this and stop them somehow."

I want to argue with that, but I can't. "So how are we going to do this? I mean, look at me. I have thrift shop clothes, and I didn't even think to get a backpack. You can't pass among the Normals looking like Little Orphan Annie."

She rolls her eyes and shoves me back. "You're on the bony side, sure, but I've got some stuff that may fit you, and I have a backpack for every day of the week. No worries. I can pick you up early tomorrow, and we'll swing by the 24-hour Family

Value Mart and get anything you still need that I don't have enough of: notebooks, whatever."

I nod at Stamp, lying back on the pavement now, looking at the stars as his feet dry on the pool deck.

"I got you, girl," she adds, reading my mind. "I figure I'll take you to school, get you situated, make sure there's no trouble in the front office when you check in. Then I'll duck out of Honors Physics in third period and come check on Stamp. I'll be back by fifth period, no worries. After school we can even swing by the pet store on Wahoo Way and grab some cat food, heavy on the lamb brains, for dinner."

She has it all figured out, down to what to do about Stamp while I'm at school and how to get us brains, at least the quick-fix kind. I don't know her game, but it's a good one and, frankly, the only one in town.

She's up in a flash, looking at the gate guiltily. "I'm supposed to do deliveries for Dad tonight, so how about I meet you in front of my house at, say, 5:30 tomorrow morning?"

I nod, and she goes without a backward glance. The gate swings shut, and I listen closely for the sound of footsteps on grass, for a car door opening or closing, for an engine to start up and slip into reverse before backing out and peeling away from the curb.

But I don't hear anything.

When I finally get up and slink toward the gate, nudge it open, and look outside, her driveway is empty and the light is still on in the second-floor bedroom.

Chapter 24
On the Night Shift

I HAVE WORK to do before school in the morning. (Wow. The thought of going to school is tripping me out.) But first, I set Stamp up in the bedroom facing the street. There are no lights to turn off, which is a good thing, and none to turn on while I'm gone, which is even better.

He harrumphs and frowns and makes all kinds of new Stamp faces. "Why can't I come, Maddy?" he whines all the way up the stairs.

"I need you here to see if any more Zerkers come down our street."

"*You* do that," he counters, leaning against the doorjamb as I ease open the blinds just enough for him to see through—and not an inch more. "And

I'll go look on the streets."

Yeah, that's a great idea. Nothing could ever go wrong with that one. Not even just a little.

"Well, but you see better from a distance," I totally lie. "So I need you up here. You'll be really helping me out."

He looks at me as we stand in the middle of the room. Between our yellow zombie vision and the orange street lamp streaming in through the slats, the air is a kind of tangerine glow.

"So what if I *do* see a bunch of Zerkers coming, huh? What do I do then, huh?"

I cringe. "Don't say *huh*, Stamp. It makes you sound mean."

He grins. "Maybe I am feeling mean."

"No, you're just feeling left out, which is different than mean."

He sighs and leans against the wall next to the window, peering outside. Then he looks back at me. "Actually, right now, I *am* feeling mean."

I chuckle. "Okay, yeah, I get that. But in general, *huh* is kind of an ugly word."

Big eye roll from Stamp. Then, an honest question: "Well, how long will you be gone?" He sounds half hurt, half pretending he's not.

I reach out and touch his shoulder and am happy when he doesn't shrug it off. "I'll be back in a couple of hours," I lie, knowing from experience that Stamp doesn't have the greatest sense of time. "You just watch the street and count how many Zerkers come, okay?"

He nods. "You're sure this is big-time important stuff, right, Maddy?"

"The biggest, Stamp."

He grunts but is already looking away, out the window, where I know he'll stand, tall and true, until he hears me walk back in the back door downstairs, even if it's two days from now.

Meanwhile I walk downstairs, sliding Vera's pen into a pocket of my black thrift shop jeans and the Eliminator into the other. I grab the a gray-and-black-striped hoodie and slip it on, creeping out the back door, through the gate, and out along the side of the house.

I linger near Lucy's place. I know she said she had to work tonight, but the house is unusually silent. Not a single TV playing, not a dishwasher grinding, not a dryer tumbling.

The light in the second-story window is the only one on. I want to look inside, but despite being dark as sin outside, it's still a little too early for me to be pushing my dead gray nose against anybody's living room window to see why the downstairs is so quiet.

Instead I stick to the sidewalk, hood up, hands in my pockets, just another surly teenager walking off another post-dinner fight with the fam. It's kind of nice, being alone and out of doors for only the second time since we snuck into Seagull Shores a week ago.

With my new ID in my back pocket and the hood covering most of my face, the night sky dark and the street lights few and far between, I feel vaguely safe. Not Normal, by any stretch, but close enough to walk around without wanting to stick an ice pick into everything that moves.

I still have a couple of twenties left over from the thrift shop till. I walk into a gas station and buy a cheap grape soda, just for the sugar. The girl behind the counter is college age, kind of pretty, and I freak for a moment until I see her talking on her Bluetooth and barely even acknowledging me.

I walk out the door with the soda and sip it while I walk, feeling almost Normal. There's not much going on at 10:30 p.m. in a place like Seagull Shores, but there's enough to keep my eyes busy.

A sushi place on the strip is still open, and I watch a family inside celebrating something: a birthday or a graduation or a raise. The grown-ups keep taking sips out of little white sake cups. The younger ones—college age, maybe—drink beers from tall glasses. They're the only ones in the place, and the guy behind the sushi bar keeps saying apparently funny things to them and bowing.

I walk down the strip. All the shops—the souvenir stands, the stationery store, the drug store, and the antiques stores—are closed, dark and quiet, except for the one dress shop that left an electric jack-o'-lantern plugged in. Its neon-green eyes stare at me as I walk past. Cars pass quietly, slowly. The streets are wide and new and lined with palm trees, and there are benches every few yards on the freshly poured sidewalks.

Seagull Shores is cleaner than Barracuda Bay, maybe even newer, but it feels a little cold and distant. At least back home people said hi to each other, and you'd always see skater boys hanging out on street corners, slouching around in their neon-pink hoodies and white sunglasses, just passing the time and whistling at the bikinied girls driving home. The sidewalks might have been a little more cracked, and there were fewer benches and street lights on the main drag, but at least it didn't feel like every trash can was going to turn into a robot and laser beam your arm off just for littering.

I walk in circles, first around the whole town, then in tighter loops, cutting out the main drag and the school and the fire department and walking around the neighborhoods, then just the neighborhood that borders where Stamp and I have holed up.

The streets are quiet but well lit, flickering pumpkins on the porches, cars quiet and cool in the driveways, the blue lights of TVs or computer screens flickering in living room or home office windows.

A few streets away from the house on Lumpfish Lane, I hear scraping behind me. On instinct, I leap into the row of bushes between two houses and stand perfectly still, watching. A minute or two later, a jogger goes by, breathing heavily, heat radiating off her in waves. She's as human as Lucy or Dad or the chick in the convenience store just now.

I watch as she glides down the street, so sleek, like a Nike ad come to life and poured into the street all glossy and glowing. Her chestnut ponytail bounces with her peppy stride, white earbuds fixed to the iPod buried somewhere in her taut white track jacket. She's about my age, probably goes to Seagull Shores Prep with Lucy.

I watch with envy until I hear more scraping.

Fast and hard at the end of the street.

I stand, hidden, the Eliminator in hand.

The scraping intensifies, shoes on the pavement, rough and clunky but fast. Faster than I would be.

Faster than I *could* be.

Human fast; living fast.

The girl is deep in the cul de sac now, running between orange pools of street light, steady in her pace, oblivious to the danger following her. I don't know if she can't hear the other shoes scraping or if she's ignoring them, but then I remember the earbuds. The street isn't very long, but I'm at the top of it, and she's at the other end.

She moves effortlessly, as if she's one big muscle in pink running shoes. I see the glints of eyeballs, yellow and fierce, under the next street light. One pair, then two, then three.

Three of them. Here. In Seagull Shores. Already. In under a week. They scrape clumsily along the sidewalk, lurking in the shadows, but they can't hide their eyes, hunting her like a wolf pack.

I inch closer to the street but not entirely away

from the safety of the thick hedge. I'm close enough for the Zerkers to sense, if they cared to, but judging by the scraping and sniffing, it's clear they only want fresh meat.

I'm torn between leaping out and confronting them, but they're Zerkers. I'm no wimp, but I'm alone.

I've never been alone before. Not really. There's always been Dane around to help or Stamp or at least the Sentinels lurking in the background.

Now it's just me. I'm Vanished. No one to help me, no one to hear me, no undead cavalry to rush in and save me at the last minute. Stamp is three streets away, too far to see what's going on. Besides, he's so literal I know he's looking down on only our street, period, because I told him to. Even if a mushroom cloud flared just to the left of his field of vision, he'd ignore it.

I stand there, watching the girl, her face blissful and serene, so happy and carefree. They strike faster than I would have expected and in tandem. While the third lurks in the shadows, the boy—Astrid or Harrington or whatever his name is—still in his running shorts, strikes her high on one bare shoulder, crunching down so hard I see a flash of white bone beneath the spurting blood and the torn sleeve of her track jacket.

She screams, but the girl—Chelsea or Chalice, whoever—is on her, mouth over the girl's mouth, chewing and chomping on her face.

I can't help myself. I leap from the shadows, Eliminator in hand, sprinting down the street, but I'm no track star. I'm stiff and zombie slow, watching in vain as they drag her into the shadows, crunching and chewing, branches cracking and twigs snapping.

By the time I get to the first blood splatter, they're gone. Deep into the shadows, everywhere and nowhere all at once.

I go left a few yards, smelling nothing but grass and the ocean breeze. By the time I turn back to go right, the blood trail is cold on the salt air, the dark maroon drops smaller and smaller as they disappear into a vacant lot between two streets, and a dozen more streets beyond that one.

I stand in the middle of the lot, watching, listening, seeing nothing, hearing nothing. They could be lying in the tall, unkempt grass three feet away or at the bottom of the retention pond. They could be picking their teeth in somebody's garage five streets over, for all I know.

I curse myself and turn back toward the street.

It is still and silent—the lights on in the houses, the cars dewy in the driveways—as if nothing happened.

In a beam of street light, lying on its side, laces bloody, is her shoe. I look around, waiting for someone to come out of a house, point at me, call me out, tell me I let it happen, but nobody does.

In the end, I pick up the shoe, because blood is blood and a good Florida rainstorm might wash it away. Even a good case of sprinklers could make it just another rust-colored smear on some yuppy's drive to work. But a shoe is hard to hide and just gets people talking.

I bring it home with me, cutting across backyards and houses to double-time it to the house on Lumpfish Lane.

I put the shoe under the kitchen sink, just in case. I don't know why. I don't want anyone finding it, but I can't quite bring myself to throw it away either.

I climb up the stairs, suddenly sad and lonely and ashamed and in need of some company.

Stamp is there, standing guard, just like I thought.

"See anything?" I ask a little too loudly.

His eyes get big at the sudden noise. "Nope," he answers, kidlike. "You?"

I shake my head, feeling it's less of a lie than

actually saying no.

"Should I keep looking?"

I reach for his hand and drag him away from the window. "No, we've done enough for one night."

We stand in the middle of the room, hand in hand.

"So what now?"

I smile and lead him downstairs. "Let's put our feet in the pool. You like that, right?"

He nods and follows me onto the deck.

Chapter 25
School Daze

"How'd it go?" Lucy is waiting for me on a bench outside the library. She's facing the back door to the office as I walk out, admiring my new student ID.

Madie Swift

11th grade

Transfer

B-Lunch

Next to my vital signs is my ghoulish picture, shaved head, pale face, thin lips, drawn eyes.

I hand it to Lucy as she rises, smoothing out the green-and-blue gingham pleats in her skirt.

"I think they took pity on me. Maybe they think I'm dying or something."

She shrugs, handing the ID back. "You look edgy; that's all. Maybe if you would've let me put on a little blush, some eyeliner, it wouldn't look so bad."

"Been there," I say, thinking of Hazel and the clown makeup she applied my first morning as one of the reanimated. "Tried that. Epic fail."

She studies me critically, fixing the lapel of my maroon school jacket. "A little lip gloss." She fumes. "Something. I mean, I didn't go to all this trouble just so you could stumble around like something out of a haunted house."

"Maybe I'll just scare the Zerkers away," I huff, shaking off the guilt from last night.

We walk toward our lockers. "I'm pretty stoked Tony was able to slip your school records into the central computer like that."

"Tony?" I stop at a bulletin board outside the guidance counselor's office.

"My brother," she explains, joining me.

"Not for nothing," I complain, "but they weren't exactly themselves in there this morning." I point to the latest Missing poster, stapled next to the first two. "Emlyn James," it says, next to the yearbook photo of the pretty chestnut blonde the Zerkers bushwhacked while she was out jogging last night.

Maybe it's just me, but in the picture her eyes are quietly judging me. "I think this latest missing kid has them more than slightly distracted."

"I heard about that," Lucy says in that intense voice of hers.

I turn, looking down at her. "Did you know her? Emlyn, I mean?"

She shrugs and tugs me away from the bulletin board, toward the commons area, where the slamming of lockers and squeaking of shoes gives me déjà vu all over again. "She was on the school newspaper, I think, but we didn't hang out, if that's what you're asking."

The halls are full and not full. By that, I mean they're so wide that even with a few hundred kids all getting ready for homeroom, it still looks half empty.

The lockers are alternating blocks of green and blue, the school colors.

Lucy stops at a blue block and points to the green block one row over. "You're down there, I think."

I walk until I find the locker on my school schedule, fiddle with the combination, and open it up. I open Lucy's loaner backpack, which is maroon and pretty sweet, and dump some notebooks, extra pens, and cute locker magnets on the top shelf. If the Zerkers are already out snatching joggers off the street before midnight, I doubt I'll be here long enough to hang any candid snapshots on my locker door, if you know what I mean.

Lucy walks up.

I smile. "Thanks again for taking me back-to-school shopping this morning."

"How's the uniform fit?" She tugs at the safety pin keeping my gingham skirt around my waist.

"So far, so good."

She looks almost cheerful, a rarity. Her hair is clean and straight, her face not very made up but young and healthy. I'm suddenly jealous of her aliveness. We're standing there inspecting each other, BFF style, when a trio of girls walk by.

I smell anger and then fear. They're angry; Lucy's afraid.

She kind of shrinks back, and I turn just as one of them yanks the books out of her hands. They tumble to the floor, and Lucy scrambles to her knees to pick them up.

Mean girls. Already. Okay, I get it.

The one in the middle's in charge: red hair, alabaster skin, tall, curvy, flawless, smiling for miles.

Next to her a girl with mocha skin and

straightened hair puts her hands on her hips, licks her lips.

The blonde who shoved Lucy's books to the ground examines her fingers. "I think I chipped a nail."

They laugh and laugh as I inch forward.

From the ground, still on one knee, carefully shuffling her homework to avoid standing, Lucy hisses, "No, Maddy, it's not worth it."

I turn to her and grin. "Trust me. It's *so* worth it."

The redhead reaches out a warm hand. "Nice look," she says and ruffles the close-cropped hair on my cold head. She jerks back as if she might get scabies. "What'd they do, let you off the cancer ward for the day?"

Her BFFs echo her laughter.

I step toward her, hands at my sides. I've got to give her credit: she doesn't even falter. "That's the best you got?" I growl. "Cancer jokes? So lame."

Finally she squints. "Watch who you're calling lame, Schindler's List."

I shake my head and grab her tie, yanking her down to her knees. She hits the tile floor with a quick thwick-thwack of kneecaps on the shiny floor. She grunts, palms on the tiles. I shove my foot into the small of her back so that she's lying facedown in seconds flat.

I gently kneel next to her, eyeing her friends already backing away, as I whisper into her bright-pink ear. "Let's just skip the two months of emotional bullying and cut to the chase, okay, Ginger? Just 'cause I'm new here doesn't mean I haven't seen your kind before. From now on, Lucy and I are off limits, okay?"

"Bitch," she hisses, trying to get up.

I shove her back down with—no lie—my chill, gray pinky. "Try and get up again, and I'll use my whole hand."

She shakes her head but doesn't move.

"Say it with me, Ginger: Lucy and I are off limits."

"Screw you, trash!"

Quick like, I push a finger against her side, pressing, pressing, until I can feel a rib starting to give way under my fingernail.

She does too. I can hear it in her voice, feel it in the way she goes still, no longer resisting with every ounce of her strength.

"Okay, okay," she grunts. "From now on, you and Lucy are off limits. Fine, whatever, just let me—"

I hoist her up midsentence and spin her around so she can see the rest of the students, staring, openmouthed, eyes laughing at her. Her friends are nowhere to be seen.

"Now go find your friends. They're probably in the bathroom, changing their thongs."

Lucy shakes her head as I help her up next. "Wow," she says.

"You're welcome."

"No, I mean, wow, how stupid. I thought you wanted to pass here. All you've done is make a huge spectacle and an even bigger enemy on your first day. Not even in your first ten minutes!"

Her face looks angry, but her eyes are grateful.

"Like I said," I grunt, "you're welcome, Lucy." But I know, even as I turn and stomp off, she's right.

She catches up to me and walks me to my homeroom, straightening her skirt the whole way there. I think, because her legs are so short, she has a thing about her skirt, like a fixation. I wish I could tell her she's beautiful, human and flawless, warm and full of bloody cells, so quit sweating the small stuff. But Normals don't think that way. I know I never did.

We pause just outside of Mrs. Fillibuster's room. "Don't get me wrong," she says, moving toward her own homeroom just down the hall. "It's not that I'm not grateful. It's just . . . you know how this works. They won't come back at you. They'll target me when you're not around. What am I supposed to do then?"

"Fight back," I say. "She's weak now, wounded, embarrassed. She won't want to risk being shown up again."

"That's easy for you to say," she whispers, walking out of range. "You don't feel pain."

She has a point. Maybe it was stupid. But I couldn't help it. Sometimes I forget the rage inside. Just because I'm not a Zerker, just because I've never been bitten, doesn't mean I don't feel the sometimes uncontrollable, undead fury of being threatened, even if by a Normal.

Besides, am I going to pass up the chance now that I'm finally strong enough to bully the bully? Not likely.

I turn around, about to walk into homeroom, when I suddenly smell it.

Zombie. Not Zerker flesh; zombie flesh, like my own. There, coming toward me, blonde and fresh-looking, swinging her almost Normal hips, is a familiar face.

"Courtney?"

Chapter 26
Concerned with Courtney

"Maddy?"

I step out of the classroom, ignoring the big human eyes watching the drama in the doorway. Screw it, Normals; I've got bigger zombies to fry.

I grab Courtney's arm and drag her down the commons to the first girls' room I see. Inside, I do the whole push-every-stall-door-open thing, and before I even press the last one, I smell smoke.

It's locked, and when the smokers hear me rattling the door, they cough out, "Chill. We'll be done in a—"

I snap it open with one good yank and say, "You're done *now*."

But even a shaved, tie-loosened, sleeves-rolled-up

chick like me isn't enough to interrupt these nicotine freaks. Two of them, both nearly identical with straight black hair, pigtails, glossy maroon lipstick and skull earrings (so not edgy). They stare at me, dull eyed.

The one with the cigarette starts to speak, but I reach out, grab the smoke by the lit end first, and snuff it out between my cold, dead finger and thumb. Suddenly, with no cancer stick to distract them, they take to staring at me. I guess that's enough to do the trick, and they scram, inching past the broken door lying crooked on its hinges, a corner touching the floor.

The minute they're gone I look back to find Courtney leaning casually against the sink.

"Go block that door," I tell her.

She looks at me as if I've just gone Zerker. "Block it yourself."

I cock my head.

She stares at me, not moving an inch.

But I do. I take two steps forward and watch her flinch just a bit. That makes me smile. "Look, Courtney, this isn't Sentinel City, okay? And even if it were, you're just Sentinel Support, so I'd lose the 'tude unless you want me to do to your face what I did to that chick's cigarette."

She smirks.

Just as with Ginger out in the hallway, the rage bubbles up, threatening to spill over any second.

"Big talk for someone who just got Vanished, Maddy." She's still leaning there, blonde hair limp and long, face pale and drawn, but still so human-like it makes me envious for the days back in Barracuda Bay, when I was fresh and young. Did Dane want me then only because I was newly undead?

Is that his type?

Behind her is a mirror, water stained and brightly lit. I catch my face, hair, skin, eyes in the reflection, and even I'm scared of me. But Courtney's not. At least not yet.

"Yeah, I got Vanished, and you know what that makes me? The kind of zombie who has zero cares to give about a wannabe Sentinel like you. What else are they gonna do to me? Double Vanish me? Rekill me?"

She starts to creep back a little because I'm moving closer. "As far as the Council of Elders is concerned, I don't exist. As far as the Sentinels are concerned, I don't exist. The Keepers? I might as well be a Zerker."

Now we're about two feet apart, so close I can smell the nauseating perfume she's saturated her school uniform with. "So if everyone I've ever cared about thinks I'm a Zerker, what makes you think I care about doing insanely violent things to you right now?"

She makes a move, not toward me, but to the side—the wrong side, away from the bathroom door.

I sling her back to the other side, one handed, the way you'll see fighters do when one guy is trying to get out of the corner of the ring he's being pummeled into.

"Stop," she shouts.

It's so unexpected, I do. "I'll stop," I add, watching her there, between the sink and the exit, "when you block that door and tell me what the hell you're doing here—"

Just then the door flings open, and I roll my eyes, about to give her major now-you've-done-it face, when a guy walks in.

Not just any guy, either.

The guy.

Chapter 27
Smokin' in the Girls' Room

"DANE!" INSTINCTIVELY, I run to him. Our embrace is uneven, with me clinging to his chest as he reluctantly reaches around me, momentarily at least, until his clutch turns to an insincere pat on the back.

"Okay now," he mumbles, finagling his hands up against my shoulders and gently prying me off of him like some rock star wriggling away from his groupie. "There."

I see a flash of embarrassment flit between him and Courtney, one of those how-pathetic-*is*-this-chick looks I always dreaded being the cause of. But even now, as it's happening to me, I so don't care. I shove him back so I can wedge my pathetic,

Vanished self between him and Courtney.

"What is going on?" I grunt, pushing him a little more.

He flashes a look at Courtney. "Block the door."

She makes a soft cluck but scuttles off, wedging her arm against it as if the Zerkers were already trying to get in. Courtney and I share a look, and suddenly I don't know what to think. My anger is gone, but I can't quite feel sorry for her either.

I turn back to Dane. "Fine. Now the door is blocked and we're all here, one happy little undead family, so tell me what's going on."

He wastes no time. "The Zerkers are here. You know that, right?"

I freeze-frame. How much does he know I know? Does he know I sat in the bushes watching the Zerkers attacking Jogger Girl until it was too late for me to do anything about it? Does he know about Lucy and the missing jogger? About the thrift shop and the sixty bucks and the grape juice and the cat food?

"Yeah, yeah," I rush. "I saw the Missing posters and put two and two together."

He kind of softens. "Just like Barracuda Bay, right?"

I blink, and we could be back there in any

bathroom, talking about Bones and Dahlia and Chloe and Hazel. All of them gone, no more. Dane and I gone, no more, as well.

I lower my voice. "Not just like."

It wouldn't hurt so much if he didn't look so epically stunning in his stupid school uniform. It's like he was flippin' *made* to wear this thing. The white, collared shirt hugs his chest; the tie sets off his deep, dark eyes and hollow cheeks; his stubbly hair looks punk rock next to his maroon blazer with the sleeves rolled up. He even manages to make pleated khakis sexy.

He looks to Courtney, who doesn't have the good grace to even pretend she isn't using every bit of her new zombie hearing to snoop on us.

"Forget all that," I surprise myself by saying. "We're here, it's now, whatever. So the Zerkers. What now?"

He shrugs. "Same as it ever was. Courtney and I are here to scope things out, make sure they don't get out of control."

I look from him to her. "You. And Courtney. Are here. Period?"

He looks uncomfortable. "Well, Florida is big, and we still haven't located Val, so we're all the

Sentinels could afford to send right now."

I shake my head. Just thinking of what happened last night, three Zerkers plus Jogger Girl, who, if they didn't totally devour her, is one of them now as well. We're outnumbered.

I look at him, then at her, and something strikes me. The uniforms, the cockiness—this isn't their first day at Seagull Shores Prep. "Wait. When exactly did you guys get here?"

He avoids my gaze. "A few days ago. Why?"

"Are you . . . Are you not surprised to see me, Dane?"

"A little, yeah, but you were on foot, so how far could you go?"

Okay, that kind of makes sense. Still, something is fishy.

But now it's his turn to quiz me. "Tell me Stamp's not here, in school with you."

I get vaguely protective all of a sudden. "No, he's not, but he could come if he wanted to."

"No, he couldn't."

I nod. "No, he couldn't."

"So who's watching him, then?"

"Lucy."

He and Courtney do their eye flick thing again.

"Who's Lucy?"

"Lucy Toh. She lives next to us. She got me my fake ID and a school schedule." Then I kind of stare at him, as if he's the worst Sentinel on the plant. "I mean, look at me. How do you think I went from Vanished to attending a human high school in less than a week? You think I could do that all by myself? Do you even care if I had to do it all by myself?"

Whoosh. All of that goes over his beautiful head. "A Normal?" He looks at me as if I've just broken about 24 zombie laws.

But I'm not even technically a zombie anymore, so who cares? "Yeah, but—"

He brushes past me, roughly, so roughly I want to grab his tie as he walks by and yank it off—through his neck.

"Unbelievable," he says. "Courtney, get to . . ." He turns back to me, snapping like he's some advertising executive and I'm his secretary and we're in his office dictating a letter. "Where are you and Stamp staying?"

"One-four-six-five Lumpfish Lane," I offer happily, anything to get rid of Courtney. "Why? Where are *you* two staying?"

"None of your damn business," she answers for him.

The door swings open, and without another word, Courtney slips through it.

"Where are you staying?" I ask again.

"There's a warehouse downtown—abandoned, whatever. We've been camping out there." He pauses from pacing the room and flashes me a crooked grin. "Why? Is your place better?"

"Not for her, it isn't."

"Come on, Maddy. Let's not—"

"Not what? Not talk about something that's unpleasant for you?"

His eyes soften. "I meant not now."

"Not now? Then when? We couldn't do it during Keeper training. I missed you when they Vanished me from Sentinel City, and now a Zerker might come in the girls' room any minute, so we can't do it now. When are you going to break up with me, Dane? I mean officially?"

He looks younger suddenly in his maroon uniform jacket. More vulnerable, though I know he's not. Just the opposite, in fact.

"It's not like that, Maddy. I still have feelings for you."

"No, you don't. If you did, if you ever did, you'd grow a pair and break it off now and quit making me do all the work."

He starts to speak, then simply nods. "You're right. I'm sorry. About everything. You, me, Courtney, Val, your Dad, Vera, the way it went down back at Sentinel City. I wanted to be there. Really, I did. But my time isn't my own anymore. I'm a Sentinel now. I have to go where they send me."

"And Courtney has to go where they send you too?"

He nods.

"Funny, Dane. I don't remember Sentinels ever showing up with support before. Do you? At least not with girl support."

He shrugs. "It's kind of your fault, actually. Ever since Barracuda Bay and what you did back there, and then Val and how you handled her, well, they're planning to let girls do more around Sentinel City."

I throw my hands up. "Lucky me. I'm so glad I could make it so all the pretty young zombies get to come in and steal everyone's Sentinel boyfriends. I am so proud of myself right now. You wouldn't even believe it."

"It's not like that. It wasn't like that."

"Then how was it? Honestly, I'm curious."

Ugh, I hate myself right now. I sound so shrewish and petty and, worst of all, so desperate. But I can't help it. It's like I *have* to know, no matter how irrational I sound. He has to explain it so I can understand it, or it will never make sense.

"I don't know. It just happened, I guess."

I want to strangle him, hug him, choke him, and kiss him at the same time. How can he do this to me? How can Dane, whom I fought so hard for, whom I loved so hard, just walk away from it all so quickly? And expect me not to make a big deal out of it?

I stand speechless, my back to the sinks. The bathroom door cracks open, and I slam it shut. Harder than I expected to. The sound echoes through the room, through the halls, through the whole school probably. I don't care.

Dane looks at me harshly. "Stop drawing attention to us. It's called *passing*, remember?"

"Yeah, Dane, I remember. 'Cause you taught me how to do it. *Remember*?"

He straightens, getting ready to leave. "Yeah, well, a lot's changed since Barracuda Bay."

"I guess so."

We stand there, hearing the mumbling outside.

"What now?" I ask, holding it in place.

"Now we go find the Zerkers and take them down."

"We?"

"Yeah, we. What, you're going to let them turn a bunch of Normals just because you went and got yourself Vanished?"

"I didn't think I was allowed to do that anymore."

He smiles, breaking my heart all over again. "Yeah, well, I officially deputize you."

Chapter 28
Brain Tease

Lucy drives us home. She's got a fairly newish car. At least it still smells new. Dark green, four doors, it's a compact but feels bigger. A little sluggish on the gas for my taste, but zombie beggars can't be ride-home choosers. I called shotgun because, hey, I found her first.

Dane sits behind Lucy. Sorry, scratch that, rewind. Dane *slumps* behind Lucy, doing his best sullen teenager of the living dead act all too convincingly.

It's pretty frigid inside the car, and I don't mean the temperature, although, yeah, clinically speaking, a commute home from school with two reanimated passengers is technically rather cold.

We've left school too soon. That's because no

one listens to me. I told her to let some cars out first, let the traffic die down. But Lucy's so anal, she just had to race out as soon as we were strapped in. Now we're stuck in a long line, crawling away from Seagull Shores Prep down Pelican Row toward the main drag, where we'll peel off on Wahoo Way and inch toward the house on Lumpfish Lane.

We sit there, going nowhere fast. Dane slumps lower with each passing minute. Lucy nervously taps her steering wheel. I think idly how nice it would be to live somewhere without cheesy street names that don't sound like they come straight off a bait store inventory list. It will probably never happen, but it would be nice for a change.

Courtney is already at the house, watching over Stamp, and God knows what those two have been talking about since Dane gave her her walking papers during homeroom.

I've kind of felt bad all day about the look on her face, trying to stay brave even as she knew it was a losing cause. The crumbling kind of disappointment flickering there, just below the surface as she turned from the door and did as Dane asked. The flash of anger at the way he turned back from her without another word, just expecting her to do his bidding.

I've got no love for the kind of girl who will mack on your man and smile all the while, but I have just as little love for the guy who will turn around and treat you both like crap when it suits him. Dane was never supposed to be that guy.

And even now, a part of me still thinks he isn't. Despite all the evidence to the contrary.

"Awkward much?" Lucy asks when no one's talked for a few minutes.

The radio is on but low, some classical, baroque, all-Vivaldi all-day BS station she's got on her presets. I tried fiddling with it on the way to school, but they're all adult-oriented anyway—smooth jazz and talk radio and that malt shop memories stuff Dad would listen to at his desk in the Cobia County Coroner's Office—so I just leave it alone.

"Sorry," Dane says first, because I'm still too ticked at him to talk. To anyone. "I guess it's been a while since I've been around a Normal."

She snorts in her dorky way, which makes me smile. She even drives dorky, all sitting up in the seat, two hands on the wheel, 10 and 2, looking left and right every few seconds even though we're barely moving. "First time anyone's called me normal all year, especially a boy."

It falls flat, and that makes me even madder. "Sorry, Lucy," I grunt. "It's not your fault. We've got baggage."

Dane snorts and slumps some more. I don't know how. His knees are already pressed against the back of Lucy's seat as it is. If he slumps any lower, his kneecaps will be massaging her shoulder blades in no time.

"It's not about our baggage, Maddy. It's about bringing a Normal into this. No offense, Lacy."

"Lucy," we both correct him.

Then I say, "I didn't bring her into this, Dane."

And she says, "I came to her."

And we give each other a short Thelma-and-Louise you-go-girl nod. That is, before she turns away and looks out the windshield, as if we might do major damage going 2.67 miles per hour.

"Why?"

I turn around. "Who are you asking?"

He nods toward Lucy.

I nudge her gently. "He's talking to you."

"Why what?" She gives him a glance in the rear-view before quickly pinning her gaze to the back of the school bus in front of us.

"Why did you come to Maddy? What made you

approach someone you thought could be a zombie in the first place? I'm just curious because, for most people, that would be a turnoff."

"She's into it," I answer for her, because I know that whole turnoff thing was a jab at me anyway. "Knows all about us. I mean, not us us, like you and me and Stamp, but reanimated persons in general."

"It was also a bit of dumb luck," she adds, as if I'm making her sound even worse than dorky. "I mean, of all the houses in Seagull Shores, she showed up next to mine."

I look at her.

Dane looks at her.

I look back at Dane, shrug. "It was foreclosed. I thought it would be safe. Plus, it was like way late. Who knew she'd be up, staring out her bedroom window, the whole time?"

Dane shakes his head and looks outside.

We're moving now, slowly but surely, turning onto Wahoo Way and finally speeding up.

"I still don't like it," he says softly.

We both ignore him. What's he going to do about it now anyway?

Lucy parks in her driveway, and we shuffle out. "Just give me a sec," she says over the hood of her car as I stand and stretch my legs. "I'll just blow off my folks and be back over and we can—"

"Don't bother," Dane snaps, brushing past me toward the back gate. "I'll take it from here."

"Hey!"

But he's already gone, tromping along the grass, heading toward the gate at the back of the house.

I turn back to Lucy, who looks like she's been standing in line for the last *Twilight* premiere only to get snubbed by Edward when his publicist whisked him away at the last minute.

I wave it off. "Don't worry about him. He's just grumpy. I really appreciate everything you've done, Lucy. I mean, the ID and the school schedule—"

She nods before I can finish and walks away from all our living dead drama. She looks so alone and vulnerable at that moment, standing there between her car and the front stoop.

Suddenly, I think of that robust jogger the other night, so alive and sleek and sweaty, and what the Zerkers did to her in record time. That was only three streets away.

I call out to her, in a near panic. "Listen, Lucy, this isn't a game."

She turns around, comes back to the car, leans

against the roof.

"Those pictures you took?" I say. "They're real. And they're not like us. Those kids are gone. Your friends—"

"They weren't my friends."

"Or classmates, whatever." My voice is a little tight now, impatient. "Listen. I'm just saying, they're not human anymore. They're double-extra-superbad zombies, not like me or even Dane. And they're close, and they don't sleep, and all they care about is what's under your hair. So are you working tonight?"

She looks back at her house, dark as ever, except for that same stupid light in the same second-floor window. "Yeah."

"Well, be careful. Can someone come with you?"

"Maddy, I'll be in a car. I'll be fine."

I want to remind her she'll be out of the car for a few minutes each time, that that's all it takes, and that her car isn't exactly a tank or bulletproof and certainly not Zerkerproof, but she's already drifting away, back to her front stoop, clearly still stung by Dane's thoughtless words.

"Can you come over? Later, I mean, when you're done? Would you mind? Would your folks mind? Just so I can see you're safe?" I force a chuckle and crack a bad zombie joke: "It'll make me not sleep better."

She smiles, one foot on the front stoop, long white socks up to her knees. "You're sure the Grinch won't mind?"

"Do you care if he does?"

She doesn't answer, just drags her pink-and-black, skull-covered messenger bag up the steps and disappears inside, into the dark and empty foyer.

I turn and stomp through the back gate, finding the pool deck empty and hearing voices from inside the living room. I open the sliding glass door and see black duffel bags lying all over the place.

Courtney is still in her school uniform, but she's gone all Britney and loosened her tie and put up her hair, and her jacket is carefully folded atop the kitchen counter. She has a black bra underneath, and I just have to snort. Even in the afterlife, this chick is all cliché, all the time.

Dane is stacking plastic to-go containers in the fridge.

"That doesn't work, you know." I lean against the counter. "The power's off." But even as I say it, I can see the fridge light on and hear it humming.

"Not anymore," Courtney says, ponytail bouncing along with her not-yet-deflated zombie breasts.

(Two more reasons to hate her.)

"How? I've been here for nearly a week, and nothing. When did it get turned on?"

Courtney stands a little taller, her bra pressing against her stiff white uniform shirt, unbuttoned to the third. "That's what Sentinel Support does. I'm not just another pretty face, you know."

She didn't . . .

I can't even.

I won't.

"Great, well, try not to turn all the lights on at once, huh? The place is supposed to be deserted, remember?"

She shoots me shade.

I turn to Dane, who hands me one of the to-go boxes. I take it, not because I have no shame but because I'm hungry and, even through the clear plastic, I can smell the fresh brains. I've been mentally drooling over them ever since I walked into the house.

We feed standing up, right there in the kitchen. Plastic fork in my hand, fresh brain on my tongue, down my throat, the juice on my lips, the fire in my dry, dead veins, the sizzle in my cells.

This isn't the repackaged, remodified, reconfigured stuff we get in the mess hall twice a day:

brain bars and brain smoothies and the rest. This is pure, unadulterated brain. Do I know where it came from? Animal or human? No, and I'm not going to ask. It's brains, and it's in front of me, and that's all I need to know.

I slump until I'm sitting on the kitchen floor, the way I used to do as a Normal when Dad was working late and I had a bad day and came home and spooned chocolate chip mint ice cream down my gullet.

Dane gently takes the empty container from my hand, and I smile weakly.

"How long?" he asks, washing it out in the sink and turning it over to dry on the counter.

"Since I fed? Since the day before I got Vanished, I guess." My voice is soft and hazy, like the field of vision through my fluttering eyelids. "We had some cat food along the way, but you know how that goes."

"Cat food?" Courtney stands above me, hands on her hips, jutting out her chest. "Gross."

Dane shrugs. "It'll do in a pinch. It's better than nothing, Courtney."

"Still." She sniffs. "Nasty."

He gives me a minute, then reaches down and

helps me up.

I don't thank him. Instead I say, "That was rude, what you said to Lucy earlier."

Courtney huffs, the seeds of jealousy already sprouting. "Who's Lucy?"

"The Normal," we both say at once.

He turns to me. "It's for her own good. You know that. You were careless to include her in the first place."

Sca-rew this guy all of a sudden.

I stare at him, disbelieving. "She came to *me*. She saw us and came to me. By then, it was too late. What did you want me to do? Tick her off? Alienate her like you just did?"

"Better she gets ticked off and stays away than you encourage her and she keeps hanging around until one of the Zerkers gets her."

I shrug. "I figured I could protect her."

"That's not your job anymore."

"Maybe not as a Keeper but as a human. I mean . . . Well, you know what I mean. Isn't one of the zombie laws to always protect Normals from the Zerkers?"

"That's just it, Maddy. You're not bound by zombie laws anymore."

I feel like I've been punched. It's one thing to hear the Council of Elders say it, but Dane? "There's a higher law, Dane. You and I both know that. I can't just turn that off because I'm dead."

He shakes his head. "We don't have time for philosophy. We're here now." He points to Courtney and the duffel bags. "We'll take care of this. You and Stamp just stay out of our way."

Stamp. I look around, don't see him. "Where's Stamp?" I ask Courtney.

She flinches, her nostrils flare, and she looks at the stairs. "I sent him to his room."

"He's not a child!" I spit, stomping away.

"Then he shouldn't act like one!"

Chapter 29
Time-out

STAMP LEANS ON the windowsill, staring at the street.

"Stamp?" I ask, though I've been in the room for nearly a minute now. And I know he knows it.

"Where were you?" he asks, finally turning around. His broad shoulders hit the off-white plastic blinds, and they explode with a rattle-tattle like a machine gun.

Neither of us blinks.

I keep my voice level and calm. "I told you I was going to school."

"All day?"

I nod. "I should have been more specific, Stamp. I should have said I'd be at school all day."

He nods. "I wouldn't have even cared so much, if it wasn't for that girl downstairs."

I stifle a chuckle. "You mean Courtney?"

He nods, then elaborates. "Uh-huh, the blonde with the big . . . you know." He holds his arms out in front of his chest the way kids will signify big bazooms without actually saying something as stupid and cheese ball as *big bazooms*.

I snort. "Yeah, well, that wasn't my idea."

"At least Lucy plays with me."

"She does?"

"Yeah, I mean, she talks to me like I'm a regular person and asks me all kinds of good questions."

I cock my head. "Yeah, like, what kinds of good questions?"

He shrugs, looking slightly antsy, like maybe this is all boring grown-up talk and he'd rather go back to discussing something more interesting, like big bazooms. "Big-people questions, like where I'm from and how I'm doing and what I like about you and what you do at night and . . ." His voice trails off, as if that's too much to remember all at once.

"She asks about me?" I don't know whether to be flattered or concerned.

He nods again, bored with me, looking out at

the street. "A lot of the time she does." He turns to smile at me. "It's okay, though. I don't mind talking about you that much." He snickers, like this is some inside joke he has with himself.

I want to ask more, but I hear clomping up the steps. Heavy clomping. Dane style. I listen and don't hear any Courtney-style clomping. He enters the room cautiously, as if maybe he thinks we're talking about him.

Stamp has turned away from me again, looking out the window as I told him . . . two days ago. I wonder how long he'll stand there, doing the same thing. Until I tell him to stop, I guess.

Dane walks to me quietly, eyes questioning.

I look at him and try to smile, but it's hard. Being in the same room with him and Stamp is at once so familiar and so ruined.

Still, this isn't about me. I clear my throat. "Stamp? Someone's here to see you."

Nothing.

I try not to take it personally because he does move a little slow these days. I try again. "Stamp?"

Finally he turns cautiously, and when he sees who it is, he smiles. "Dane!" His voice is warm and familiar, in a way he almost never uses for me.

"Hey, buddy." Dane walks over.

Like magnets, they get drawn to each other until they're so close I guess instinct takes over, and they hug. Whoa. I didn't see that coming. Stamp seems a little uncomfortable at first, maybe because Dane probably didn't say ten words to him the whole time we were in Sentinel City together.

But then, we haven't been *together*, not really, since Orlando. And even then, Stamp and Dane were never BFFs.

But right now, my dead, shriveled heart is pretty close to pumping again. This moment makes me think of family, and what that word means, and how once upon a time I thought I'd never need anyone else but these two. And now, neither one really belongs to me anymore.

Stamp is locked in his own mind, a shadow of his old self. Every choice Dane has made since we moved to Sentinel City has taken him farther from me. Suddenly I realize my adopted, undead family is breaking apart even as I struggle to keep it together.

When they separate, only Dane looks vaguely uncomfortable about it.

Stamp nods. "I missed you."

I swear I can feel Dane's heart unshrivel like

the Grinch's.

Then dude totally ruins it: "Maddy did too."

"Stamp!"

"Did so. You said you did! A hundred times, even!"

Dane chuckles. He looks at me and says, "I missed you guys too."

Gheez, where's Courtney when you need her?

Ah, spoke too soon. Soft footsteps announce her presence.

"Knock knock," she says right behind us instead of actually having knocked on the door.

I turn around and grimace.

"There's someone downstairs with Chinese food."

"Finally!" I snap, zipping out the door.

Lucy is standing at the front door, a bag from Lop Sing's in her hand, a dopey smile on her face. She's in this maroon velour jumpsuit thing that's formfitting in some places, lumpy in others, trying to be funky but not quite cutting it, like something out of a *Cribs* episode. It makes me flinch a little.

"Are you done already?" I say, dragging her inside.

No one has followed me down, so it's just us in the kitchen.

She looks a little squirrely. "My dad saw that new Missing flyer and told me to take the night off.

They're going to stop delivering until they catch whoever's doing this, so I thought Stamp might like some more moo shu."

I take the bag and slide it onto the counter, then look upstairs. I don't hear footsteps, and I can't imagine anything worse than spending the evening watching Dane and Courtney cuddle and coo while Stamp watches out the window for Zerkers, no matter how many times I tell him to stop.

When I look back at her, she has some paper in her hand. "More Missing posters. They just dropped them off at the restaurant. I know a few of them. I mean, they're all kids from my school."

I take them, give them a cursory glance, see three more yearbook photos, and blanch. I set them on the kitchen counter, next to the first two. They're all so young, and I know they're all gone. And I can't help thinking it's all my fault.

Again.

The house grows claustrophobic as I hear footsteps upstairs. I just . . . I want out. Now. I want to be doing something, not just waiting and waiting, as Dane wants us to do.

"Can we go?" Before she can answer, I shuttle her back outside. "Do you mind?"

She shrugs. "I know Dad wanted me home now, but it's so early and I didn't come bribe you just to sit on the sidelines and watch Seagull Shores get infested, you know?"

That's a pretty good answer, as answers go. She starts for her car, and I gently guide her past her driveway, down the street.

"That won't help you if trouble comes," I say.

She looks back at her car wistfully, as if she may never see it again, but nods and follows me down the street just the same.

"Trust me." I chuckle. "You're tooling along, thinking you're immune, and then you come to a road all blocked by burning cars and overturned ambulances, and there's nowhere for you to go, and suddenly you're stuck, a sitting duck. Better to be on your feet."

"Really?" she asks, catching up to me.

"Really."

I stand at the intersection of Lumpfish Lane and Snapper Street, looking left, then right. I chew on my lip and turn to Lucy. "Is there someplace we can sit and not be bothered but not look weird doing it?"

She squints, thoughtfully looking over my shoulder. "There's the playground in Center Square. It's not far from here but close to downtown. It's supposed to be closed after dark, but as long as you're not acting the fool, nobody will bother us."

We walk slowly toward downtown Seagull Shores. It's dark but still early—9:00 or 10:00 probably. I mean, early by zombie standards.

Lucy doesn't seem tired. Just the opposite, in fact. As we get closer to downtown, she ducks into a Stop N Go and buys two bottles of cheap grape soda. I don't know if it's a coincidence and she likes that junk too or if she's seen the empty bottles around the kitchen at the house on Lumpfish Lane.

It feels good, sipping and walking with someone other than Stamp for a change. It's something you would do with a friend, which reminds me: in all this time, I haven't seen or heard her say one thing to another human soul. Haven't met her parents, haven't even seen her swap high fives with another kid at school.

The walk is slow and casual, the night air cool but not brisk. Here and there, orange or purple or green Halloween lights blink in a storefront window or a jack-o'-lantern flickers on a front stoop.

I sip the cold, sugary soda, feeling it in my cells.

The silence between us is comfortable.

I put the cap back on my soda and clear my throat. When she looks at me, I ask, "So I'm not sure how to say this without sounding insensitive, but how are your friends doing with all these other kids going missing?"

She smirks and sips some soda, her upper lip tinted purple until she licks it. "Is that your majorly awkward way of asking why I don't have any friends?"

I snort.

The park comes into view, still a ways away: a vast opening just off Main Street, clean white sidewalks and a manicured lawn and benches and swings and monkey bars.

"I guess so, yeah."

She shrugs.

Our shoes pad on the sidewalk. From an open window somewhere, maybe even an early Halloween party, the strains of "Monster Mash" twinkle in the air.

"You could say I'm not very good at being popular." She tosses me a vaguely embarrassed look. Then she juts out her chin. "Plus, we just moved here not too long ago."

I nod. That would explain her loner status in the halls, the lack of friends knocking down her door, and the quiet cell phone.

Then again, I get the feeling that even if Lucy had lived here since birth, she still wouldn't be getting texts at all hours, sharing BFF stuff like which boy is cute and who dumped who and, OMG, did you see who they just voted off *American Idols Who Think They Can Dance* last night?

Which is cool and actually quite familiar. If it hadn't been for my own BFF, Hazel, back in Barracuda Bay, I probably would have been a lot like Lucy. Probably a lot less annoying and anal but most likely just as unpopular and vaguely restless and all kinds of lonely. I mean, when you're actively seeking out the living dead as your friends of choice, you know you're not quite socially adjusted.

The park is quiet, dark, and big. We stand at the mouth of it, looking at the empty benches and the tall and not-so-tall palms dotting the nice green lawn. There is a gurgling fountain in the middle, a walking path of rust-colored pavers, and a swing set—all sterile, like something off a brochure cover.

We sit at opposite ends of a bench by the fountain, leaning the plastic bottles of soda against the slats between us, kind of like cup holders. The air is cool and quiet, perfect for listening for Zerker noises. From here in the middle of the park, we have a view of most of Main Street and a few other streets.

It feels good to be doing something. Frankly, I don't know what else to do. At least this way if people come running out of a random building screaming, I'll be close enough to do something about it.

And this time, I *will* do something. You can bet on that.

We sit quietly for a few moments, just listening. For Zerker noises. I'm not quite sure what that might be. Drool hitting the ground? Stupid shuffling? But I'm listening for anything nonhuman at this point.

Then out of nowhere, Lucy says, "So . . . you and Dane? What's the deal?"

I chuckle, crossing my legs, and realize I'm still in my school uniform. Man, I really did want to get out of that house tonight. "We were kind of a thing for a while."

Her eyes get a little bigger. "Yeah? How a while?"

I look to see if she's poking fun or actually interested, but her face is a mask. We've got nothing better to do, so I answer. "Long enough to matter."

She nods. "Okay, I mean, but how does that work?"

"It doesn't, apparently."

"I meant how does that *physically* work?"

I roll my eyes. Stupid Normals and their morbid curiosity. "I know what you *meant*, Lucy. It's complicated, okay?"

She puts her hands up, girl talk for *Okay, okay, I wasn't all that interested anyway.*

"What? It doesn't talk about zombie anatomy in your little book there?" I tousle the strap of her messenger bag on the bench between us.

She shakes her head. "If it does, I haven't gotten to that chapter yet. Maybe I should read faster."

I snort. "I suggest skipping it altogether."

A surprisingly not-that-awkward silence follows.

Then she smirks and says, "Was it serious?"

"Yes," I moan instantly, as if it's been bottled up for weeks and just waiting to come out. Who *else* is there to talk to about it? Stamp? "It was hella serious, and I thought it would last forever, which really means something when you're undead and, ugh, now he's here with that zombie tramp, and it hurts major. I just can't believe what a monumental tool he became."

She snickers a little. "That must have felt good, huh? Getting that off your chest."

"I'm sorry." I almost gasp. "I just, you know,

being a zombie is kind of lonely and isolated."

"I bet . . . So, probably, you tend to get a little clingy so you don't feel as isolated."

I see where she's going. "Heh. No, not clingy exactly, but I see what you mean. If anything, maybe I wasn't clingy enough."

She arches an eyebrow.

I think of Dane's Sentinel training, his missions, my Keeper training, and Vera's constant demands. Of my body, my mind, my allegiance, and my time. And then there was Dad, who I tried to see every night before he went to sleep. And poor Stamp, who I felt like I should pop in on every now and then. "What I mean is," I say out loud, "if I had been a little more clingy, we might not have drifted apart."

She's nodding encouragingly, so it just kind of spills out: "Whatever. I know how it sounds, but he was so nice, to me anyway. I know he looks thuggish, and I never thought I'd be one of those girls who dug that, but that wasn't what did it for me. He was a very different person around me, with me. A calm and happy and safe person, you know?"

Her gaze goes a little far away, like maybe she does know, all too well. Then she quietly nods.

I sigh and look at my hands resting on my

green-and-blue plaid skirt. "I thought he was the one, you know?"

She nods. "Maybe he just got scared."

My lips go thin because what the hell does *she* know about it? Then again, what do I know? She could be the resident relationship expert in Seagull Shores, for all I know. "Go on."

She shrugs. "You guys are supposed to live a long, long time, right? So maybe he didn't want it to be literally till death do you part, you know?"

I scoff. Loudly. "It wasn't like we were married or anything."

She takes a sip of her soda and puts it back down. "Maybe not, but maybe it felt like that to him. Was he dating anyone when you met?"

I think of Chloe and snort. "Not hardly."

Lucy nods.

"What? What does that nod mean?"

She smiles, probably surprised by my desperate tone. Even I'm surprised by it.

"He strikes me as a lone wolf, is all. Brooding . . ."

"Go on." She's 110 percent dead-on so far.

"Well, so, sometimes guys like Dane will pull a dick move just to end it fast rather than actually, you know, tell you about it."

"But why?"

She shrugs. "Why do guys pull dick moves ever? So they're done, over and out, free to walk away. He probably doesn't even like this Courtney chick, but it's better than dragging it out another few decades with—"

I put a finger up. To her mouth.

She winces because I'm sure it's cold and she's probably going to have to gargle with cherry-scented hand sanitizer now. But to her credit, she doesn't move and even shuts up.

I remove it and turn around, pointing to the cluster of palm trees ringing the park. "Did you hear that?" I whisper so low she has to lean in. I repeat. "Did you hear that?"

"No, 'cause I was giving you all that good love advice just now."

"I thought I heard a twig snap."

"Shit." She looks around, panic clearly gripping her. "So this was a pretty stupid idea, huh? I mean, look at us here: we're like fish in a barrel!"

I shush her, but if someone is back there watching us, she's right: our goose is cooked anyway.

I slide the Eliminator from my front pocket, popping both ends.

She looks down at the two kinds of metal hissing out. Her eyes get even bigger. "What's that?"

"That's not in your book either?"

She shakes her head.

I shrug, feeling pretty smug about that. I hold up the weapon, just high enough so she can see but whoever's snapping twigs behind us can't. "It's called an Eliminator. Well, I mean, I call it that, anyway."

She rolls her eyes, as if I don't know it's cheesy. I know it, but when you haven't slept for over a year, yeah, you find cheesy things to name cheesy things so you don't go stark, raving mind. That, and I never in a million years pictured myself sitting on a park bench in another beach town showing off a weapon to some Normal chick with a backpack full of zombie books.

She nods toward it, eyes wide. "How's it work?"

"Well, the ice pick goes in the ear, killing the brain instantly. The scalpel cuts off the head, just to make sure."

She's so still I feel the need to say something more, if only to convince myself. "In theory, anyway."

Her frown tells me that was probably the wrong ad to lib.

"What? You haven't killed a live Zerker yet?"

I'm about to correct her when she says, "You know what I mean—a moving Zerker?"

"Well, I was still in training when they Vanished me, so—"

"You mean banished."

"No, I mean Vanished. But it's kind of the same thing."

She looks at me expectantly.

I sigh and look toward the palm trees, squinting into the yellow darkness but see nothing, hear nothing.

I look back at her. "Basically, I got kicked out of Sentinel City."

I kind of worry I've said too much already, but she's still listening and, besides, who is she going to tell . . . that would believe her, anyway?

"It's, well, it doesn't matter. When they kick you out, they call it being Vanished. So I never finished my training or got to actually, you know, ice pick and decapitate a real Zerker."

"So, like, you're not even an official zombie?"

I shake my head. "It's a long story—"

There. Right there. I heard another one. I stand, senses on high alert, Eliminator at my side, forget whether or not they can see it. In fact, screw that. I *want* them to see it. Stupid Zerkers.

Lucy moves too, her velour jumpsuit swishing, but I still her with a wave.

She sits, and I turn. The palm trees sway against the yellowish sky. Shadows and shapes form just beyond the line of trees behind us.

Shit, this *was* a stupid move.

Really stupid. And now I've got a Normal along for the ride.

Another twig snaps, and a leg appears, a running shoe attached, lemon-yellow jogging shorts, white hoodie, all blood splattered.

Lucy has turned around. "It's . . . It's him. Armand Suit. The exchange student." The fear rolls off her in waves.

It's one thing to buy a bunch of zombie books and slap some edgy skull stickers on your messenger bag, but to stand there staring one in the face, well, that's a whole other story.

I grunt. "It's not just him."

A second later his girlfriend emerges, dried blood all over, hair still up in a freakishly neat ponytail.

They move forward smoothly.

I think how well Bones and Dahlia, Zerkers to the core, assimilated at Barracuda Bay High. Why not these two? What's to stop them from taking a shower one day soon, putting their uniforms back on, and just showing up at school? They could say they were foolhardy, ran away, spent all their money, came home, and now they'll be all better, just let them back into school and let them do their makeup work, pretty please.

It could work, and it would work, so why are they still shuffling about like horror movie zombies, creepy and obvious to anyone foolish enough to venture out for a late-night stroll?

Suddenly a third Zerker stumbles out, a vision of creep, face scarred horribly, teeth visible on the right side of her jaw line, half a nostril missing on the same side.

And I blink to make sure. It is. It is the girl, the jogger, the one I could have saved.

Unlike the other two, who look plenty bloody but otherwise normal, there'll be no passing for her. Not in this afterlife. The right shoulder of her white track jacket is crimson, her one good eye wide and yellow and searching for brains.

"Stand," I tell Lucy.

She doesn't even blink. Just does it, and for once I don't mind the gentle whispering of her maroon velour track suit nightmare.

"Get behind me and stay there."

I should probably tell her to go get Dane and Courtney, even Stamp, but I'm afraid these aren't the only three Zerkers in town. If I let her go alone, she could run into more and not have me or my Eliminator around to help her. The last thing I want is to see Lucy one-eyed and bloody, showing up with a bag of cold moo shu at my door tomorrow.

She stands there at my back, sticking close. I keep the bench between us and the trio of Zerkers, not that it will do much good. But if all it does is buy Lucy a few extra seconds to get away, it's worth it.

The two with their faces still intact pause in front of the stand of palm trees. Jogger Girl keeps walking, stopping, turning for reassurance. The other two hiss at her. Hiss. I'm not even exaggerating. Even I cringe a little. I glance behind me, and Lucy goes pale.

Jogger Girl turns and grits her exposed teeth, walking toward me. No, more like limping. Then I realize why. Her right sock is drenched with blood, her shoe missing. *The* shoe . . . The one I hid beneath the sink the other night.

She's coming right for us.

"What should I do?" Lucy asks, fumbling for

her phone. "I'm calling 911."

"And tell them what? A Zerker is coming? By the time you explain that, we'll both have yellow eyes and matching teeth for the rest of our afterlives."

"Well, what, then?"

"Just let me handle it!" I hiss, wishing I had asked Dane for his cell number first instead of just running out of the house, half-cocked and jealous.

I look behind me, where the town is dark but the coast looks clear. At this point, screw it. I'd rather have her sprint home and get the others and stand a passing chance at living than keep her here with me. "Run, Lucy! Just get back to Lumpfish Lane. Go get the others. Tell them where I am, have them stay there and shut the door, and don't answer it until one of us breaks it down."

But she stands there, clueless. Not that I can blame her, but she needed to be gone a few minutes ago if I'm ever going to get any help. But then, that's my fault. I can't be mad at the Normal because I got Vanished and old and rusty in less than a week. I shove her, and she blinks to life, sprinting off on her short legs.

I turn to Jogger Girl, whose bloody socks squish with every step.

"Good. Now we're even."

She cocks her head, and a little drool runs out the toothy side.

I look over her shoulder and see a few others have joined the Living Dead Cross Country team. Two, three, four, five more. Two girls, the rest guys. Two are still in their school uniforms; another is in a Burger Barn uniform, as if they got him just after he clocked out. This is happening fast. Faster than in Barracuda Bay, faster than I know what to do about.

They all look young, like the faces on the Missing posters lining up on the kitchen counter back on Lumpfish Lane. I'm quite certain, if I could stop the onslaught and poll them one by one, I'd learn they're all from Seagull Shores Prep School. And who else would do that? Who else would turn only students into Zerkers but a twisted, wicked, revenge-fueled chick . . . like Val?

Jogger Girl is closer now, a soft keen coming from her jagged mouth. God, she looks worse than some of the masks we'd wear to scare the audience in the *Great Movie Monster Makeover Show*.

"Can you hear?" I ask, gripping the Eliminator, trying to keep her occupied, focused on me, on my mouth, my head, not the hand at my side. "Can you talk?"

"Yeah," she grunts, soft air moving through the hole in her cheek where I see her pinkish-white jaw muscles flex. It's a reedy sound but weird because her voice is so Zerker deep. "I just don't like to."

That airiness combined with that hoarseness— I figure probably the gash in her throat nicked some vocal cords when the Zerkers were chewing on her face.

I shiver. "Stop. You don't have to do this. I, I know there are a lot of them, but I have friends too."

She shakes her head, as if even she knows how stupid I sound. "Just don't," she says, limping faster now. "It won't work."

I raise the Eliminator, hoping she'll see it and stop, giving her one last chance. "Don't," I blurt, my voice raw with guilt. "Don't make me do this."

"Do what?" she says, three feet away now. She pauses, giving me that creepy half smile that is her full smile because half her freakin' face is missing. Her good eye narrows. "All you're doing is finishing what they started. What you *let* them start."

"I couldn't," I sputter, "take them all by myself."

She cocks her head, drool drizzling onto her shoeless foot. "That's not what she says."

"She? *Who* she?" I growl. "Tell me!"

But she's walking again. "Why should I help

you"—that whistly voice croaks from her mouth and throat at the same time—"when you never helped me?"

I shake my head, begging now. "Stop. Just. Stop."

She gives me that horror movie half smile. As if she knows what she's doing, as if she's doing it on purpose, and how can I blame her?

When she walks to the bench, just when she's flush with it, I lunge with the ice pick. It slides in a smidge past her ear, slick and stiff all the way. I feel her thick, black, oozing Zerker blood splooge across my hand, but I hold tight.

Her good eye gets big. She drools some more, quivering on the end of my weapon, hands flailing at her side. I'm there when the lights go out, standing just out of range at arm's length. She slumps to the ground, taking me with her, the weapon still half stuck in her skull.

I yank it out and stand above her. The Zerkers on the fringe creep forward now, grumbling. Then they stop.

A voice behind me says, "Finish it, Maddy."

I turn. "Dane?"

"You have to. To make sure."

I shake my head, and he snatches the Eliminator

from my hand. It's glossed with black Zerker blood, but he doesn't even pause before slicing across her throat, through her spine, until her face lands, horror-mask-side-down, a few inches away.

She looks almost peaceful now, without her exposed teeth shining.

Behind us, without much fanfare, Stamp and Courtney bend toward the playground dirt, using their cold, gray hands to begin digging a shallow grave to hide the Zerker body and its head.

Lucy stands around awkwardly, then kneels to help.

Stamp gives her a smile, like, oh, what fun it is to bury Zerkers in a playground in the night!

Dane hands me the Eliminator, nods toward the other Zerkers drifting into the tree line. With the others busy, he moves closer, wiping Zerker blood onto his khaki pants. "What did she mean just now? About what you let them start?"

I look up at him helplessly, shaking my head. "It's too late now, Dane. And I don't owe you explanations anymore."

He clenches his jaw but finally nods. "You're right. You don't. I just thought you seemed upset and might want to talk about it."

I stare at him in disbelief. "This is hardly the

time, and you're hardly the person I'd go spilling my guts to now."

He nods, scanning me from head to toe before turning his attention toward the Zerkers, who are disappearing one by one into the stand of palms bordering the park. "Fair enough," he grunts, nodding toward them. "How many?"

"Six," I count on the fly, but they're moving fast.

"Wrong," he says, pointing a blood-blackened finger at something above their heads.

There, in the shadows, lurks a seventh.

Chapter 30
Jeepers Sleepers

"WHY DIDN'T YOU go get them when you had the chance?" Lucy paces in the living room, velour sweatpants whoosh-whishing as she keeps throwing her hands in the air, soap opera style. "They were right *there*!"

"There are procedures," Dane says coolly, leaning against the kitchen counter. Behind him, Courtney casually spoons fresh brains from one of his plastic Sentinel-sanctioned to-go containers.

I wonder how she can be so poised about it. It kind of makes me wonder if the Sentinels eat the real thing a lot more often than the rest of us do.

Dane levels his gaze at Lucy and continues, "It's more complicated than that. What if there were more in there, hiding, waiting for us to rush back, guns blazing? A *lot* more? What if they wiped us out our first week in town? What if nobody were here to call in the Sentinels until it was too late? Then where would your precious Seagull Shores be?"

She paces some more, nodding. "Okay, okay, I guess. But what now? What if those goons are ransacking the town as we speak? Going house to house?"

Dane shakes his head. "We've already put in a call to the Sentinels. They're aware of the situation and on standby. But without a confirmed sighting of Val, they're not willing to commit any reinforcements. For now, it's just us."

She shakes her head, hands up in a can-you-believe-this-shit motion, but no one nods in an I-know-right way because we've all been there, done this before.

The Sentinels suck; let's face it. There's a reason undead folks call them zombie cops. Like real cops, they're never around when you flippin' need one.

Dane looks at Courtney spooning her brains. Then at me. Then at Stamp. Then at Lucy. "Listen. It's late. Your parents must be freaking out."

I watch her face, but it's fairly placid. Like, *No big deal that it's nearly midnight and I almost just got bushwhacked by a half-faced undead jogger and I'm the only person breathing in the room, and, oh, by the way, there's a chick eating brains right out of the fridge.*

He adds, "Get some rest. We'll walk the streets tonight, make sure nothing else happens. Tomorrow we'll all go to school, see what develops. Maybe one of them will show up or slip up and we can find out where they're staying and track them down."

Lucy nods, as if this is a good idea.

It's not, but maybe she doesn't know that yet.

"Come on." I grab her messenger bag from the counter. "I'll walk you home."

"No. Really. It's just next door. Don't be silly."

Dane nods at me.

"Yeah, well, we were just in the park, and look how much trouble we got into there."

She bites her lip and frowns as I slide open the back door and walk to the patio. "Come on." I stare her down, giving her no way out, waving her outside like a puppy who has to go number one.

I wait for her at the gate. Looking up, I see the light in the same second-story window, the rest of the house as dark as the midnight sky that surrounds it.

"Thanks," she says, shutting the gate behind

her. In the yellow dark of my zombie vision, I see the dirt stuck under her fingernails from digging a grave for Jogger Girl. "I'm fine. Just watch me from here. Really."

Her voice is insistent, which turns up my radar another notch.

I shake my head and take her arm a little more forcefully than I intended. I forget sometimes that she's a Normal. Then again, nothing's really been normal about this Normal since we met. Which is kind of why I want to meet the parents who spawned this little type A go-getter. Once and for all.

"I'd like to see your folks," I say, dragging her toward the front stoop. "Thank your dad for all that awesome moo shu."

"Oh, he . . . won't be home yet."

"You don't say." I knock on the front door. Pound on it, to be more exact. "Well, maybe I can apologize to your mom for keeping you out so late tonight."

"No, he and Mom . . . work late. Every night."

I nod. Try the door. It's locked. "Then I should probably stay with you, just tonight. Make sure no Zerkers get you."

I'm expecting a nervous chuckle, a shake of her

head, something.

Nothing.

She stands there on the front stoop, clutching her messenger bag, not rooting around for the key, not moving, not speaking.

I sigh, turning the knob, turning, turning until—snap and crackle—the door pops open.

I wait a beat for the sound of a distant TV or someone calling out, *Lucy, is that you, dear?* For a kitchen light to turn on or a pot of tea whistling or a grandfather clock ticking in the foyer.

Nothing.

Inside it's dark and empty. No easy chair for Dad to sit in after a long night over the wok. No TV for Mom to watch her soap operas on. No dinner table. No chairs. No Halloween decorations.

In the dark kitchen: no dishes, no forks, no knives. Just a counter full of greasy wrappers from Burger Barn and lots of crumpled soda cans. Energy drinks, mostly, their overly tall cans empty and crunched.

Like this place belongs to a teenager. Living alone. On permanent spring break.

I walk upstairs and turn halfway up.

She's still in the doorway, looking at the floor.

My voice is a mix between disappointed and more disappointed. "You coming?"

She looks up, a pained expression on her face.

"There's Zerkers out there, remember?" I remind her.

She steps in quickly, shutting the door behind her, leaning against it with her back to squeeze it all the way shut. Suddenly, I feel kind of stupid about breaking the lock that way.

The rooms are empty, all of them, except the one with the light on upstairs. There's a sleeping bag on the floor, a big shiny laptop open next to it, the screen blue, in sleep mode. There's a little dorm fridge humming in the corner, some random magazines scattered about, more zombie books, a few cell phones—the cheap, disposable kind you get in gas stations and charge with cash.

I stand in the middle, my sneaker nudging a book called *Living with the Living Dead*.

I turn to her very slowly. "What gives?"

She follows me into the room, slumps against the far wall dramatically. "I knew you'd find out." She picks lint off one of her velour knees. "I knew you were too smart to fall for it."

"Fall for what?"

She waves a hand around the room, looks up at me as if she might cry. "All of it. The stupid zombie books. Me living right next door. Really? Right next door? Not two doors down, even? Being able to hack into the school system like that dude from Facebook or whatever. The driver's license. The school schedule. Just all of it."

I try not to wince. I kind of actually *did* buy all that stuff. Man, am I unprepared for being Vanished. "You mean, no dad who owns a Chinese restaurant? No brother who can hack into school computers?"

She smirks. "What? Do you fall for every Asian stereotype?"

"You're the one who kept showing up with Chinese food, saying it was from your dad's place, jackass! You're the one who told me your brother hacked into the school board, got me a driver's license, whatever."

She looks at me, nonplussed. Her elbows rest on her knees, her palms up. "I never thought you'd believe me. I kept waiting for you to call BS on me every time I spun another lie."

"Then why'd you say it?"

"They *told* me to say it. It's only my third

assignment. What do I know? I thought maybe you understood the code or whatever."

"What assignment? Who's *they*?"

"The Keepers." When all I can do is blink and keep my jaw from hitting the floor, she adds, almost sheepishly, "I'm a Sleeper."

Now it's my turn to slump to the floor, resting an arm on her humming black dorm fridge as I lean against it. "I can't with all this living dead James Bond crap anymore. The hell is a Sleeper?"

She looks at me as if I should already know, then looks away, then back. "Don't you know? What, is this your first assignment too?"

"I'm not on assignment, Lucy, remember? I'm Vanished. I shouldn't even be here."

She looks at me, blinking.

Then I remember she asked me a question. "And, no, I don't know what a Sleeper is. Nobody tells me anything, apparently. I'm like the Rodney Dangerfield of Sentinel City."

"Sleepers are like civilian sympathizers with the Keepers. Like secret agents. Undercover. You know, kids like me go to school and sniff around, but grown-ups work in hospitals or police departments or whatever, where they can look for evidence of Zerkers."

I shake my head, not because I don't believe her but because in all that time I was training with the Keepers, nobody said a word about Sleepers. Not one. "So you don't really go to Seagull Shores Prep School?"

She gives me bitch-please face. "I don't go to *any* school. I'm nineteen."

I look at her differently. She could be nineteen. Then again, she could be sixteen. Or twenty. With her baby-doll T-shirts and hipster messenger bag and goofy barrettes and knee socks, how should I know how old she is?

I shake my head.

The dorm fridge vibrates against my rib cage. Every few minutes there's a clink like the fan is on its way out or something, and it shoots out a musty smell.

"But why? How? In what universe would you and Vera ever be in the same room together?"

She looks away, talking to the wall. "When Zerkers attack someplace, when they infest a town like, say, Seagull Shores, what do you think happens? Afterward, I mean. Once the dust settles and the fires go out and the soldiers or whoever leave. What do you think happens then?"

I look at her thoughtfully, trying to form an

answer. I should know, I suppose. It did happen to my town. But I ran so fast and so far that I never stuck around to find out what happened to those who survived.

The most I saw of what happened to Barracuda Bay after we killed the last Zerker was in my rear-view mirror. I guess I fast-forwarded through the part she's talking about. Beyond my dad and a couple of my friends' parents, a teacher or two, I never really wondered what happened to folks who lost kids or brothers or sisters or moms or dads.

When I don't answer, she stares at me with cold eyes and starts speaking with a voice to match. "Say your whole family gets wiped out and you're seventeen and you're wandering around town in some clothes the Salvation Army gave you, wondering where you're going to sleep that night, and some chick in blue cargo pants comes up to you and gives you a bag of hot, greasy Burger Barn and money for a hotel room and new clothes. Suppose she sticks around all week, checking in on you, feeding you, and one thing leads to another and, well, you do the math."

I picture Lucy as she describes it: wearing sweat-pants and a flannel shirt, maybe, thrift shop stuff like I stole for Stamp and me. Dirty and hungry, dazed and confused, wandering around. No home, no car, no money.

My voice sounds loud after staying silent so long. "So Vera, like, recruited you?"

I think of me, sitting in Sentinel City that first night, Vera sitting across from me, a file as thick as a phone book between us. She knew everything about what happened in Barracuda Bay and afterward in Orlando. Pictures, files, phone calls, bank records, pay stubs, the works. Why would it be any different if she wanted to recruit a Normal on the outside?

"That happened to you, Lucy? Your family? Zerkers?"

She nods. I think of the few missions Dane has been on since becoming a Sentinel. He never says much, but I know of a few semi-infestations that have happened since we've been in Sentinel City. There was that cluster in Tennessee back in January. And something in Georgia. That one even made the news.

"When?" I ask her. "Where?"

"It was a few years ago, up in Tallahassee."

I wrack my brain. I was still a Normal then, two years ago. "You mean that train full of hazardous waste that ran off the tracks?"

She chuckles. "Yeah, that's what they told everyone. Kind of like the way they told everyone what happened in Barracuda Bay was a school fire, right?"

I nod. She has a point. Vera always said the Sentinels were the muscle stopping Zerker infestations but the Keepers were the brains of the outfit. Maybe this is what she meant.

I look at her, chin up. "But it wasn't hazardous waste?"

"It was Zerkers. My dad was a professor at a community college up there, a feeder school for FSU. He taught graphic design. My mom was head of the nursing school there. My brother was on the lacrosse team. It was a real family affair, except for me. I was still in high school."

"What happened?"

"Kids had gone missing at the college." She pauses to collect her thoughts.

I blink twice, remembering Hazel and the Curse of Third Period Home Ec.

"Nothing like what's going on now, nothing so fast like this, but enough that Mom and Dad would talk about it at dinner, you know? Anyway, one day during classes, I guess somebody pulled the fire alarm. Everyone was in the halls, going outside, when they just started . . . feasting.

"It was the afternoon. I used to ride my bike up after school. Dad had a class break around then, and he'd take me for ice cream. My brother might stop in, sometimes with a new girlfriend. Mom was usually too busy with department meetings and such, but every once in a while she'd surprise us."

Her eyes go a little blank as she stares at the wall just to the left of me. "I heard the screaming from a block away and sirens coming. I got close enough to see Dad's car in the staff parking lot, and then a bunch of bloody people started chasing me. People but not people. Like the people we saw tonight. I was on my bike, so I could outrun them, but if I'd gotten off or fallen, we'd be having a very different discussion right now. Or maybe none at all."

We both chuckle dryly, and I doubt she even realizes she's doing it.

"I just kept pedaling and pedaling, until I was halfway across town and couldn't hear the sirens anymore. Something caught on fire eventually, a car crash or something at the college, but by the time it got put out and I tried to make it back home, home was gone, burned to the ground. I had a little cash— lunch money, pocket change. Some gift certificates left over from my birthday. I ate junk food and slept in the park and found a paper one day with the names of the dead. My whole family was listed there. All three of them. A little while later, I met Vera and she fed me, gave me a place to sleep . . ."

She's still looking toward me but not at me. I wait a beat, then two, until finally her eyes focus and she lasers them in at me. "I've been a Sleeper ever since."

"I'm sorry, Lucy."

She doesn't blink. "From what Vera told me, your story's not much better."

It kind of makes me queasy to think that Vera told a Normal about me but not as queasy as Lucy must feel, all alone in the world, with a cold fish like Vera as her only friend. And I use that term loosely since, once upon a time, I thought she was *my* friend too.

"No, but I still have my dad, you know?"

She does know. I can tell. She nods and smiles, sniffs a little but never cries. It makes me wonder how many times, if ever, she's told that story. She nods, and I don't want her to dwell.

"But what do you do? On these assignments, I mean. Where do you go?"

She shrugs. "Whatever they want, within reason.

Since I look so young, mostly I just hang around in high schools, wherever more than a few kids have gone missing in a certain time period."

"Like here," I begin, then stop myself midsentence. I cock my head. "But you said people didn't go missing in Seagull Shores until *after* we got here."

She averts her gaze. "You . . . This was a special case."

"You followed me?" I ask, feeling more creeped out by the second. "But how?" I picture Stamp and me stumbling through the sagebrush and scrub pines as we trudged down the east coast of Florida. I know I'm about as clueless as a zombie can be, but no way a chick like Lucy could have stayed on our trail the whole time.

She shakes that straight black hair side to side. "Vera followed you, saw where you were heading, and sent me here."

"Here, to this house?"

"Once they saw you move in next door, yeah. They set me up. Nothing fancy, just an address and a sleeping bag, some spending money, and they enrolled me at school. Just like I did for you. Well, they did for you."

"I thought I was Vanished. But it turns out I'm just bait."

I'm not gonna lie; her expression is kind of condescending. I can picture her back in school before Zerkers came into her life, before Vera. She was probably one of those girls I wouldn't have gotten along with anyway. You know the ones: pretty, smart, but totally focused, zero comprehension of sarcasm, and no real sense that everyone else thinks they're entitled, stuck-up biotches.

"You're not bait, Maddy. You're just part of a team."

"What team?" I huff.

I dunno, for whatever reason, that superior tone of hers has me wanting to shove her head into a dorm fridge right about now. Or better yet, into that wonky fan in the back that keeps making metallic noises every few minutes. Try being a Sleeper without eyelashes, woman!

"The team. You know: you, Vera, me."

I imagine the bliss of kicking her in the shins.

Suddenly, she's the one schooling me. "How do you think this all works? How do you think a few dozen Sentinels and some Keepers keep a lid on every outbreak, every new zombie alert?"

I hate to admit it, but she's got me there. "I honestly don't know. I guess I just assumed . . . Well, I never stopped to think about it."

She nods impatiently, as if I've interrupted her mojo or something. "*This* is how. With Sleepers. A coroner here, a sheriff, librarian, federal employee, or reporter there. It's a network of us working with them working with us."

"But why? Why would humans work with zombies? I mean, look at what happened to your family."

She blinks, as if this is the stupidest question known to man. I dunno, I'm all befuddled, and maybe it is. "That's exactly why I'm doing this. I'm not as tough as you or a Sentinel like Dane or Courtney—"

"She's not a Sentinel." Can't anybody keep this straight? "She's Sentinel Support."

Lucy gives me major WTF face. "Whatever. Jealous much? Either way, I was lost, just sitting there, and Vera mentioned this program, where people like me could help. She knew I'd seen the Zerkers and knew what was up. And more than anything, I didn't want anyone else to go through what I had, losing their whole family like that. So if I can spend the rest of my life looking out for those yellow-eyed beasts, why wouldn't I?"

"Okay, okay," I hold up a hand to physically stop her from lecturing anymore. This is worse than school. But I guess she has a point. I think of everybody who's ever lost a son or daughter, sister or brother, husband or wife, friend or neighbor. Wouldn't they *all* make good Sleepers too? And wouldn't some of them happen to be cops or coroners or mail carriers or just plain neighborhood snoops who could put in a call to Vera if they saw some yellow-eyed hooligan gnawing on the neighbor dog's brain or snatching up joggers out of the middle of the street?

I sigh, run my hand across my face, then do it again. "So you and Dane and Courtney have been laughing behind my back this whole time?"

She wrinkles her nose and looks hurt I'd even say such a thing. "What? No? Why? I don't even know those guys, and they sure don't know me."

"But you said—"

"Vera recruited me, not the Sentinels. I mean, I assume they know about Sleepers in general, right? But not any particular Sleeper, per se. Do they? Would they?"

I shrug.

"From what Vera said, the Keepers like to keep their Sleepers on the down low."

I nod, as if I have any idea what she's saying. As if I care. It's none of my business anymore anyway, except when people lie to me. "So where's Vera now?" I ask, almost relieved to hear that somebody's in touch with the Keepers.

But she frowns and kicks at the carpet like a little kid might. Or Stamp. "That's just it. All of a sudden, she's not returning my calls."

"Of course she isn't." I stand, then pace around the room in tight circles. "'Cause that would be just too flippin' easy!"

Chapter 31
The Exchange Student

I STAY WITH Lucy until morning. She gets a little sleep but not much. I get none because, well, for obvious reasons. Basically I just sit there, watching her snore as the night wears on or, when that gets old, walk the halls of the empty house.

I come back just before dawn and sit down a little louder than I should, but maybe that's because I'm lonely and wish stupid Normals didn't have to sleep so much.

She wakes up quickly, as if she was never even asleep. Just sits up from a dead slumber and smiles shyly and reaches into the dorm fridge and grabs some gross-looking energy drink in a double-long can with neon-bloodred letters down the side.

I try to read them sideways as she guzzles. They say Level Up or Level Out, and it's not very good branding because I wouldn't even know what to ask for if I walked into some random Stop N Go to ask for one. She lets me have a sip, and I think it may be my most newest favorite thing on the entire planet.

I finish it off, and she scowls.

That's it. Her wake-up is complete. I have to admit, I'm more than a little impressed.

We talk a little and, in the end, decide not to bring up the whole Sleeper thing to the others. Dane; Courtney; Stamp, naturally. What would it solve? Either they already know and are keeping it from me (bastards!), or they don't need to know because screw the Sentinels anyway. What have they ever done for me except turn the man I wanted to spend my afterlife with into a workaholic player? Let them figure out about Sleepers on their own time.

We take turns with the shower and dress in our school uniforms just like roommates.

We walk out to the driveway and meet Dane, who looks all freshly scrubbed and fifty shades of gray. He's spiffy in his school uniform, and of course that makes me love/hate/love/hate him all the more.

I try to hide it by being all businesslike.

"Anything else happen last night?" I ask, hating the reporter tone of my voice.

Lucy notices and, like any good BFF, arches an eyebrow, which is universal girl speak for *slow your roll.*

Naturally, I ignore her and stare stone-faced at Dane. He shakes his head.

"Nothing?" I ask.

"What's that supposed to mean?"

"Nothing. I mean, it's just weird that they went all Greasers versus Socials last night and then didn't show up again."

He looks from Lucy to me. "Well, we could have used a little help scouting the town, but we never saw anymore."

I soften my tone a little. "Maybe they were tuckered out."

He sniffs. "Maybe."

Ugh, this is going worse than I thought. I turn toward the back gate of the house on Lumpfish Lane, where Stamp and Courtney look longingly after us, both for very different reasons.

Dane nods toward his blonde bimbo. "She's babysitting again."

"Don't say it like that," I scold him. I wave at Stamp before sliding into the passenger seat.

"Why?" he asks from his spot in the back.

"He doesn't like it. That's why."

Lucy starts the car and pulls away, waving at Stamp.

"Okay, then." He's looking out the window. "I won't."

The town is eerily silent as we drive past. The streets are serene. It feels like Christmas morning, when everyone's still home with their families, not going anywhere for a while, the stores closed and parking lots empty.

But it's not. It's just a normal weekday in October, seven something in the morning when it's usually not so Deadsville.

"It feels like today," Dane says, staring out the window, and I know exactly what he means.

Lucy and I share a look.

"What does that mean?" she asks, putting her blinker on to turn up the long, two-lane street that will take us to Seagull Shores Prep, even though there's no one behind us.

Dane shrugs. "It just feels like something is going to happen today."

She looks at the rearview mirror. "Well, so, where are all your buddies?"

He doesn't look back. "I told you, Lucy. There is protocol to be followed. We're following it."

"Did you not see what I saw in that park last night? What more proof do you need for your precious protocol?"

He sighs, not fogging up the window the way a Normal would. I wonder if he misses that the way I do; I wonder why I care. "Six Zerkers we can handle, Lucy. That is, if they keep to themselves. They don't want an infestation any more than we do."

"How do you know?" Lucy snaps.

"Look, kid, there are Zerkers in every town all the time. Usually it takes something major to set them off this way. Until we find out what that is, until we have confirmed proof that Val is their ringleader, the Sentinels aren't going to send reinforcements to help us. Period."

She looks at me, hands tight on the wheel. "Is he right?" she says.

"He's the Sentinel. I'm a free agent now, remember?"

She keeps looking from me to the road, from the road to me. I figure she won't stop until I answer and we'll do nobody any good if we run into a light pole on the way to school.

"But, yeah," I say, "that sounds about right.

Sorry, but for now, it's just us."

I sneak a peek at Dane, fiddling with his thin uniform tie. He slips a hand into his pocket and pulls out a generic cell phone. The kind we'd always get at the Stop N Go around the corner from our apartment in Orlando so nobody could trace our calls. And look how well *that* turned out for us.

He kind of holds the camera up so Lucy can see it in the rearview mirror. "I spot Val, snap her picture with this, send it to Sentinel City, and we're all good. Instant cavalry."

"How instant?"

Dang, this chick needs to be on *Jeopardy*, stat!

Dane looks back out the window at the gray, silent morn. "An hour or two, no more."

I shake my head and murmur, "A lot can happen in an hour, Dane. Let alone two. Especially with someone like Val."

He sighs, as if he's schooling some would-be Sentinel on his first day. "That's protocol, Maddy. What do you think the teams do all day, huh? Wait around on the town border for a whistle from us? The Sentinels are in other cities, looking for Val as well, on the off chance she's not in Seagull Shores."

"Okay, okay, I'm just not looking forward to

spending an hour alone with Val if she's already turned six or seven kids into Zerkers, you know?"

He sports a cocky grin. "Trust me, this time you're not alone."

Lucy and I give each other a little can-you-believe-this-guy look as she pulls in at the school.

She slows down to a crawl, and I see why. Even the student parking lot looks fairly deserted.

"What is it?" Lucy asks, mostly to herself as she finds a sweet spot right near the school building. "Senior Skip Day or something?"

I look back at Dane, but he's already getting out of the car, keeping his cell phone handy.

I grit my teeth and follow them to the quad. We're betting against a full-scale infestation on a $19.99 cell phone? Nice. Sure. Why not?

I shake my head and wonder why Dane bothers with the Sentinels anyway. I mean, I used to think it was like this vast army of well-trained, elite assassins, like G.I. Joe or SWAT or the Stormtroopers or something. And though they look badass with their black berets and new shoulder pads and double Tasers, really they're kind of stupid.

And I'm not just saying that because Dane is one and I'm still mad at him. I'm saying that because they'll dangle kids like me and even Stamp as bait, waiting on the sidelines while Val, or someone like her, is busy turning Normal kids into her Zerker mini army. I mean, those kids may not mean anything to the Sentinels, but they meant something to somebody.

Those two joggers were just a couple of lovesick kids out for a morning run, and because the Sentinels have some stupid protocol, Val or someone was able to turn them without any interference.

I know the Sentinels can't be everywhere, and they'll never be able to catch all the Zerkers all the time, but hello. They couldn't send more than Dane and Courtney to sniff out Seagull Shores? I'm not flattering myself, but they know Val and I go way back. Wouldn't that at least warrant another team or two, just for grins and giggles?

I sigh and follow along. I keep seeing the face of that jogger as the Zerkers devoured her. What would have happened if I'd stepped from the shadows one minute sooner? Would she have survived? Could I have saved her? What if I'd jumped out two minutes sooner, as she was passing the bushes?

Better to spook her and have her run away than stand there silently waiting for the Zerkers to come. Was I any better, lying in wait, watching it all unfold, than the Sentinels are now? Isn't that what they're doing: sniffing around other towns, waiting for a call from Dane to let them know the bait worked, that *I* worked, that Val is here and so are a dozen or so new Zerkers?

I shake my head at the hopelessness of it all. I should have stayed Vanished. I should have walked away from Sentinel City, never looked back, and let Val come and get me alone, the way she's always wanted. At least then it would be only me and her and nobody else—not Armand, not Cecile, not Jogger Girl or Lucy or anybody.

I should have sent Stamp away right away. The minute those Sentinels dumped us out of that van, I should have cursed him and kicked him and shoved him until he was alone as well. Then he wouldn't be here, waiting for Val to take her revenge.

How, after more than a year as a zombie, could I still think like a Normal?

When we get to the hallway, it's full but not full. Maybe it just feels that way because everyone is talking about the new Missing posters lining the bulletin board outside the library. So many now that they dangle off the bottom with Scotch Tape. I count a dozen, easy, and half of them look like the faces lurking in the shadows last night.

As the crowd drifts away, I move in for a closer look. I tap one and nudge Lucy's shoulder. "Isn't this the chick who laughed while the other one knocked books out of your hand my first day of school? The redhead?"

She nods, averting my gaze, cheeks red.

I check out the redhead's name, finding that, not surprisingly, it's not Ginger after all. "Gingham Thompson," I say out loud, trying it on for size. "Well, that's kind of close."

Lucy looks at me, concerned. "Are they dead?"

"Were those the creeps in the park?"

She looks away again, pointing at Gingham's poster. She frowns and looks at a few more. "Maybe this one and him."

The images all blur together. Young, fresh-faced kids in yearbook photos. Every poster full of hope, listing as many details as possible. "I would guess they're all gone but not dead. You know what I mean?"

Lucy nods, but her eyes are still empty.

"Either way, they're not coming back. You know that, right?"

Dane has been so silent I almost forgot he's been standing there the whole time. "Well, I have a feeling they're coming back, Lucy, but not alive."

He points to the posters for emphasis and looks directly at me. "This is a lot more than went missing in Barracuda Bay."

I turn to him, the posters making me mad. "Have you seen it happen this fast before?"

He shakes his head. "Usually the Zerkers lie low, take it easy. If they need to feed, either they make sure the victim never comes back or they make him one of their own. But they do it slowly, one every few months, so nobody gets suspicious. This? This is purposeful. Ten, twelve kids in a week? You don't turn that many kids if you don't want to get found out."

Lucy starts out looking nervous. Then, as Dane keeps talking, she looks mad. "Do you guys even know what you're doing?"

"Yes," we say, but even as we do, I sense we both know we're lying just to make her feel better.

"Just to be sure," Dane says, grabbing Lucy's messenger bag, "we all stick together today."

"I've got a Chem Lab final," she moans.

"Then so do we."

She looks shocked that we'd even suggest this. "You guys can't just audit any class you want. This isn't college."

Dane taps the bulletin board and gives her his best haunted, scruffy-headed, hollow-cheeked living dead face. "A dozen of your classmates went missing within a week. Do you think your teachers are going to care if a couple of friends stop in to check out what your Chem Lab or AP English classes are like?"

She shrinks back a little but, to her credit, doesn't look to me for help. "Okay, fine. Just back off." She inches toward her locker as we follow. "But, you know, I've got a rep to think about after you guys are gone."

Even I snort at that one. Didn't Vera teach her anything in her Sleeper training? I don't really know what Sleepers are, and even I know she's way off base.

"Lucy, do you understand what's happening here? You'll be lucky if you can still spell *rep* after the Zerkers get through with this place. Seriously, find another gear because we're way past neutral now. There's a very good chance half the people you consider friends won't be here by the time it's all over. You know that, right?"

She nods but doesn't say anything more as we shadow her to her locker. I look around, watching kids listlessly shuffle around. They're looking at empty lockers, talking about who's not here and why.

Little mumbles reach me from the row Lucy's in:

"I heard the reason there's no Missing poster for Mona is that she went to visit her boyfriend in college."

"Byron? Byron skips every Thursday. What are you talking about?"

"Sally's mom kept her home today. Until they catch whoever's doing this, anyway."

"My mom wanted me to stay home, but no way I'm missing pizza day!"

We're still a little early, and you can tell the kids who are here kind of just showed up rather than sit at home for another minute of hearing their parents tell them to be careful.

I spot a flash of red hair in the distance and tug on Lucy's maroon jacket. "Isn't that Ginger?"

She looks, then nods. "That's not her name. It's Gingham."

I watch the girl, pale as ever. She doesn't look all that different, actually, save for the flat, lifeless hair and dull, yellow eyes. As she walks by, other kids murmur and whisper in her path. I get the feeling from the vacant sneer on her waxy, pink lips that she kind of likes all the attention. Are all Zerkers drama queens?

My back is to Dane when I say, "So the first

Zerker has officially made it to school."

I hear the snap of a cell phone picture being taken, and then he says, "But not the only."

I feel her before I see her.

Chapter 32
One-Armed Bandit

"Val."

She walks up, big as you please, Ginger/Gingham not far behind, a few other Zerker lackeys in too-big jackets bringing up the rear.

She sees Dane snapping pictures and smiles. "Make sure to get my good side."

"Sure thing," he says, and I can see him dialing his stupid outdated cell phone cockily.

She darts forward, not for the phone, but for the locker door. She slams it on Lucy's arm. I don't hear anything crack, but Val's not giving up. I clutch the pen in my pocket but quickly do the math: I electrocute Val, who's holding a metal door against a Normal's arm. Hmm, I'm no physicist, but even I know that's probably not a great idea.

And I'm pretty sure Val knows it's not as well.

"Ummmppph," Lucy grunts, struggling not to cry. She looks at me, eyes half shut, chin trembling, nodding as if she wants me to know it doesn't hurt any more than getting your arm caught in a locker door by a crazy living dead psychopath should.

"Val," I try, moving closer to Lucy if only to let her know I'm still here. "Leave her out of it. It's us you want."

She ignores me, shoulders even boxier than usual in her maroon jacket. "Give me the phone, Dane." Val's voice is wet gravel on a cold, December day. "Do it now, or I will slice this Normal's arm off and beat her senseless with it."

Dane looks past Val to me. "I can't."

"You can," I say. "Look at this place. It's crawling with cell phones. You can snap her picture later."

He shakes his head pitifully. "You don't understand."

Val smirks and leans a little harder on the door. I hear a tear and see Lucy's jacket rip, crisp white dress shirt just a bit bloody underneath.

"Damn it," Dane hisses, handing it over just the same. "Damn it."

Val drops it and crushes it under a black army boot. As she focuses on her dramatic moment, I yank open the locker door and it slaps the side of her head.

Ginger gasps, but Val raises a hand as I yank Lucy out of her grasp and a little farther away from the action, just in case.

"It's fine, Gingham," Val says. "We've got all day to get her back. And we will. Just you wait and see."

Her hair is spiky, of course, and for effect she rubs the side of it where I hit her. A few random Normals are watching, but if they're waiting for fireworks, then they don't know Val very well. That's just not her style.

Not yet anyway.

A balding adult ambles over, sweaty and wearing bad shoes that make him look uneven. "Everything all right here, people?"

We all mumble and nod.

"Gingham?" he asks, recognizing only one of us.

"Yes, Mr. Frankenmeyer," the redhead answers sweetly.

"Who are all your new friends?"

Before she can answer, Val waves a printed schedule. "I'm the new exchange student. From

Sentinel City."

"From where?" he asks, reaching for the schedule as Val subtly draws it out of reach.

Just then, the first bell of the day rings, and he looks mildly alarmed. "Well, fine, then. Run along, and don't be late for class."

"We won't," Val says in her best brown-nose voice.

Then he's off, leaving us alone. Lucy slides out of her jacket, dumping it in the bottom of her locker and grabbing a spare she keeps on a hanger, just because she wouldn't be her if she didn't.

"Wait," I mumble, looking at her arm.

"It's fine," she snaps, probably embarrassed at being the only soul in the cluster who's actually able to bleed.

But I keep a firm grip just to make sure. It's a scratch—two scratches, really, where the door hit and then where it hit again. I grab her old jacket, tearing out a strip of black lining and wrapping it around the gashes. "There."

She looks at me, eyes red, chin a little less quivery now. "Thanks."

"We'll be fine, okay? We'll get through this. *You'll* get through this."

"That's right," says Val, slinging an arm around

my neck roughly and squeezing it just to remind me who's boss around here. "Just one big, happy family. That's what we'll be today, right, gang?"

Dane smirks. "Val, the first chance we get, we're so out of here."

Val reaches for Lucy, but I yank her away. "What?" she says anyway. "And leave all these yummy, smelly humans here alone?"

Val levels her big, wide, crazy gaze at the commons, which is crawling with living beings, Normals, who, in less than a bite or two, could be Zerkers.

Dane stands an inch higher. "Why do you think there are two of us?"

So far, so good. Then again, this is Val we're talking about here. She smiles. "And why do you think there are two *dozen* of us?"

Dane says, "Two dozen, my ass. We saw six last night, not counting the one Maddy dispatched."

Val sneers, letting us know she was there, hiding in the shadows all along. "With your help, of course. Right, Dane?" She cuts me side eye.

I say, perhaps a little too boastfully, "I won't need help to take you all by myself, Val."

"I know." She smiles. "Been there, lived through that. Which is why this time I made sure to bring my own little army with me. Or, should I say, make one while I'm here. Did I say two dozen? I might have underestimated just a smidge."

Dane and I shoot each other panicked glances as Val nods toward the light-blue double doors at the front of the school. "Outside, just across the street, behind a bush, or in the stand of palm trees that line the PE field, are my friends. Like Gingham, here, and her friends too."

Gingham looks back at me as if we're equal or something.

Behind her, the random Zerkers Val let come to school with her chortle and snort and try to play Normal. They fail miserably.

I smile back, imagining how it would feel to shove Gingham's hair down her throat.

Dane says, "No way you've turned that many Zerkers already."

"You know how this works," she purrs, clearly in her glory. Clearly having thought this through on a million different lonely nights while pacing in her cage back at Sentinel City. "I follow Maddy here into town a few nights ago and, just my luck, I find a few unfortunate joggers to turn. Once they're sentient, they bite two friends, and they bite two friends—and pretty soon good-bye, Seagull Shores, hello, Zerker Central."

Dane keeps his smile fixed on, but as the next bell rings and Lucy leads us to her homeroom, I can see little cracks in his armor. The way he walks too quickly, talks too loud. He's panicking, like me. He just doesn't know how to cover it as well.

Or maybe it's just never happened to him before.

The classroom is mostly empty, and the teacher is a young guy, handsome in a preppy way, tall and thin, wearing khakis and a pink Oxford shirt, sleeves rolled up. His face is kind and you can tell he was a jock or at least popular as a younger dude. It's easy to picture that's how Stamp would have looked someday.

That is, if I had never come along.

He smiles as we stumble in. "Whoa there," he says good-naturedly.

We slump into seats like the Technicolor street punks in the Charles Bronson *Death Wish* movie.

"Lots of new students today, huh, Lucy? And, Gingham, aren't you supposed to be in Mrs. Hammersmith's homeroom?"

Gingham puts her feet up on the seat in front of her and sighs.

The teacher laughs a little nervously, but it's

clear he's waiting for an answer.

To give him one, Val says, "I'm an exchange student, and Gingham is my student aide for today."

The guy is clearly cool, far from dumb. But again, Val has this effect on people. Even if you don't know what she is, you know this: she has nothing to lose and won't mind taking you down with her when she implodes.

"Uh, okay," he stammers, looking quickly around the room as if we're supposed to cheer him on or something. "Well, is this some new protocol? You're not my first exchange student, but you're the first one to get her own student aide. You must really rate."

Finally, the recognition Val's been waiting for. "Yes, yes, I do." Her tone is all, *I'm bored with this. Get on with it.*

He cocks his head.

She stares right back at him.

Finally, he blinks and shrugs. "Okay," he says, stretching the word out. "Well, I assume you have a class schedule, so if you'll walk it up here, I'll—"

"Gingham will bring it."

Suddenly his face is severe, his voice going a few octaves lower as the rest of the class watches. "You'll bring it, Miss . . . ?"

She doesn't answer, at least not right away. She stares back at him, crazy eyes going several notches crazier.

He doesn't back down. I'll give the dude that. He just stands there, hand out, not trembling, just waiting.

Suddenly Val stands up, all five feet nothing of her, and slinks toward the teacher.

He leans against his lectern, hand still out as she rises on tippy toes to whisper something in his ear.

Dane nudges me and nods toward the girl's purse next to me.

I nod and reach in, looking for a cell phone. I eventually find it on her desk, next to her notebook. Witch!

Val turns without another word and sits down. We don't hear from the teacher for the rest of homeroom. Not even to call roll. Which is kind of nice because Dane and I aren't in this class either.

Chapter 33
Zombie Skip Day

I<small>T'S LIKE THAT.</small>

All damn day.

Val never lets us out of her sight. It's like being trapped, with no bars or wires, no locks or keys, just her steely-eyed stare and stupid spiky hair. Poor, Normal Lucy's a foot or two away, in constant danger of being bitten and turned into the living dead.

And not the good kind.

But it's not only Lucy. In every classroom, flesh-and-blood kids in their ill-fitting uniforms watch us, but thanks to Val, they're too afraid to ask about us. And they're warm and full of blood and brains and meat, all a Zerker could ask for.

I imagine us getting up every few seconds,

Dane and I, and tearing Val limb from limb, but it wouldn't even matter. Whatever she's done, however she's done it, she has her Zerker lackeys trained. Even if we could get Val alone, by the time we turned around, a jawbone in each hand, half the class would be Zerker-izing right before our very eyes.

What makes my undead blood boil isn't so much the threat of Seagull Shores turning into the Prep School of the Living Dead, although it should, but that Val knows the trap she's laid. She knows its brilliance and is enjoying every last minute of it.

She'll sit there, tapping her fingers on her desk, Lucy in the middle and Gingham on the other side: the reanimated bookends from hell. And any second, on a whim, she could bite her, or straight-up punch a hole in the side of her head.

Meanwhile, she's being sly with her big eyes scanning the room every 0.00017 seconds. Every time I'm close to snagging a cell phone, Gingham calls me out. Or Val catches me outright.

The bell rings, and I look at the clock on the wall behind the silent teacher: 10:15. It must be third period. Chairs squeak, and the Normal children can't get out of class fast enough. Meanwhile, Dane and I stick close together, watching as

Gingham wrenches Lucy out of her chair and Val follows closely.

"The hell?" I finally ask Dane in the halls, just out of earshot of a gaggle of Normals stringing by, eager to get clear of our motley crew.

"What else can we do?" he grunts, bumping into everybody he can, the world's worst pickpocket hunting for a cell phone, and still coming up empty-handed. "She's got Lucy, and every other kid in this school, on her own personal lunch menu."

I groan and follow Val obediently.

Lucy looks over her shoulder at me, offering a weak smile.

I send one back, but I don't know how long I can keep faking that I've got this, that it's all under control. That I know what the hell I'm doing.

I just want to run away from all this, the Eliminator in my hand, slicing off Zerker heads all the way back to Stamp. I want to forget about Lucy and the kids at Seagull Shores and everyone I don't know and never will and just turn into a Wonder Woman head-blitzing zombie badass, but I can't. Every time Gingham yanks Lucy around, I know I can't.

And I hope Stamp understands that. If he can.

If he's still around to understand anything.

I keep my pen handy, just looking for a chance to strike. One jolt from that sucker, and she's out like a light and maybe, just maybe, I can get to Gingham before she bites Lucy or anyone else. But it's Val we're talking about here, and she's quick and slick. Every period, it seems, there are more of them around her.

It's not only Gingham anymore but a guy or two as well, a few random girls with yellow eyes and vacant expressions. Every class we walk into, more and more have turned. But it doesn't work like that. They take time to be functioning. To get dressed in maroon jackets and skinny little ties, crooked though they may be. You don't just bite someone in third period and by fifth they're solving quadratic equations. No, uh-uh.

"She's been at this for a while," Dane whispers as we walk into Chorus, Lucy's next class. "She—" He stops in the doorway.

Val shoves him hard, but the teacher doesn't stop her. Doesn't even quake at the sudden burst of violence. Because the teacher's one of hers—one of *them*. Now I know why Dane never finished his sentence.

"Mr. Phillips?" Lucy asks, eyes wide.

Inside, a dozen kids, a quarter of them undead,

sit quietly. The living ones are quivering; the undead ones are literally licking their chops.

"Screw this," I shout, pulling Lucy out of the class.

She leaps along with a yip and emerges on the other side of the door. I turn and see Val's double-wide crazy eyes until the door shuts, obliterating that god-awful image of her stupid spiky hair I want to mow down with my own teeth.

Dane is right behind me but not following.

"Dane," I shout, heading for the front office, as far away as I can go.

He nods, waving me ahead. "I'll be right there."

I stumble backward. Lucy, at my side, keeps me steady as I watch Dane launch into Gingham, who stands just outside the closed Chorus room door. Even from two classrooms away, I can hear something crack.

Something big or at least pretty important-sounding.

Chapter 34
All That and a Bag of Chips

"WHERE ARE WE going?" Lucy asks, out of breath. I hear Dane's sloppy footsteps as he races to catch up.

"The office, teacher's lounge, whatever. Somewhere with a phone. Somewhere we can call 911!"

Lucy inches forward on her flesh-and-blood Normal legs. "But last night you said the cops wouldn't believe us."

"They won't believe this," I say, passing the board with all the Missing posters on it as Dane finally catches up. "But we'll call in a bomb threat or something. All we need are warm bodies."

"And their guns," Dane grunts, stumbling beside us.

He's not alone.

Val is at his back, some of her new Zerker buddies along for the ride. Minus Gingham, of course.

We stand just outside the office, never sure if she's going to bite Lucy or sic the Zerkers on us but ready for anything and nothing all at once.

Val's smile is infuriating. If I didn't think her Zerker goons would devour Lucy in the time it takes me to crack my knuckles, I'd love nothing more than to wipe that smile right off her face. Literally.

"Here. Let me help!" She cracks open a glass box on the wall next to her and slams down the fire alarm. Instantly, the commons fill with noise and, a few seconds later, bodies, not all of them living.

The office door swings open, and secretaries, principals, assistant principals, and counselors flee, trudging past us toward the front doors. Kids follow them: office aides, some alive, some not.

Those who are not stand in front of the office door, blocking it.

Val joins them, beaming that triumphant smile.

"What the . . ." Dane murmurs, watching them flood by, too many yellow eyes to count. He shakes his head. "Holy hell."

"Here." I haul him inside the teacher's lounge,

figuring there's gotta be a phone or two in there.

Lucy is warm and breathing heavy between us, messenger bag clutched tight against her shoulder as if it's hiding some nuclear weapon or something.

I slam the door behind me, feeling Val or one of her Zerker pals clanging against it. "Dane, hurry! Find a phone. Call someone. Lucy, get over here!"

She comes to my aid, but I forget she's only human. And small and soft. The door bangs against our shoulder blades.

Finally, on the far wall, Dane finds a phone. A pay phone. "Are you kidding me?" he says. To the phone. He punches the wall next to it, still conversing with the immobile phone. "Unbelievable."

"Well, hurry!"

"I don't have any change," he says. To me, not to the phone this time.

I dig in my pocket, finding only the Eliminator on one side and Vera's pen on the other.

"Don't look at me," Lucy grunts. "I didn't know they even had those things anymore!"

Dane twists and turns, eyes closed, groaning, like he can just create dimes and nickels out of sheer frustration.

"There. Dane, look! The vending machine."

"What about it? Does it sell cell phones?"

The door is silent for a moment. Lucy and I look at each other, faces all, *Oh, snap, are six of them getting ready to sprint across the commons and knock it down at once?*

I use the relative silence to shout at Dane. "It will have change inside, you stupid dork!"

He shakes his head and nods and walks to it, quickly grabbing the sides and shaking it.

This guy, honestly. Did he become a zombie before they invented vending machines?

"Dane. The coin box inside. Grab—"

Suddenly, there's a rumble. Violent and low. Not at the door but on the other side of the wall. No. Not on the other side. *In* the walls.

Dane fiddles with the vending machine, fingers trying to pry it open, unable to move its bulk.

Lucy clings to the door, as if that's any help.

I stand in the middle of the room, listening, feeling the pounding, and trying to find out where it's coming from—

Something cracks. There's a jumble of dust and plaster, and the vending machine slams into Dane, knocking him over and pinning his arm to the ground.

Val emerges, spiky hair filled with dust. She

kicks through the last of the drywall like Kool-Aid Man. Then she kneels on the back of the vending machine, triumphant as flippin' always.

"What do we have here?" she asks, shaking her head.

I look at Dane. From about his shoulder down, his arm is covered by the vending machine.

She sees it, smiles, and rocks the massive metal box. It can't hurt, not really, but if his whole arm comes off, well, he won't be much of a Sentinel then.

"Stop, Val," I shout. "Get off."

Val snickers as I reach into my pocket. But it's hard because Lucy clings to my side like a second skin.

Suddenly the door she was supposed to be blocking swings open, and Gingham limps in. One arm at an odd angle, the maroon sleeve of her uniform jacket missing, she snatches Lucy, who screams.

Gingham, voice like sandpaper, laughs. "Scream all you want, brainiac. There's no one left to hear you!"

Dane grunts, trying to wriggle his arm out from under the massive vending machine, but Val rocks it again.

Lucy squeaks, biting off a scream, and Gingham stretches her arm behind her back.

"Stop, okay? Just stop," I sputter.

Gingham smirks and squeezes just a little tighter.

Lucy manages a few words: "Stop. Helping. Me. It's. Not. Helping. Me!"

I turn, looking back and forth between Lucy and Dane.

"Drop it," Val says, sliding off the vending machine but leaning on it so Dane can't ease out while she's not looking. Which seems impossible because it's like she's got eyes in the back and on both sides of her head.

"Drop what?" But even as I ask, I'm cringing, thinking maybe I whipped out Vera's pen. But when I look down, I see I'm holding the Eliminator, ice pick side out.

I don't even remember doing that.

Still, I want her to think it's all I've got, so I bring it closer to me protectively.

How did this go so wrong so fast? How did she get the drop on us so soundly? Again?

"Ah, ah, ah," she teases, wagging a finger and rocking the vending machine.

Dane winces with each motion. A few more of those or one big jump, and he'll be able to count on only five fingers from now on.

I smirk, as if it's exactly what I wanted when I hear Lucy scream, "Maddy, look out!"

I half turn in time to see Gingham, with her one good arm, shove me to my knees, right at Val's feet.

I smile, using the graceless fall to tumble and toss the Eliminator halfway across the room.

Val rolls her eyes at this obvious display. "Gingham?"

The redhead dutifully limps toward it, slow as molasses, which works just fine for me.

In a headlock, Lucy grunts and slides along by her side.

We share a look, and in her eyes is utter fear. It makes me wonder how long she's been a Sleeper and what training she had for the job, if any.

Then again, look at me. All the Keeper training in the world couldn't stop Val from surprising me so thoroughly, even though we were pretty much expecting her this whole time.

"Let's go, Val. Come on," Dane spits, grunting with his arm pinned. "Do what you're gonna do to us, and let the Normal go."

Val gives me a can-you-believe-this-schmuck look.

On my knees, I look at her, hating that I look subservient but definitely wanting her to think I'm right where she wants me to be.

"Why would I want to hurt you two?" she purrs, stroking my cheek.

I pull away. "You know why," I seethe. "We all know why."

Gingham has retrieved the Eliminator, and Lucy's kneeling in front of her. Gingham turns the weapon over and over, calling out to Val, "Hey, look at this. I think I like it."

Val smiles. "Good. It's yours." She looks at me but talks to Gingham: "When it's time, I hope you'll figure out how to use it."

The two cackle. Seriously. Like the witches they are.

I'm trying to ESP, *Don't worry; I'll take care of these two*, to Lucy, but Val grabs my ear.

"Pay attention to *me*, Maddy."

I twist away, half expecting her to be holding my ear in her fingers. Fortunately, it's still attached to my head. For now.

"This was never about rekilling *you* two," she says to me and Dane via me. "It was about making you suffer. And the best way to do that is to kill the ones you love."

I smirk. "You had the chance to kill Dad when you broke out of Sentinel City. Why didn't you just do it then and be done with it?"

"My sentiments exactly!"

Ugh, she has this dramatic way about her I've

forgotten I can't stand. I mean, as big of a part as Val has played in my afterlife, it's amazing how little face time we've had over the past year.

Her eyes get twice as crazy now. The veins stand out above her open collar, her black tie loosened and dangling. And with her spiky hair—*blech*—she's like the annoying schoolgirl from hell.

She's leaning there, Dane's arm pinned, waiting for me. For some kind of response.

"I . . . I don't know what that means."

She frowns, disappointed that I ruined some big moment she's probably been planning for weeks. Months, even.

"I mean, Maddy, I didn't want to finish it right then. I wanted it to last and last and last. Killing your dad would have been too easy. I know that now. The people you spend the most time with, the ones you'll have around forever, are the undead. I see that now."

She winds down her soliloquy and looks at me pointedly. "I went about it all wrong last time. This time I made sure you were all together: every undead person you cared about." For emphasis, she taps a boot on Dane's trapped shoulder.

"Fine, great, you've made your point. So get it

over with. Kill me now, and—"

Dane interrupts, outcroaking me, looking like he just lost a wrestling match with a vending machine. "Just kill *me*, Val. You know you want to. That's what this has all been about from the very beginning."

"Don't flatter yourselves." She chuckles in a villainous way, those eyes getting even wilder. "Like I said, it's not you I want." A pause and she takes her foot off Dane, looks down at me.

"You know, Maddy, here's an idea: why not just surrender for once? You know, stop being the good guy for a change." She looks back at me, points at Lucy. "Just give us one willingly. Just give us Lucy, and we'll call the whole thing off."

"Yeah, right," I spit.

"I mean it this time. I will take Gingham and Lucy here and the rest of my horde, and we will walk out of town, no questions asked."

Dane looks as if he's considering it, which I know he can't be. He turned out to be the afterlife's worst boyfriend, but he can't be as bad as this. "And what happens to her? Lucy, I mean?" he says.

Val shrugs. "What do you care? You trade me one measly, skinny Normal, and you get to save the rest of Seagull Shores. No big fight to the death, no big climax, no—"

"No." My voice is low. "I don't care how many promises you make, I will never willingly hand a Normal over to a Zerker."

"Maddy, listen . . ." Dane's eyes plead with me.

"No, Dane. And, no, Val. There is no surrender. There is only you and me and win or lose. Only one of us is walking out of here in one piece."

She tries to look bored, but I can tell she's disappointed. At least just a little. Then she looks at Lucy to say to the only Normal in the room, "You see, I gave you a chance."

Lucy's voice is resigned as she grunts, still in Gingham's clutches. "I haven't had a chance since you all got to town."

"All righty then." She sighs, settling in, leaning against the machine, as if she's got all day. And I suppose she has. She turns back to me and licks her lips in anticipation. "All day, you've been watching me, waiting for me to do something. And all day, every kid I've turned and every kid they've turned has been heading toward the house on Lumpfish Lane to finish what I started back in Barracuda Bay."

"What's that?" Dane asks.

But I already know. I already knew the last time

Val and I faced off like this.

She looks at me, as if she can read my mind. Or maybe just because she wants to see my face when I finally realize why she's here. "Ask her."

"Stamp," I say, still on my knees at Val's feet, gripping Vera's pen behind my legs. I look at Dane. "Courtney."

He looks from me to her and back to me. "But why?"

I shake my head and answer for her. "It's all so simple. All along. Bones. We took her brother from her. All she ever wanted that whole time in Sentinel City was to find a way to hurt us as badly as we hurt her. Stamp for me. And now Courtney for you."

Dane turns to her, smiling up at her gross face uncertainly. Even I can see it, and I know Val can. "Courtney's a Sentinel," he bluffs. "And Stamp? He's half Zerker. They'll never fall, no matter how many of your kind you send."

Val sneers. "She's Sentinel *Support*, Dane. And he's half Zerker, all dimwit, from what I could see from my cage next to his. I doubt they lasted past first period. I doubt, if you ever get back to Lump-fish Lane yourself, you'll find more than a couple of toenails and a few IQ points lying around."

Dane grunts, squirming like he'd wring his own arm off just to get the chance to grab her by one leg and toss her around the room like a rag doll. Which he totally could, if he weren't buried under a ton of old metal filled with glazed honey buns and powdered donuts.

"Call them off," he says, the tendons in his neck standing out now. "Get . . ." he grunts, running out of steam. "Get over there and stop them, and we'll do whatever you w—"

"Like hell," Val says, launching into another soliloquy.

And that's when I jab Vera's pen into her ankle.

She squeals, not from the pain but the shock that I had something other than the Eliminator up my sleeve.

Before I can press the power button on top, she grabs my hand.

"Nice try." She sneers. She studies the pen, seeming familiar with it. I try to think if I've ever flashed it at her in her cage or if maybe one of the Keepers did when apprehending her in Barracuda Bay. Or if maybe she's like the zombie Michael Meyers and knows everything and anything and will never, ever, re-die.

"Go ahead." She smirks. "Squeeze that button,

and we'll both fry."

I smile cockily, not even caring anymore what happens to me, as long as nothing happens to anybody else. "That's the general idea, dumb ass."

Her eyes get big but not for long.

Suddenly my finger is on the button, grinding it down, and she sizzles like a piece of bacon. But . . . so do I. Our teeth clatter, and our muscles tense, and our bones shake, but I've had a little more practice with Vera's pen than Val has, and I watch her eyes flutter back in her head until mine do too.

I squeeze until I can't feel anything else, and the world goes dry and cold and black.

The next thing I know, someone's kicking me.

I kick back, grunting, fried and angry and disoriented, until I hear, faintly, as if it's in the next room: Something, something, ". . . it's me."

My eyelids open, and I see the break room ceiling high above, water-stained tiles and fluorescent lights and yellowed tape, probably from where they've hung Christmas ornaments or paper snowflakes in the past. I look left and see Val, splayed out unnaturally, eyeballs smoking and one leg bent at an odd angle.

To my right, Dane is still kicking me.

"Stop it." I say. "Stop now."

I stand, wobbly, as if I've just stuck my finger in the world's biggest light socket after drinking six cases of cheap champagne. "How are you still jammed under there?" I slur, reaching down to help him. I just assumed the click on Vera's pen would solve everything. "Push harder," I tell him.

"I've tried that." He gasps. "Don't you think I've tried that?"

I look around the room slowly. Things are blurry still and rough around the edges.

Lucy is struggling with Gingham, but after whatever Dane cracked in her, it's hardly a fair fight.

Still, we don't have much time. Val will be up soon, and in my condition, I'll need his help if I'm going to finish her for good.

I find a chair with metal legs and jam it into the back of the machine, pounding furiously, until I can feel the thin metal panel give way. Then I jam it in some more.

"What are you doing?" he asks.

"Just wait!" I feel like I'm hungover and he's asking me for directions to Toledo at the top of his lungs.

The back panel is crushed in the center, the seams lifting at the sides.

I toss the chair to the floor and tug one end of the panel until it peels off like wrapping paper.

Inside the guts of the machine, it's just a patchwork of those spiral rings the treats hang from. I grab a couple: sleeves of powdered donut thumping down. I reach for three of the metal rings coiled together and tap, tap, tap them against the glass of the vending machine. It shatters all over, chip bags ripping, stale cookies flying as I wrench half a dozen more spirals out and toss them away to give him room.

When there's enough space, I tell him, "Reach in and pull yourself through."

He does. Just like that. He pops up, like a rabbit out of a hole. He's favoring one arm, twirling it like a swimmer before the 400-meter backstroke, but grinning just the same. "Who *are* you all of a sudden?"

I look at him, teeth still smoking, probably from Vera's pen. "I'm badass; that's what I am."

He shakes his head. "You're power drunk is what you are."

Val stirs, kicking one leg out, and I reach for the nearest metal coil from the vending machine. It's like one long corkscrew. Just as she's opening her eyes, I jab one in, straight through an eye socket and her skull and—boom—into her cerebral cortex.

Lights out, Val.

Nighty-forever-night.

I keep jamming it down until I hit the floor, then keep pushing it straight through the linoleum.

Dane tries to pull me off. "Come on," he says, as if he knows jack squat about Zerker killing. "Let's go. That's enough."

"That's what every stupid good-looking kid says in every stupid bad horror movie film." God, when will I talk right again? This is nuts. "I'm not being that. I'm not being her. Help me."

"Help you what?"

I shake my head, as if it will clear the fog, and you know what? It does. It really does. "Tear her apart, Dane. What else?"

He looks from me to Lucy, who's sitting on Gingham's back, repeatedly bashing her head into the tile floor.

"Don't look at me," she huffs, eyes cloudy with violent intent and mouth upturned in a curious smile. "I'm busy!"

Chapter 35
SpongeBob Square Stamps

THE SCHOOL IS silent. Even the fire alarm's quit ringing. It must be on a timer or something. Having been trapped in the teacher's lounge with a maniacal Zerker spewing the world's largest guilt trip, I suddenly can't remember hearing it go off. Or ringing, for that matter.

The halls are empty and bloody. Some of it's red: Normal blood. Some of it's black and gooey: Zerker blood. Lockers are open, and backpacks and books and papers are scattered everywhere.

"What happened?" Lucy asks, clinging to her messenger bag as we leave Val and Gingham and their various body parts behind.

"Val got what she wanted," Dane says, stretching

345

his injured arm. "A town full of Zerkers."

"You mean . . ."

"Full infestation," I say, limping beside her. "*Day of the Dead* stuff, all right."

Dane stops at a classroom, shoving the door wide open. Inside, the chairs are overturned, a bloody handprint on the chalkboard. He turns back and looks at me, then at Lucy.

She looks pale, drained, scared in a way she didn't back in the teacher's lounge, scrapping with Gingham like a straight-up Sentinel wannabe.

"We're about to find out," I say, grabbing her sleeve and guiding her toward the student parking lot.

It's a mess of open car doors and bloody sneakers and purses. Her car is there, right up front, pristine and waiting, as if we were the only ones still stuck inside when everyone else got out. We get inside, finding our familiar seats by now: Dane in the back, me riding shotgun.

Lucy turns the key and, after all that's gone wrong, after all we've screwed up, I'm surprised the car actually starts. We pull out of the lot, dodging vehicles parked every which way: on the school lawn, out in the street, windows broken, one hood up as if somebody stopped to check the oil in the middle of a zombie infestation.

"Jesus," Lucy says, both hands on the wheel as she goes as fast as possible toward the house on Lumpfish Lane. "Jesus."

A tan, drab van passes us going about twice as fast, in the opposite direction, nearly plowing into the Go, Seagull Shores Spartans! sign across from the school.

Dane and I look at each other.

Sentinels.

Two more vans race by, careening after the first, tinted windows unable to hide the grim, gray faces.

"But if Val crushed your phone, who called?"

"Don't look at me," Dane says, favoring his arm. "Maybe Courtney got through."

"Maybe," Lucy mumbles, turning off the main drag toward the house. "Maybe one of the cops around here is a Sleeper too."

Dane barely notices. "A what?"

"Forget it," we say at the same time.

"Look at this place," Dane adds. "It's a war zone. Hell, they could have been watching CNN in the day room back in Sentinel City and seen it live and in person."

"Lucy," I say through gritted teeth, nudging her

shoulder. "Let's go. Pick it up."

I picture Stamp, wondering if we're too late. Wondering if we were too late by second period or even when Val walked us into homeroom when the day started.

Lucy slides onto a sidewalk to avoid an overturned ambulance and says, just as grittily, "I'm trying!"

I attempt to see the world, her world, through her eyes. But I can't. It's pretty screwed for both of us. Despite being a Sleeper, is this her first real encounter, up close and personal, with the living dead? "Okay." I pat her rigid arm. "Okay, I know you are."

We see the first Zerkers in a shopping center, feeding on . . . something. Two of them wear school uniforms; one of them looks like a housewife.

Lucy slows down while I shoot Dane a look.

He quickly shakes his head.

"Keep going," I urge, looking away.

She flashes panic. "But shouldn't we help?"

"Whatever they're feeding on," Dane explains from the backseat, "was done the minute they bit into it. It's too late for them. It might not be for our friends. Please."

But it is. Too late for them, I mean.

After drifting through a town full of overturned

cop cars and fog, fire, and steam, Zerkers shuffling and occasionally feeding, we pull up in front of the house on Lumpfish Lane.

There's no one here but a few Sentinels.

"Anything?" Dane asks, going to the nearest one. It's amazing, and a little disturbing, how quickly he slides back into Sentinel mode.

I don't wait to hear an answer, but I can sense, as I walk past them into the living room, what he's saying. And it isn't good.

Zerker blood is everywhere, but I also see Tasers on the floor, shoulder pads torn in two, scenes from an epic battle between the good zombies and the bad. How long the Sentinels were here, I can't say, but it doesn't look like they all made it out re-alive.

I stomp upstairs, and it's more of the same in every room. Shattered glass, broken closet doors, blood and more blood—all black. I look everywhere twice, even under the kitchen sink, and there's nothing, nobody anywhere.

I drift downstairs, empty inside. To think of Stamp, spending his last minutes alone, without me or even Dane at his side. For better or worse, we're all he's ever known of the afterlife. And we let him down, all the way. This whole time, he was the bait, not us. If I'd been smarter, if I'd thought a little more about someone other than myself . . .

How long did he hold out before they ganged up on him, tearing him apart or feasting on his flesh or toying with him, Courtney by his side, trying her best but doomed from the start?

Why did we go to school and leave them here to their fate? Why couldn't we have just thought a little more, planned it out? Maybe if Dane and I hadn't been still ticked off over what happened back at Sentinel City, we would have. I'd hate to think that Stamp got the shaft again, the soggy corner in this limp love triangle, just because we wanted to see who could find Val the fastest.

Dane is waiting for me at the foot of the stairs, Lucy at his side. They look up at me expectantly, and halfway down I realize they're waiting on me for some news, any news. I shake my head and keep walking past them, toward the sliding glass doors. Shattered, half open, splattered with still-drying black goo.

I just need a minute away from people, the living *and* the dead.

There is movement out in front of the house, a car or truck or van screeching to a halt like something in the bad B movie that is our afterlife. Doors slamming, boots clomping, voices shouting. I ignore it and keep walking until I hear Vera's voice.

And then this: breathing.

I turn, expecting her to be yelling at Lucy or Lucy yelling at her, a real Sleepers versus Keepers catfight going down. Instead I see Dad, lab coat clean, back straight, moustache combed, a white beret atop his balding head.

A white beret? Dad? He swore he'd never wear one. So what now? I mean, they don't exactly hand out berets for nothing. Especially to a guy who the Elders think let a Zerker escape in the first place.

"Maddy!" He sees me, comes running, spryer than ever, a healthy, strong human.

Mortal.

He smells like hotel room soap and drug store cologne and gas station coffee, and I can't get enough as I nuzzle into his chest. God knows I can't cry, but he cries enough for both of us.

He pushes me away, a first, and looks at me. Really looks at me, gripping my shoulders, kind of shaking me for emphasis each time he wants to make a point. "When Vera came to ZED to get me, when she told me what had happened here, what was going on, I thought . . . I thought I'd never see you again. Again."

We laugh, the sound of naked relief. It seems like every few months, Dad and I are thrown into some ordeal where we think we're never going to see each other again. Again!

Then some of his words cut through the nervous laughter.

"Vera? Came to ZED?"

He nods emphatically, taking his hands off my shoulders to straighten his stiff white beret. It's more off-white, I notice now, like his long lab coat.

I look to Vera, rigid in her own blue beret, her voice neither kind nor judgmental, merely factual. A zombie Spock without the ears. "When Lucy told me you were here in Seagull Shores with Stamp, I thought we'd have more time. I thought maybe your dad could help somehow, knowing Val the way he did from his studies. I didn't think she'd move so fast."

Behind her, Dane clears his throat. "None of us did."

Next to him, Lucy nods grimly. "We wouldn't have left them here otherwise."

Vera ignores them, even her teacher's pet, Lucy, and looks at me. "I'm so sorry, Maddy." She doffs

352

her trademark light-blue beret and troubles it in a circular motion, like a Frisbee, in her cement-gray fingers.

"Don't apologize to me," I say, staring into her eyes. "Apologize to—"

"Stamp!"

They all say it at the same time. Dane. Lucy. Dad.

I turn and see Stamp and Courtney lurching out of the canal. Dripping wet, seaweed and algae falling off them in clumps, little fish flopping at their feet as they clamber onto the dock behind the house.

Never have they looked more like the living dead, rising from the sea, water streaming off them, hair wet, clothes sticking to their gray skin. They look at one another, brush seaweed off each other's shoulders.

We run across the patio, onto the grass, and down to the dock.

"What took you guys so long?" Stamp asks, smiling, then clearly remembering and frowning, whisking water from one eyelid. "And where did all those Zerkers go?"

Epilogue
Bon Voyage

THE SENTINELS COME, and the Sentinels go. They move around silently, diligently, like giant black ants. Body bags line the back of drab, tan vans just as they did in Barracuda Bay, in Orlando, in every town I've ever passed through since I became the living dead.

Val was right about another thing, I suppose. Everywhere I go, everyone I meet, every friend I make or town I settle into, I put the folks I love in danger. Even random citizens like the guy who sold me grape soda at the Stop N Go or Gingham and her wannabe mean girl friends—their life spans are cut short simply because they popped into my life, if only for a few seconds.

I'm straight-up bad news, as if the Grim Reaper is my shadow or something.

What would Seagull Shores look like right now if I hadn't decided willy-nilly to set up shop here for a few days? Last week at this time it was just another random, generic, seaside beach town: souvenir shops and snow cone stands and surfboard street signs and a town square that looked like something out of a Norman Rockwell painting.

Now it's smoking and sirening—just another gutted city, like Barracuda Bay before it. And who knows what will come next? Who knows how many Zerkers got away this time? Or how many Val sent away to do her dirty work, spreading her hate and virus and gurgling black blood?

A dozen? Two dozen? Three?

I guess we won't know until the Missing signs start showing up in the next few days or, depending on her master plan, weeks. I shake my head and watch the last Sentinel drag the last body bag full of Zerkers out the front door of the house on Lumpfish Lane.

Dad is back in his element, running the show pretty much. There are jars of Zerker blood samples to precisely fill and label. I think he's happier than ever. Not about the death and destruction, obviously, but the chance to put his mind to work to stop this from happening the next time or the next or the next. He may have lost a daughter to the living dead, but he's found his calling.

He catches me looking, starts to move toward me, maybe give me a hug or a smooch or a high five, something. But he looks at the sample jars and bags, big black glove on each hand dripping with stuff, and he stops, shrugs, and turns back to his work.

I chuckle to myself. I guess seeing him happy is better than a hug anyway, right?

Dane is back in uniform but not a school uniform this time. His sleek black shoulder pads gleam as he fishes out Zerker body parts from the swimming pool, Courtney at his side, Stamp at hers. They, too, work with purpose or, in Stamp's case at least, pleasure. Pleasure at being included, at being wanted, at being necessary.

Ever since they spent an entire school day clinging to the bottom of the dock, hiding from the Zerkers that Stamp spotted from his vantage point upstairs, he doesn't seem to mind having her as his babysitter, and she doesn't seem to mind being one.

He splashes Courtney with the pool skimmer and, where just a few days ago she might have Tased him without even thinking twice, now she snorts and nudges him gently in the ribs.

Dane, looking only mildly perturbed, tells them both, "Grow up." But even so, it's a playful growl, like when he used to tell me and Chloe the same thing back in Barracuda Bay. Dane told me he loved me maybe five times in our brief year or so together. Six, tops. But I felt like every time he growled at me to grow up, he was kinda saying it then too.

From the patio, I look into the house. The Sentinels are all gone, but one Keeper remains. And a Sleeper, to boot. Vera and Lucy confer in the kitchen, plotting their next move, speaking softly so the rest of us don't hear. I watch, useless, still Vanished, a nobody to everybody.

I see Lucy's messenger bag, crumpled on the floor, forgotten, slumped against the bottom of the kitchen counter. Inside is, basically, her life: wallet, cash, credit card, ID, iPad that's not an iPad, a couple of *Living with the Living Dead* gag books, a barrette or two, protein bars, probably one of her addictive caffeine drinks. Next to Vera, she looks so young and ambitious, so eager to get on with her next assignment or help out here. So deadly serious about assisting the living dead.

And Vera, beret spiffy on her shaven dome, dark eyes studying a map or something on the kitchen counter, so eager for an apt pupil.

The kind I never was and now will never be. I walk closer, and only Lucy looks up, eyes crinkling in a soft smile. She sends me a curt nod before returning her attention to whatever Vera is pointing at.

I reach down and pick up the messenger bag. It occurs to me that I'm still in my school uniform, and that feels kind of right.

I slide the strap under my maroon lapel and wedge the bag part into the small of my back so it looks as inconspicuous as possible. I don't even know why I bother. As I back out of the living room, away from the kitchen, past Dad and his symphony of gross-filled jars, nobody looks up, nobody questions, nobody dares.

Only Stamp, waving the pool skimmer like a second hand, notices me. "Hi, Maddy. Wanna look for fingers in the pool with us?"

"Gosh, I'd love to, but . . ."

Dane focuses on me for a hot second. "But what?"

I turn away, toward the sailboat I've been studying ever since Stamp and Courtney rose from the canal like creatures from the black lagoon. "But . . .

I'm leaving."

Dane looks into the house, as if maybe he wants to alert Vera or something. "You can't just leave," he says, dragging an arm out of the pool and rolling down his black sleeve.

"Why not?"

He blinks twice.

I don't move. "I'm supposed to be long gone already, so this just makes it official."

He kind of can't argue with that.

Courtney is more specific. "But where would you go?" I look at her to see if she's being pissy, as in, *Catch you later, reanimator.* But her head is cocked, eyes expectant.

"I have no idea." I chuckle. "Left, I guess."

She snorts. "You mean north?"

I shrug and offer her a smile, since it's probably the last time I'll ever see her. "Sure, whatever."

I step forward, from the pool deck to the grass that leads down a sloping hill toward the dock. It's still spotted with dead or dying crabs and minnows and crunchy, dried seaweed from their underwater hideout.

The sailboat rocks gently in the canal, drifting back and forth against three white buoys tied to the dock. I hear footsteps behind me as I quickly slide the messenger bag under a seat cushion in the boat.

When I turn, Stamp is on the dock, his lanky body leaning against a piling. He wanted to wear Dane's school jacket after we dried him off, so he looks vaguely sporty, like something out of an '80s prep school movie starring Rob Lowe and Phoebe Cates.

Dane and Courtney stand just behind him, heavy zombie feet sinking into the tall grass.

"Maddy?" Stamp says. There's a look in his eyes I've never seen before, not even when he was a Normal. "I thought . . . you said we were a team."

"We are, buddy," I lie, stepping off the boat. I hug him, but he clings to the piling. "Hug me back right now," I say, pulling him forward. "Or you'll regret it later."

He nearly crushes me, which is saying something considering I just punched my way through a vending machine to save Dane.

He looks away as we part.

"How did you know to hide in the water?" I ask.

He tries not to smile, but he's never been very good at being humble. "Your dad told me to protect you, right?"

I wait for him to go on, then realize he's actually waiting for an answer, so I nod quickly.

"Well, when I saw all those Zerkers coming down our street, I knew the only way to protect you was to stay alive. And the only way to stay alive was to hide. And the only place to hide was"—he risks a cautious look over the side of the dock—"down there."

I hug him once more. "That's good thinking, Stamp."

He doesn't quite push me away, just sort of squirms out of my grip, like a teenager who's getting too old to hug his mom in front of the other kids when she drops him off at the mall. I can't say I blame him. "Yeah, well, now you're here and you're leaving, so I can't protect you anymore."

I smile and whisper in his ear, "Look around you, Stamp. There are lots of people to protect around here."

He does. He looks around at the people gathered near the dock. Only when I see a smile tickle the corner of his lips do I back away. Slowly but not quite reluctantly, I get back in the boat.

I'm there when he's done looking around and tries to find me.

Courtney arrives gently at Stamp's side. For once, I'm grateful for her nosiness, even her timing. "She'll be back," she says to him softly while looking at me. "She just . . . She just doesn't want to cause any more trouble right now."

Dane flashes her a withering look, but I smile. I couldn't have put it any better myself.

Stamp shakes his head. "But your dad said . . . Your dad said that I—"

"It's okay, Stamp." Dad appears, black gloves sticking out of one of his lab coat pockets. "You did exactly what I asked you to do."

This is too much for him. "I did?"

Dad puts an arm around Stamp's shoulder, which is not so easy since he's shorter than him. "Look at her, my boy. Why, she's better than ever."

I give Dad a questioning look, and he nods. "Do you know how to drive that thing, dear? I'm afraid, for as long as we've lived in Florida, I've never taught you how to sail."

"Do *you* know?" I snort.

He shakes his head. "I was always so busy." He points a thumb over his shoulder, and even now I can sense he's eager to get back to the work that makes him so happy.

I look at the sail, bundled up tight, and frown. Then I see two oars. "I'll just row around for a little while until I get the hang of it."

He looks confused until Vera sneaks up to his side, blue beret popping up out of nowhere. "She'll be fine, Dr. Swift. We trained her well."

He rolls his eyes at me, but there's a new sense of camaraderie between them that I've never seen before. Like something happened when I wasn't looking.

"You know where you're going?" she asks.

Lucy creeps up to join the group on the dock.

I smile. "Not a clue."

Vera waits a beat. "That's not such a bad thing, Maddy."

I shrug.

Lucy kneels, untying the bowlines. "You sure you know what you're doing?" she asks quietly, as if we don't have an audience.

"Hell, no." I snort.

She chuckles, leaning in for a quick hug. "Take good care of my identity." She winks, nodding toward the strap of her messenger bag poking out from under the seat cushion. Then she shoves me gently away from the dock.

As the momentum pulls me out into the canal, I watch Dane walk away from the group to the very edge of the dock.

He says not a word. He doesn't even wave. But as I

struggle with the oars—they're longer than I thought and heavy and awkward, getting them in their little metal holders and then sticking them in the water without them sliding all the way through and floating away—he's still there every time I look up.

The others drift away one by one. Dad first. A scientist, after all, he has the facts: *Maddy is going away for a while; she knows I'm safe, we've said good-bye; I have jars full of Zerker thumbs to label.*

Vera next, with Lucy close by her side. They have work to do. The Zerkers won't all go away just because I'm taking a break from hunting them down.

Courtney goes, and, though I pretend I'm not watching, I see Stamp look after her, then at me, before offering a quick wave and shuffling off. And that's okay. That's good. He's found a new buddy, someone who will maybe teach him how to shine Sentinel boots and stitch up torn berets when this is all over and done with.

Good for them both. Good for everybody.

Finally, when I've drifted the wrong way down the canal while I get my sea legs, I row back up the other way. Dane is still there. The pool deck is empty. Maybe Courtney is spoon-feeding cold brains to Stamp inside or something. Or maybe they've already got a head start signing up Stamp for Sentinel Support.

Either way, the busier he is, the happier Stamp will be. And all I've ever wanted all along was for Stamp to find happiness in the afterlife. If it takes a ditzy blonde who has the same IQ as he does, well, so be it.

The water laps gently against the oars as I glide forward, coming close to the dock but not too. Dane looks into the house behind him, as if for permission, then walks toward the water's edge.

"Room for one more?" he asks, his sleek shoulder pads glinting in the afternoon sun, looking for all the world like a young Darth Vader, minus the helmet and cape.

I chuckle. "Not this time, player."

He nods, leaning against the last dock piling. "Stamp's not the only one who'll miss you, Maddy. You know that, right?"

I'm tempted to swirl my oars in the water, turn around, or coast or just drift a while, but I know where temptation leads and even dead hearts can be broken more than once. "I guess so."

He blinks twice in the afternoon sun. "I screwed up, huh?"

I can't tell if his tone is regretful or cavalier, and it's not just because I'm inching past as he says it. I nod and keep moving, the oars gently lapping as I near the end of the canal.

As I turn left—sorry, north—out of the canal, heading up the east coast of Florida, I cast one last glance back at the dock. Yes, he's still there. Yes, he's still watching, arm casually on the piling, waiting, I suppose, until I'm out of sight so he can wipe his hands and get back to the rest of his afterlife.

Finally, turning toward the wind, I answer him: "Big time."

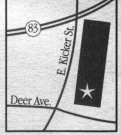

ZOMBIES Don't Cry

BOOK 1 IN THE LIVING DEAD LOVE STORY SERIES

Rusty Fischer

Maddy Swift is just a normal girl—a high school junior surviving class with her best friend and hoping the yummy new kid, Stamp, will ask her out. When he finally does, her whole life changes.

Sneaking out to meet Stamp at a party one rainy night, Maddy is struck by lightning. After awakening, she feels lucky to be alive. Over time, however, Maddy realizes that she's become the thing she and everyone else fear most: *the living dead*.

With no heartbeat and no breath in her lungs, Maddy must learn how to survive as a zombie. Turns out there's a lot more to it than shuffling around 24/7 growling, "Brains." Needing an afterlife makeover is only the beginning of her problems. As Barracuda Bay High faces zombie Armageddon, Maddy must summon all of her strength to protect what matters most—just as soon as she figures out exactly what that is.

Trade Paperback
US $9.95 / CDN $11.95
ISBN# 9781605423821

ZOMBIES Don't Forgive

BOOK 2 IN THE
LIVING DEAD LOVE STORY SERIES

Rusty Fischer

Maddy Swift was just a normal girl—a high school junior surviving class with her best friend and hoping the yummy new kid, Stamp, would ask her out. When he finally did, her whole life changed. On her way to the party, she was struck by lightning and awoke with no heartbeat and no breath in her lungs. When Barracuda Bay's homecoming turned into zombie Armageddon, Dane helped Maddy and Stamp escape undead.

Now Maddy, Dane, and Stamp have fled to Orlando, where they work at a theme park, hiding in plain sight with their jobs in The Great Movie Monster Makeover Show. But all is not well as the three BFFs of the Living Dead cohabitate 24/7 trying to avoid curious Normals (humans), vengeful Zerkers (bad zombies), and equally lethal Sentinels (zombie cops).

While Dane and Maddy draw closer, Stamp drifts away—straight into the arms of a mysterious blonde with a permanent scowl. The girl puts their whole afterlife in danger, and before long Maddy's ready to hunt her down to separate her from her head!

Trade Paperback
US $9.99 / CDN $9.99
ISBN# 9781605426365

VAMPLAYERS

RUSTY FISCHER

At the Afterlife Academy of Exceptionally Dark Arts, the vampires in training follow one of two tracks: they become either Sisters or Saviors. Of course, everyone wants to be a Savior, swooping into infested high schools in matching red leather jumpsuits and wielding crossbows, putting down swarming vampires with deadly efficiency.

But Lily Fielding is just a Sister—a Third Sister at that, a measly trainee. When Lily and her two Sisters, Alice and Cara, are called out to their latest assignment, she figures it's just another run-of-the-mill gig: spot the Vamplayer (part vampire, part player), identify the predictably hot, trampy girl he's set his eyes on, and befriend her before the Vamplayer can turn her to do his bidding.

Finding the sleek and sexy Vamplayer, Tristan, and his equally beautiful and popular target, Bianca, is easy. And when Lily meets the adorably geeky Zander, she too falls under a lover's spell. But this assignment turns out to be trickier than most when the Third Sister must battle the baddest vampire of all.

VAMPLAYERS

Trade Paperback
US $9.95
ISBN# 9781605424491

MEDALLION

P R E S S

For more information
about other great titles from
Medallion Press, visit

medallionmediagroup.com

Read On Vacation

Medallion Press has created
Read on Vacation for e-book
lovers who read on the go.

See more at:
medallionmediagroup.com/readonvacation

MMG SIDEKICK

Do you love books?

The **MMG Sidekick** app for the iPad is
your entertainment media companion.
Download it today to get access to
Medallion's entire library of e-books,
including **FRE**

MMG Sideki

to get access to TREEbook™ enhanced
novels with story branching technology!

GREGORY LAMBERSON

THE JULIAN YEAR

Every day, 20 million people are becoming homicidal maniacs.

TREEbook™ enhanced

Available on the
App Store